Elisabeth Hobbes grew up in York, where she spent most of her teenage years wandering around the city looking for a handsome Roman or a Viking to sweep her off her feet. Elisabeth's hobbies include skiing, Arabic dance and fencing—none of which have made it into a story yet. When she isn't writing she spends her time reading, and is a pro at cooking while holding a book! Elisabeth lives in Cheshire with her husband, two children and three cats with ridiculous names.

Also by Elisabeth Hobbes

Falling for Her Captor
A Wager for the Widow
The Saxon Outlaw's Revenge

The Danby Brothers miniseries

The Blacksmith's Wife
Redeeming the Rogue Knight

Discover more at millsandboon.co.uk.

BEGUILED BY THE
FORBIDDEN KNIGHT

Elisabeth Hobbes

MILLS & BOON

First Published in Great Britain 2018
by Mills & Boon, an imprint of HarperCollins*Publishers*
1 London Bridge Street, London, SE1 9GF

© 2018 Claire Lackford

ISBN: 978-0-263-93289-8

Printed and bound in Spain
by CPI, Barcelona

To Emma and Jules
for many years of silly jokes,
Dylan impersonations,
bottles of wine and camping trips.

Chapter One

Yorkshire—May 1071

'Tell me, madam, where is my bride?'

Gilbert du Rospez flung his arms wide in a gesture that encapsulated frustration, surprise and disbelief. He turned a circle around the brightly lit hall, then once again faced the impassive woman sitting on the dais.

'I have travelled from York to Haxby in appalling weather, and at risk to my safety, with the sole intention of meeting your daughter and now I discover she is not here!'

From his place at the left side of the hall Guilherm FitzLannion hid a frown as he watched his liege lord and childhood friend grow increasingly irate. The journey from the city to this manor house was manageable within half a day on foot, and on horseback had been even faster. The Galtres Forest had provided shelter from the sudden May rainfall and there had been no sightings of any trouble. Gilbert was merely attempting to impose his status on his audience and, as usual, he showed no sense of how to do it with poise or effectiveness.

With his even features, chestnut hair cut in the fashionable style and a slim frame, Gilbert seldom failed to charm anyone he raised his soft brown eyes to, but if the glowing youth was hoping to make a good impression on his future mother-in-law he was failing. From her seat above them, Emma, Countess of Haxby, continued to look down her nose with an expression of disdain.

'Perhaps you should have checked before setting out on such an—' Emma smirked openly '—*arduous* journey whether it was one worth making. My daughter has not lived with me for almost two years.'

Her blue eyes became flint. 'I sent her away in the winter of sixty-nine when your King marched to retake York from Edgar and his allies. I did not want her in the city when he was wintering there.'

Your King, Gui noted. He had not expected her to call William 'the Great', but this open disdain was a clear signal. If Gui had wondered which claimant to the throne of England Herik of Haxby's widow might have supported in the tumultuous events five years previously, this was the evidence to confirm it. She either believed the oath-breaker Harold's claim had been valid, or perhaps she had supported the Aetheling in his failed attempts the previous year to take York back from Norman control.

Gui flexed and bunched the fingers of his right hand and ignored the creeping itch in his left wrist. He looked at Gilbert to see if the nobleman had also picked up the inflection. Doubtful. Lady Emma would have to openly call William 'the bastard' for Gilbert to notice her hostility.

'I know you have sent her away. You are telling me nothing I don't know and I believe you are being intentionally unhelpful!' Gilbert gazed on her with eyes full of injured dignity. 'The question is, to where did you send her?'

Gilbert's voice was rising and a blush was creeping up his throat. Any moment now he would stamp his foot. Gui noticed a shift in the stance of the attendants standing at either side of Emma's chair. The two men were middle-aged and wore short swords buckled at their waists. Emma must have considerable influence to be allowed to keep armed guards after William's determination to bring Yorkshire's defiant inhabitants firmly under his yoke.

Gui and Gilbert carried swords so Gui doubted they were in any real danger. Part of Gui relished the idea of drawing English blood and teaching these northern curs that they were under the rule of William of Normandy. Another part grew clammy with cold sweat at the thought of taking arms in battle. The sword had never been his preferred weapon, but he no longer wielded the bow that he had loved since his youth.

In any case, William had decreed that was not the way things were to be done. England had been taken by force and subjugated by brutality, but would be held and secured through marriage and creating alliances.

Gui was growing tired of listening to the demands and refusals going back and forth. It was time to intervene and smooth the path for his lord as he had done so many times before. That was why Gilbert had brought him today after all, not to fight. He was no use in that respect any longer.

Gui swallowed the bitter bile that caused his stomach to twist in self-loathing. He cleared his throat and stepped forward to stand beside Gilbert.

'Lady Emma, it's time to put an end to this

nonsense. Be gracious enough to tell us where the maid is. Now.'

Emma raised an eyebrow in surprise. Her watery blue eyes raked over Gui. She blinked, but did not outwardly show aversion at the sight of him as most women did. Gui felt a grudging touch of admiration for the woman who faced down these unwelcome visitors in her house and lands with such assurance.

'Who are you to speak so boldly on a matter which does not concern you?'

What must she think of him in comparison to the noble knight he now stood beside? He was a head taller than Gilbert and with a broader frame. He bore a nose that was slightly crooked after a break during his childhood, and his time in William's army had left him with a scar that split his lower lip into two uneven parts and eyes that were charcoal smuts from frequent sleepless nights. He felt like a rough tree trunk beside a tower of polished oak.

He thanked his stars that his greatest disfigurement was not immediately apparent to an onlooker and folded his right arm over his left, masking the padded leather glove he always wore. He turned his eyes to meet the widow's gaze, *boldly* as she had called it.

He gave Lady Emma a smile, knowing that

even when he meant it—which was rare these days—his scarred grin was more likely to provoke repulsion than kindness.

'My name is Guilherm FitzLannion, my lady. I am no one of import.'

No one. Not a man of rank, simply an archer who had followed his friend and lord to England to seek his fortune and failed to find it.

Gilbert clapped a hand tightly on Gui's shoulder and gave him a wide smile. The sorrow in his eyes was replaced with a warmer expression.

'Gui is my closest confidant and my advisor, Lady Emma. He reminds me that I need to temper my speech at times and perhaps now is such a time.'

Emma flashed Gui a look of understanding that took him by surprise. Perhaps she had spent the years before widowhood smoothing the path of a rash nobleman.

Gui bowed his head. 'Sir Gilbert does me too much kindness. I would add my petition to his, however. Delaying this affair simply to provoke us will solve nothing. Whether or not you accept William as King, he has spoken on this matter.'

He gave another crooked smile, took a step back and waited.

'She is with her companion—a foundling left

with us as a child—at the priory at Byland near Elmeslac,' Emma said after a long pause.

Her voice caught. Her eyes were blank, viewing something other than the room before her. Were her nights plagued by bad dreams as Gui's were? Did she hear the same cries?

'Sigrun was already of fragile temperament and is not strong in body or spirit,' Emma continued. 'She narrowly escaped defilement, first at the hands of the rebels, then by men such as yourself who came to take back the city. Despite his determination to break our shire, I believe William of Normandy respects the sanctity of holy orders enough to allow a maiden to be safe in a priory from abuse and slaughter.'

Her voice dripped with contempt. Having travelled from the south through the ruins of what had once been prosperous villages, Gui found it hard to blame her. He studied his boots, ashamed of his countrymen, though he had not taken part in such dishonourable exploits.

'My heart aches for the maid's distress, but if you have sent her away you must fetch her back,' Gilbert blustered.

A gleeful smile flitted across Emma's lips.

'That is out of the question.'

Gilbert growled deep in his throat and tensed his shoulders. Gui laid a restraining hand on his friend's forearm, foreseeing a return to the hostilities he had hoped were ending.

'You are making this harder than necessary, my lady,' he cautioned.

Emma rose from her seat and walked slowly to the men. Her attendants stayed at their stations, but both stood poised to act if the need arose. Did these men of the north think Normans so dishonourable that they would attack a woman in her own home?

Emma stopped before Gui.

'I am a poor widow with few resources. I do not have the means to escort my child here safely and she cannot travel alone, not while bands of rebels and outlaws roam through Yorkshire. It is simply not safe.'

'Your daughter will come to no harm,' Gui assured her.

'You thought York was safe after FitzOsbern was given the garrison in the city, but Edgar and Sweyn of Denmark proved you wrong! Yorkshire may rise in rebellion again at any time.'

'Now Alan Rouz holds the estate as Tenant in Chief, Yorkshire will not rise again. William has seen to that. Barely a village stands between here and Durham.'

Gui and Gilbert had marched with Alan the Red of Brittany to take York back when the Aetheling had attacked for the second time. Rouz had been granted land and William had decreed that Gilbert was the man to marry the sister of the young *eorl* who had taken arms against him.

Emma looked from man to man. Approaching her late thirties and therefore at least ten years older than either man, she was still an attractive, elegant woman with full breasts and a gently curved belly. Where once he might have taken his time to appreciate her beauty, Gui remained unmoved, simply noting that time and her troubles had not diminished her looks.

'I agreed to allow my daughter to marry you, Sir Gilbert,' Emma said coldly, 'but I do not have to like it. Nor do I have to aid you in the process.'

'You did not agree. You were given no choice,' Gui pointed out. Neither was Gilbert, he thought ruefully. 'A marriage was settled in return for your lands not being devastated after your son joined with the Aetheling's forces.'

Emma's eyes filled with hatred. Gui shrugged. A daughter's virginity was a small price to pay in return for the guarantee of safety for those who lived on her manor, especially when the girl would have been doubtless married off to some straw-haired *eorl* in any case.

'Sigrun is a compliant and dutiful maiden and will do what is required of her. If you wish to marry my daughter go and bring her here your-self!' Emma lifted her chin. 'I'll send word ahead that the prioress should expect the noble Gilbert du Rospez to come claim his bride. Until you marry her, this house is mine so leave it now. Both of you.'

She turned on her heel and vanished behind the thick embroidered hangings into her private quarters, leaving Gui, Gilbert and their escort standing alone. Her attendants moved silently to stand before the curtain and block entry.

Gilbert spun on his heel and marched out of the building with as much dignity as the departed woman. Outside he sagged against the beam of wood at the corner of the building and sighed.

'That woman is impossible. How dare she be-have to me in such a manner?'

This was Gilbert through and through. Veer-ing between tongue-tied shyness and wild out-bursts of bullishness. Managing him took all Gui's efforts.

'We have invaded her land and now you wish to claim her daughter as your wife. Did you ex-pect to be greeted with open arms?' Gui asked.

'Wish to marry her daughter! *Wish* to?' Gil-bert threw his arms up. 'The wish is not mine. You know that, Gui. It is as much a penance to me as a reward. I don't want to marry an English mouse who by her mother's own account might be feeble-minded!'

Gui doubted that Gilbert had the urge to marry any woman. His mind was consumed entirely with thoughts of riding or breeding his beloved horses. Give him a kindred spirit and he would waste the night in enthusiastic discussion, but with a woman he was useless. Gui strongly suspected he was still a virgin.

'Calm yourself. You might not want the girl, but you do want this.'

Gui gestured at the imposing house and the fields surrounding it, his throat catching with envy. It was built in the old style from tall planks of oak with wicker fencing surrounding a courtyard. To own such a home would be the greatest thing Gui could imagine. Gilbert shrugged him off and stalked to his destrier and the mare Gui had hired in York.

Gui followed him. 'You'll be a man of means with land here. Plenty of room to breed your horses. It's better than being the second son of a nobleman in Brittany, even if it does mean marrying an English mouse.'

Much better than being the son of a vassal in that nobleman's fief, too. Although Gui had accompanied Gilbert from Brittany at the behest of his friend, no one had offered him land, much less a bride for the part he had played in the conquest.

'You know where the girl is now. All you need to do is go fetch her and the matter can be settled. You can have her back here by midsummer's day. That would be a good-omened day for a wedding.'

'I can't go fetch her. I'll be as useless persuading the girl to leave the priory as I was compelling her mother to retrieve her,' Gilbert said gloomily. 'Besides, I've been offered an opportunity I'd like to take.'

'Which is?' Gui prompted.

'I've been invited to hunt on the Earl's lands in the west. One of the men going breeds good stock horses. I told him I'd be there. There are good deer to hunt. You should join us.'

Gui's jaw clenched. He jerked his head to his left arm. 'And how would I bring them down with no means of drawing a bow?'

Gilbert's eyes lit and he pointed a finger at Gui. 'My friend, I have a solution. Go to Byland in my place. Bring the girl back for me while I am away.'

Gui gave a short laugh, then stopped short. He scowled. 'You actually mean that, don't you?'

Gilbert swung himself into the saddle. 'Why not? It should be a simple matter. If you don't intend to come with me, you have nothing better to do with your time.'

Gui had planned to spend his immediate future visiting as many of York's drinking dens as he could and passing into oblivion. Traipsing halfway across Yorkshire to collect another man's bride did not hold any appeal, even if that man was his oldest friend. He mounted his horse, gathering the reins in his right hand.

'We'll make arrangements within the week,' Gilbert mused.

'My lord! Gilbert! I said no.'

'Of course you did, but you'll do it anyway.' Gilbert exuded confidence, displaying the easy charm that had failed to work on Lady Emma. 'I could command you as your liege lord, but I know I won't have to. My good friend. I ask a lot of you but I'll reward you, too. You'll need a better horse, of course. Better clothes, too. It will cost me dearly.'

Gui rolled his eyes. He was ambivalent about horses, something Gilbert found incomprehensible.

'I imagine Lady Emma will see it as a personal insult if you send a messenger in your place.'

Gilbert pouted. 'It's the daughter I have to marry, not the mother.'

Gui gave him a stern look. Diplomacy was not Gilbert's strongest feature.

'I suppose you're right,' Gilbert conceded. He broke into a trot and they skirted around the edge of Lady Emma's land towards the forest path. Gui followed, uneasy on horseback and watchful for signs of trouble Gilbert might ignore.

As they reached the edge of the forest Gilbert pulled his reins sharply and turned to Gui.

'You go *as* me!'

Gui drew his horse to a halt, momentarily puzzled.

'You go in my place to Byland,' Gilbert clarified. He smiled. 'Take my name. Lady Emma is sending word I am coming, but the Lady Sigrun and I have never met. She won't know you aren't me. I'll even give you my seal to wear to add to the deception.'

He trotted on, lost in his plans, talking half to himself. 'It would cause difficulty if she discovered the deception halfway home. Swear to me that you will take my name until you return here with my bride.'

'I haven't agreed yet,' Gui pointed out. 'She'll discover I'm not you on your wedding night. What will she do when she finds out she has been deceived?'

'She'll be uncomplaining if she's as timid and

compliant as her mother says,' Gilbert answered. He smiled. 'Court the girl on my behalf, Gui, but do not let her know what we have done. When she arrives here she will be more amenable to the thought of marriage. If I went to bring *your* bride back, I can see that would be a problem, but as it stands…'

He left the thought unfinished. Gui ended it for him.

'As it stands she will take one look at you and thank God she does not have to marry a one-handed, scar-lipped, crook-nosed beast after all.'

Gilbert had the grace to look abashed. 'That isn't what I meant.'

It had been, but Gui had long grown accustomed to Gilbert's unwitting tactlessness. The offence was never meant. Besides, it was true. A wife of his own had seemed an unobtainable dream since his injuries.

'You really don't look as bad as you imagine,' Gilbert said. 'If you were wealthier, a woman would look past your injuries anyway. When I am master of this manor I'll have the power to grant land. If you do this for me, I'll grant a portion to you. I'll make you my reeve. My second-in-command.'

Gui gazed around him. Lady Emma's land had been spared the worst of the harrying that had all but destroyed the north. A river ran through the flat plain that lay barren, but in time could be brought back to life. It reminded him a little of home and the farmer's son in him awoke. To be master of his own lands under the fiefdom of his friend would be a good thing to be.

Gilbert had been spinning tales of riches and power for them both since they had left France. They had so far failed to appear, for Gui at least, and this could be the opportunity he craved to rebuild his life and start afresh. All for making a journey of a week and escorting a girl to her home. What could be simpler? His lips twitched into a smile.

'I'll bring your bride,' he agreed. 'I'll take your name if I have to. I'll do whatever it takes.'

Gui raised himself high in the saddle and rolled his shoulders back. It was now mid-afternoon and he had been riding all day, but the final stage of his journey was almost complete. He had reached the highest point of the hill and stopped beside the stone marker, and could make out the roofs of the priory nestling in the dip below. It stood along the opposite bank of the river that wound lazily between hills and back towards York, passing by the remains of a couple of desolate villages and vanishing periodically into knots of trees.

He pulled at the neck of his cloak to loosen it. In the three days since he had left York the spring weather had changed steadily for the better and the new wool was still stiff and itchy in the unexpected sun.

Not that he was complaining about his new attire. Gilbert had been so grateful for Guilherm's agreement he had presented Gui with the new cloak, two fine linen undershirts and a new tunic of light wool with a deep band of embroidered braid along the thigh-length hem. A new buckle adorned the worn leather belt Gui insisted on retaining along with his old boots and gloves. They were by far the finest clothes Gui had ever possessed and how he looked exactly like what he was supposed to resemble: a knight of middling wealth hoping to make a favourable impression on his bride.

He could almost believe their plan would be a success, and as he rode he passed the time making idle plans for the crops he would plant and the house he would build when the promised land was finally his. It wouldn't have to be a big house; he would be living there alone after all. Best not dare to dream too big—a companion to share his life with was so unlikely that the pit of loneliness that made his heart ache soured his thoughts.

He brushed his hair back from his forehead where it had become damp with exertion from the ride. Despite all Gilbert's coaxing Gui had steadfastly refused to shave his head in the same style as the knight, and had kept his dark-brown hair longer than fashionable so it skimmed his jaw and framed his face. Sweat pooled beneath his arms and the linen clung to his torso. He frowned. It would not do to arrive at the priory looking so travel stained. No doubt the prioress would provide the means to bathe, but sunlight turned the river silver and to Gui it was a more appealing prospect. He turned the horse towards the river and in a lazy walk he made his way down the hill to one of the bends where trees would afford him some privacy in the unlikely event he encountered anyone.

Gui tethered his horse to a tree close to the river where she could drink as she wished or take shelter from the sun. He unbuckled the short sword he wore at his belt and stowed it alongside the bow and quiver of arrows he could not bear to part with, which were wrapped in leather and strapped to the pannier. He stripped off his clothes, gritting his teeth in frustration as he worked the buckles and laces with his right hand. He paused before removing the padded glove on his left hand, but in this isolated spot no one would cast their eyes on his affliction so he removed that, too.

Naked, he plunged into the river, which proved to be deeper than he had expected. He stood, gasping and shuddering, toes curling in the silt as the chilly depths closed around him to his waist. When he became accustomed to the cold, he swam under the surface with powerful strokes and emerged downstream when he could no longer hold his breath. He scrubbed at his hair and body until his flesh stung, wishing he had the means to scrape the bristles from his jaw that had become a rough beard. He resembled one of the Yorkshire Norsemen the longer he wore it.

The sun was still warm, lessening the worst of the chill. He lay back in the water and closed his eyes, taking deep breaths of the sweet-scented air. He drifted along with the gentle current, allowing the water to caress him, feeling knots in his muscles loosen as the current and weeds played around his body. For what was almost certainly the first time since stepping foot in England, Guilherm felt truly at peace.

'That'll do until I come again next week.' Aelfhild tightened the knot holding the bandage on Brun's leg. She wiped the greasy balm from her fingers, pulled the threadbare blanket back over the old man's legs and smiled. 'Try to move a little if you can or you'll get more sores. That poultice will help ease the discomfort.'

'You're a good lass, Aelfhild. You'll make a good wife to some man,' Brun rasped.

Her first thought was that she'd rather be a good nurse, and her second was whom would she marry anyway; now Yorkshire's men were in short supply.

'I don't think a foundling with no dowry would be many men's first choice,' she sighed.

Brun started to answer, but coughs racked his frame. 'I won't be sorry to go, but you've made these months more comfortable,' he wheezed.

'Don't talk like that! You've got years ahead of you,' Aelfhild lied.

A film of tears covered Brun's eyes. 'Weeks. A month or two, perhaps. I didn't think I'd see this year come when *they* came to burn the village. My home is gone; my sons are dead. I'm ready to join them.'

They. The Normans. They'd lain waste to the villages all around Elmeslac, and further afield if tales were true as the new King's vengeance for what had happened in York. For the people daring to try to regain their city. Aelfhild's throat tightened with hatred. If she ever met a Norman she'd drive her knife through his black heart!

Brun was her final patient. She began to pack up her bag of poultices and medicines to stop her hand straying to the brooch she wore concealed beneath a fold in the neck of her shapeless tunic. She would not think about the man who had given it to her or her eyes would fill with tears, too.

She left the dimly lit hut where the remaining villagers lived together: the old and the young, those who had escaped the killing. She began to make her way back to the priory, considering herself lucky to have a home however much she hated the confining walls. She stomped along the rutted track and tried to ignore the fields that should have been thick with growing barley. Her boots were sturdy and she set a good pace up the hill, only pausing for breath when the top came into view. The breeze was warm as it caressed her cheeks, a sure sign that spring would be hot this year. She felt perspiration rising on her face and neck.

Aelfhild's skirts billowed around her and she shook her head, enjoying the sensation of the wind's kiss upon the back of her neck. She ran the last few paces to the top of the hill, then spun around, arms wide and head thrown back. She laughed at her foolishness, as she realised what she must look like. She did it again, sure no one was watching, for who was there left to watch her now?

Her stomach growled. Breakfast had been gritty bread and sour cheese, and supper was nothing worth anticipating. The river glinted in the sunlight, winding through the valley. Aelfhild had time to spare before she had to return to the priory and her spirits lifted. When such feeling came upon her she could forget her country was under the yoke of the Conqueror, could forget she had not seen her home for almost two years and the walls that now confined her.

She was thirsty and hot. The river could satisfy both those needs and she could even try to catch a fish to supplement the meagre diet at the priory, using the method Brun described when his mind wandered to his youth.

Anticipating the cool water swirling around her legs, Aelfhild hastened her steps as she neared the river where it bent towards her side of the bank, skipping and occasionally spinning in circles in the sheer joy of being alive. The world was empty. She could even bathe completely naked if she chose, though would not go that far. If her swim was ever discovered, Aelfhild would no doubt receive the customary whipping from one of the sisters, but there was no one to see and no one to tell. It would be her secret and hers alone.

Chapter Two

It was only when he heard a high female voice singing that Gui realised he was no longer alone.

He tensed. The voice was coming upstream from the direction where Gui had left the horse. He had drifted much further than he had realised. He rolled over on to his front and lowered himself beneath the surface until only his head from nose up was visible and searched for the owner of the voice.

A girl was making her way through the field towards the river on the opposite bank from Gui's horse and clothes. She wore a grey cloak and grey tunic with a veil that covered her hair and shadowed her face and had a bag hooked over her girdle. She moved with purpose, making quick progress, which was why she had come upon Gui so quickly. As she neared him she slowed her pace. Once or twice she spun in a circle, arms raised wide, and did a handful of dance steps, humming in a carefree manner that Gui envied.

It was so rare to see anyone who appeared untouched by what had taken place in the country that Gui was transfixed. He raised his head to better watch the girl as she cavorted around, seemingly oblivious to her surroundings. Perhaps she was a simpleton to be behaving in such a way: one of those poor unfortunates for whom time and place had no meaning. Gui shook his head ruefully. He almost envied her that, too.

As she reached the curve in the river almost opposite Gui's horse the girl dropped her bag to the ground. Still humming, she removed her shoes, unbuckled her girdle and dropped it beside them. She moved slowly, languorously stretching her arms in a manner that sent shivers running over Gui and causing more goosebumps to rise on his skin than the chill of the water had alone managed. The girl unpinned the veil from her hair and revealed a thick plait of pale-blonde hair, the colour of sand from his homeland.

Slowly, and completely unaware of Gui's presence, the girl pulled her billowing grey tunic over her head to reveal a closer-fitting linen shift beneath. Gui froze, acutely aware that he was intruding on something private, but unable to leave. He could not return to his horse without alerting the girl to his presence and for both their sakes he did not want to do that.

At first Gui had mistaken her for a child: partly because of her manner, but mainly because she was so slightly built. Now she was closer he could make out the shape of small breasts beneath her shift and the blossoming curve of hips as she twisted and bent to unlace her shoes.

She was more woman than child.

Faced with this new evidence Gui gulped in surprise. He lowered himself further beneath the water, conscious of his own nakedness. Fortunately for Gui's composure the girl did not do as he had done and shed every layer. She hitched up the skirt of her shift and waded purposefully into the water to her knees. Just as Gui had done she shivered in the cold. Beneath the water Gui grinned to himself in sympathy as another shudder racked his body.

The girl paused her song and giggled to herself. Unexpectedly she ducked under the surface to her neck and came up again in one fluid movement, now soaked to the skin. She gasped aloud in a series of breathy panting noises that reached inside Gui to a time when he had been capable of causing women to make such sounds. His guts twisted with longing as he looked at her, transfixed.

The curves that were now apparent beneath the thin cloth indicated she was even closer to womanhood than he had at first supposed. True, her breasts were small, but her waist was shapely and the wet tunic clung to her legs. Through the fabric Gui could make out the dark triangle of hair where her legs met, and the pink of her nipples. Despite the cold water Gui felt himself hardening. He almost choked on the cold water in surprise at the unexpected awakening of an urge that had lain dormant for so long.

The girl had not spotted Gui or the horse. She waded to the edge, but instead of climbing out she fumbled with her belongings. When she turned around Gui realised she was holding something in her hand. She unwound it and Gui caught a glint of metal before she dropped it into the water and began staring intently down with a look of concentration on her face.

She was fishing.

Gui was transported back across years and the sea to his home in Brittany where he had done similar as a boy in the river that ran through Gilbert's father's land and an ache stabbed his heart.

He tore his mind from the memories that were simultaneously comforting and painful to recall. This might be his only chance to slip away. Keeping low in the water, he eased his way slowly towards the bank, taking care not to splash. He was roughly halfway there when his horse spotted him and whinnied in greeting.

The girl straightened up and turned around. She raised her head and in doing so her eyes slid over Gui who was half-crouched in the water. They fell instead on the horse. She became rigid, eyes moving around from side to side as she searched along the bank for the owner. Still she failed to see Gui who was almost beneath her nose, holding himself equally still and barely daring to breathe. Instead of turning and fleeing to the opposite bank, as any sensible person would have done, she started wading towards the horse. And towards Gui.

'*Kac'h!*'

Gui swore under his breath. He was faced with two choices. To duck beneath the water and try to swim out of her way, or to surface and reveal his presence. If it had just been his own possessions at stake he might have risked leaving them, but Gilbert's seal ring was in the saddlebag where Gui had put it for safety during the journey. He could not risk it being discovered and taken.

In the brief moment he had before the girl waded straight into him he made his decision and rose from the depths to face her.

Water cascaded off Gui's body as he pushed

himself to the surface. His hair clung to his face in tangles, half-obscuring his view. The girl began screaming at a volume and pitch that her previous soft humming had not suggested she was capable of. Still she did not make any attempt to run but stood, eyes wide and fixed on Gui. They flashed to his face, then downwards over his body where they settled at the level of the water. Her mouth widened and she screamed once more.

'Serr da veg! Loukez plac'h!' Gui bellowed. Stop that, you foolish girl!

He realised too late that he had spoken in his own tongue, the Breton dialect that even Frenchmen struggled to master at times. To her ears it must have sounded like meaningless babbling.

In any case, it didn't stop her cries. He would have to stop her forcibly if necessary. He plunged towards her, holding his right hand up towards her in an attempt to silence her screams before half of the shire came running to discover the cause of her panic.

The girl made a lunge at him as he neared her, fishing hook outstretched. He had expected her to retreat to the far bank, not attack. Surprised at her ferocity, Gui flung himself to one side. The hook gouged the length of his left forearm, drawing blood and leaving a deep scratch. He roared in pain and whipped his arm away viciously.

His toe bashed a half-buried rock and he lurched under the water. Instinctively, he reached out to steady himself and grasped hold of the nearest object. It turned out to be the girl's outstretched arm. His fingers closed around her wrist as he went back and then she too was slipping below the surface.

With his eyes closed Gui could only feel rather than see what took place. The girl's legs tangled with his, shift floating loose. He felt bare flesh against his shins and she fell face forward on to him. Through her shift Gui could feel her small breasts, the hard nipples straining against his naked chest. Her sharp hipbone brushed against his groin, sending a tremor through his entire body and causing him to swell despite the icy water. He had not been this close to a woman for longer than he cared to remember. In any other situation this would be the most arousing sensation imaginable, but now he focused his energy on breaking through the surface once more.

He rolled so that he was on top of the girl and grasped her firmly round the waist with his right arm, holding her close to him as he straddled her. Feeling for the riverbed with his feet, he pushed upwards, taking the girl with him.

They came up, both gulping for air. The girl pushed herself violently from Gui, kicking his shin for good measure. Almost as soon as her lungs were full she began screaming once more. She looked from his face downwards whereupon her eyes opened wide and her mouth became a perfect, pink oval of alarm.

With mounting horror Gui realised that although he was standing waist deep in the river, the water was not particularly murky. The half of him that was below the surface must be clearly visible to the girl. He instinctively brought his arms round to cover himself in a belated gesture of modesty. He realised too late that his disfigured left arm was now on full display instead and put both arms back behind his back.

The girl screamed again. She was similarly attempting to cover her body with a two-handed version of the dance of modesty Gui was performing. Gui dropped to a crouch so that the water came to mid-chest and his lower half was less conspicuous. He kept his left arm behind his back, suspecting that the sight of his deformity would cause her further panic.

The girl settled for covering her breasts with one arm and the dark triangle between her legs with the splayed fingers of her other hand. Gui did his best not to stare at what she was trying to hide, but she drew more attention to her attributes than she concealed.

Now she was seemingly satisfied with their attempts at modesty, the girl's screams became words.

'Leave me alone, *dweorgar*!' she cried.

'Stop screaming,' Gui ordered. His brain caught up with his ears. 'What did you call me?'

'You can speak!' the girl gasped. Her eyes grew wide with surprise.

Gui frowned, his earlier suspicion that she was mentally deficient creeping back into his mind.

'Of course I can.' Her accent had been broad, with the flat vowels of York. He'd understood her words, but it had not come naturally. 'If you mean in your tongue, then why not?'

The girl took a careful step backwards, folding her arms tightly across her breasts. To Gui's relief she didn't scream again, but widened her eyes and jutted out her jaw assertively. Their eyes locked and Gui recognised terror brimming in hers below the confrontation.

'What are you? *Swartalf*? A *dweorgar*?' she demanded.

'What did you call me?' He recognised the Danish words for elf and dwarf and barked a laugh at such a preposterous accusation.

The girl looked furious. 'Don't laugh at me, monster!'

Her voice was deep. Hoarse from screaming.

'Are you a child to believe in such things?' Gui mocked. 'I'm no monster. I'm a man.'

'Well, you look like a beast!'

Gui pictured what he must have looked like, rising from beneath the surface, his frame broad and towering, the dark spread of hair on his chest darkened further by the soaking and with traces of waterweeds clinging to it. His hair had obscured his eyes so she would only have seen his scarred lips and crooked nose through the matted locks and beard. It was no wonder she believed him to be some unearthly creature.

Humiliation coursed through him, reddening his face and heating his blood. He stopped laughing and raised himself higher in the water, pushing the hair back from his face.

'I'm a man,' he repeated firmly.

Gui shifted his right hand before him in an attempt to create a sense of decency, but not before the girl's eyes had flickered rapidly down. Her eyes slid over his body once more, examining him and flickering to the area of his body that could be guaranteed to prove his claim. As he concealed his most intimate parts she brought her head sharply up again to settle on Gui's face with a look of mortification. Her skin was very pale like most of the women in these northern parts and now bright streaks of red flashed across each cheek. He wondered if she was a virgin. She had certainly known where to look for confirmation of his masculinity. He spread his hand wider in front of his cock as the speculation about her innocence caused a throb of lust that necessitated a little more concealment.

Presumably satisfied that he was what he claimed to be, the girl had recovered enough to glare at him.

'You were spying on me!'

'I was here first!' Gui exclaimed, stung by the accusation.

'You were watching me at any rate. How long were you there?'

Gui heaved an exasperated sigh. 'I don't know. I was enjoying the peace before you came upon me. I was trying to get back to the bank without you spotting me. That's my horse you saw.'

It was at this point Gui became aware that during their underwater tussle they had inadvertently swapped positions. Now the girl was between him and his belongings, and he stood in the middle of the river, preventing her reaching hers. At some point while they had wrestled beneath the water she had dropped her fishing hook. Gui could see it glinting on the riverbed halfway between them.

'I'm not going to hurt you,' Gui assured her.

'You tried to drown me!'

'No, I didn't!' This was becoming tiresome. 'I slipped and you were the nearest thing to take hold of. If you hadn't screamed, I wouldn't have had to come near you at all, but you were making enough noise to wake a dozen *korrigans*.'

Her forehead wrinkled.

'Water creatures,' Gui clarified. His forearm stung where she had razed him with the pin. He wiped away the blood she had drawn. Her eyes followed his movement and a hint of triumph filled them.

'The only one who has caused injury so far is you. Are you sure you aren't a *korrigan* sent to tempt me to my watery death?' he teased. It struck him that if he was to drown, doing it in the arms of a creature as alluring as this one would not be the worst end he could imagine.

The girl looked outraged.

'I'm nothing of the sort! What are you doing here?'

She eyed Gui haughtily, then her face changed into an expression of hatred that Gui had seen so many times. 'You're Norman, aren't you?'

The tone she used implied this was worse even

than if he had indeed owned to being a dwarf or other monstrous creature. He'd been met with hostility and hatred since arriving in England so that was hardly a new experience to Gui. Nevertheless his jaw clenched.

'I'm Breton, but I expect to you it makes no difference.'

She blinked at the ferocity in his voice and opened her mouth as if she was intending to scream again. Perhaps she was not as alone as Gui thought. They were close to villages, the fields must be tended and bands of outlaws roamed the countryside. There were plenty of men who would not hesitate to slit the belly of a lone Frenchman in vengeance for what William's army had done to the north. Gui did not relish the idea of dying naked in a river that was increasingly feeling icy. He lowered himself into the water a little, bending his legs to take the weight on his thighs and held his right hand out in supplication.

'I'm travelling and wanted to bathe because the day was so warm. Just as you did.'

Uncertainty filled her eyes. The colour struck Gui for the first time and once he had noticed it he could not tear his gaze from a blueness so pale the irises almost blended seamlessly into the whites. Her sandy hair stuck to her face in long tendrils and she looked more of a sprite than Gui first thought.

'I mean you no harm. I'm twice your size. If I'd wanted to rape or kill you, I'd have done it by now.'

The colour drained from the girl's cheeks as he so casually spoke of the deeds she must have been dreading. She unwound her arms from across her body and shifted into what she clearly thought was a fighting stance, fists raised and feet spread apart. Gui recognised the bravado he had seen in enough fights in taverns to know she would probably swing for him if he got close enough.

'You're safe with me,' he said. 'Wrestling un-willing girls into submission isn't my idea of pleasure. Especially not in water as cold as this.'

'Why should I trust you? You've taken my land and killed my countrymen.' Her accent was becoming broader as her fury rose. 'Men like you intend harm to everyone they meet. All you know is how to destroy and hurt. Where is your army now? Did they forget you?'

William's soldiers must have passed this way on their march to Durham a year or so ago. Per-haps the girl believed he was one of them. Gui ground his teeth. He heard once more the screams of battle, smelled the iron scent of blood and the smoke of burning buildings. Would she believe him if he told her all he longed for was a life of peace far away from the memories that haunted him? Despite the cold water he was standing in, sweat broke out across his back and in the pits of his arms. He stepped backwards.

'I'm travelling alone. Are you alone also?'

She eyed him warily, then nodded. Irritation surged in Gui's chest.

'If you think the country is so dangerous, why are you dancing around in fields and singing to yourself?'

He jabbed a finger towards her, his temper rising and mingling with an unexpected sense of protectiveness towards the silly girl. He wondered again if she was a simpleton to put herself at such risk.

'Why are you bathing and fishing if you fear you might be set upon at any moment? Who knows you are here? Who would search if you don't return home?'

His volley of questions came as rapidly as the arrows he had once loosed. She folded her arms defensively across her small, firm breasts.

'No one knows I'm here.'

She snapped her mouth shut. Gui watched with private amusement as she realised the stupidity of what she had just admitted to a naked stranger, even one who had professed benign intentions.

'I'm doing nothing wrong,' she added, a shade too defensively.

Something struck Gui. Wherever she was supposed to be and whatever she should be doing, it wasn't fishing and bathing. The breeze whispered around Gui's body, raising the hairs on the back of his neck.

'I have somewhere I need to be and I suspect you do, too. The water is getting colder so I suggest we both get out. On our own sides of the river, of course.'

She nodded slowly, glancing behind him to where her heap of clothes lay. She shivered and tightened her arms around herself. Her pale lips trembled and she looked colder that Gui felt. The breeze was becoming stronger and her soaking wet shift must offer little protection.

'Go on. Get yourself to where you need to be.'

She took a step towards him, then stopped and stepped back.

'You're in my way.'

'And you're in mine.' Gui grinned. 'What do you propose we do about it?'

'Close your eyes while I walk past you.'

'No. I doubt I'm going to see anything more

than I already have. You go one way. I'll go the other.'

He took a step to his left. The girl did the same and they circled round each other, wading in a wide arc. As soon as she was close to her own bank the girl turned and waded in long strides that sent deep ripples around her back towards Gui. He stood and watched her. Water lapped against his belly, caressing him like fingers.

The girl heaved herself on to dry land, giving Gui a perfect view of her rounded buttocks as she pulled herself up. She gathered her clothes and bag and turned back to look at Gui. He averted his eyes, not wanting her to know he had been so openly admiring what he saw, but when she did not move he looked up. They held each other's gaze briefly, then the girl was off, running away through the grass, a white slip among the greenery.

Gui watched until she turned a bend and was out of sight. He looked down and the sun glinted on metal on the riverbed. He bent to pick up her fishing hook, which turned out to be a horseshoe-shaped brooch of silver with the pin twisted at the tip. The design was like others he had seen both men and women wearing in York. Gui closed his fist over it and waded to the bank.

He tugged his fingers through his hair to remove the knots as best he could, then dressed. He examined the scratch the girl had given him with the brooch. Blood seeped out in places where the wound was deep and he hoped he would escape infection.

The last thing he did—the last thing he always did when he dressed—was to spread out the leather thongs that were sewn to the cuff of his padded leather glove and push the padding until it formed the shape of the hand it replaced.

The stump where his hand had been removed was no longer puckered and red as it had once been, and far less unsightly than the horrific scabbed wound when his hand had been amputated in the aftermath of the victory at Senlac Hill. Gui could look at the ruin of his arm without recoiling even if no one else could. That it caused his stomach to tighten in despair until he felt physically nauseous every time he thought of how his life had changed since that dark day was something he was resigned to.

He ran his fingers over the end of his left wrist, musing on the fact that when faced with the choice, he'd rather the strange girl had seen his nakedness than this mutilation. He pulled the glove over the stump and tightened the laces of the high cuff, winding them around his forearm to secure it in place. He held his arm up before him. Hidden in this manner no one could tell that beneath the leather was nothing more than thickly wadded wool.

He put his head in his hands—hand—hand and glove. He still caught himself referring to them in the plural at times. The girl had thought him a monster and that had been without appearing to have noticed his deformity. How much worse would she have thought him if she had seen that? He looked across the river, but there was no sign that she had ever been there. He fixed the brooch to the left shoulder of his tunic as a memento of his curious encounter and folded the neck over it. He pulled his cloak on, fastening that awkwardly at his right shoulder.

The day was growing late. He had spent much longer than he had intended to in the water and he still had a way to go down this side of the river before he came to the ford and was able to take his horse across. He heaved himself to his feet and unhitched the reins from the branch. The mare snickered in greeting, pushing her velvet nose against Gui's shoulder. He nuzzled her neck, smelling the earthy warm scent of horse. Rather than mount immediately he walked on foot back to the road, occasionally glancing over his shoulder at the river.

He would be at the priory before curfew even

if he walked. He cast a final glance across the river, wondering where the girl had come from, or was returning to, and whether she would learn from her adventure not to go dancing about the countryside alone when there were men such as him roaming it.

Chapter Three

Aelfhild ran, not caring she was soaking wet and dressed only in her shift, which tangled between her legs and slowed her down. Not caring the stones in the grass hurt her bare feet and her plait was becoming a knotted rope down her back.

She ran until the river was safely out of sight and with it the alarming man in the water.

She threw herself on to the ground, her heart thumping, and dropped her bag beside her. To her horror, her legs began to shake. She clamped her hands on to her knees to stop the shameful reaction and stifled a sob. She had no time now to indulge her emotions, not when she should never have stopped to bathe in the first place and would be missed if she did not return to the priory soon.

She gathered her shift in her hands and wrung the water out as best she could. When she had decided to swim she had thought she would only be in the water briefly and would have plenty of time to dry herself. She shuddered, imagining what might have happened if she had taken the shift off and swum naked as she had briefly considered. As the man in the water had.

Her knees had stopped shaking, but at the memory of the muscular form rising before her the trembling began again and a curious fluttering filled her belly. Aelfhild unrolled her dress and dragged it down over her head. The shift would have to dry beneath her tunic as she walked and she would have to suffer the damp. Her hand slid to her collar and she gave a cry of dismay.

Her brooch! She had dropped it in the water when the Norman had pulled her under. Her lip quivered. The brooch had been a gift; the only token she had to remind her of a man who had once been dear to her, but she could not go back to search for it now. The man might still be there and even if he wasn't she would be missed if she took that much time. She would have to try to slip away at another opportunity and hope it would be on the riverbed where it had fallen.

She pulled on her stockings and shoes and sped across the fields, arriving at the priory from the rear. She could enter via the main door, but the portress would raise her eyebrows at Aelf-hild's dishevelled appearance. She strode instead to the tree with overhanging branches. No one but her seemed to have discovered its use as a ladder, but then again, no one except her seemed inclined to leave the priory.

The timbered building loomed above her. Aelfhild shivered at the idea of re-entering the dim confines. She hid behind the wall and pinned the veil on, hiding the tangle of hair beneath it, then went inside to find Sigrun. With less than a year between their ages, Aelfhild had been raised to be part-maid, part-companion to Sigrun under the watch of Lady Emma, who had shown more kindness to the foundling than she had any need to do. In a house with three boys, the two girls had bonded and mistress and servant were as close as sisters.

Sigrun was in the small cell in the dormi-tory that the two girls shared, praying as she most often was. Most inmates of the priory— sisters, nuns and women sent there like Aelfhild and Sigrun to be shielded from the horrors of the conquest—spent their days sewing or clean-ing, gardening or taking alms to the nearby vil-lages. Sigrun spent much of hers on her knees; hands clasped, eyes closed and motionless, leaving Aelfhild to ensure practical tasks were completed.

It was rare that Aelfhild felt her lower status too hard and she willingly took on Sigrun's chores. If Sigrun's heartfelt prayers were heard by any gods listening, Aelfhild's soul might reap a little of the benefit, too.

Aelfhild stood in the doorway, reluctant to disturb the devotion that was more sincere than most she had witnessed. When Sigrun finally stirred and opened her eyes she turned to Aelfhild with a serene smile, indicating a peaceful soul that Aelfhild envied.

'I heard you come in, Aelfhild. You didn't have to wait there. You wouldn't have interrupted me. You might even have joined me...'

Sigrun left the suggestion hanging. Aelfhild ignored it as she always did, but returned the smile. She sank on to her cot in the corner and leaned back against the cool stone wall. Sigrun's expression changed from serene to anxious. She joined Aelfhild and took hold of her hands.

'What's wrong? Did something happen in the village?'

The morning had been so overshadowed by what had occurred since that Aelfhild had almost forgotten she had left the confines of the priory to take medicine to Brun and his neighbours.

'No, nothing happened in the village. Brun seemed in so much pain he barely recognised me, but he slept after he had drunk a draught.'

She rummaged in her chest for a dry shift, removed her veil to let her hair free and pulled her dress over her head.

'You're soaking wet!'

Aelfhild peeled the damp linen shift from her skin and hung it on the peg by the narrow slit of window. She wriggled into the dry one and followed it with the dress. She grinned at Sigrun; less perturbed by the memory now she was home and dry.

'Not any more. It was so hot and the day was so fine that I decided to stop to bathe. I thought I might try to catch a fish.'

Sigrun looked horrified. 'You shouldn't have done that! If anyone finds out you'll get another whipping!'

The last whipping had been five days ago when Aelfhild had retorted sharply to the wrinkled nun who had tugged her hair for making too-large stitches in her embroidery. She frowned at the memory and rubbed her calf even though the wheals had subsided days ago.

'No one will find out if you don't tell anyone,' she told Sigrun sternly.

Aelfhild found her comb and began to tease

the knots from her hair. Sigrun took it from her and continued the task. Aelfhild twisted her hands in her lap, then turned to her mistress.

'There's more. There was a man. In the water.'

Sigrun stopped combing and clutched Aelfhild's arm.

'Did he hurt you?'

Her fingers settled on the same spot the Norman had grasped her. Aelfhild shuddered as she remembered the lurching terror as they had sunk down and the unsettling pressure of his muscular arm enveloping her, holding her tight against him and dragging her back to safety.

'He didn't hurt me. He was bathing like I was, only I didn't see him at first so we surprised each other.'

Her stomach squirmed as she recalled the sight of him emerging from the river, water streaming off him in a cascade as he rose above her, dark hair on his head and torso. She waved her arms to try describing the size and shape of him and capture the broadness of his body, the sense of tightly packed muscles that had reminded her of a horse or ox.

'He had dark hair that masked his face, his nose was crooked and his lips were scarred. I thought he was a river monster, but he was just a man after all.'

She broke off as her cheeks flamed. He had most definitely been a man. The—the—conspicuously large *thing* between his legs had been proof of that. She'd felt it pressing against her as they had tumbled together in the river, tracing a path from her inner thigh to hipbone. At the time the sensation had been unsettling, but now as she recalled it the odd fluttering filled her lower belly again and a pulsing ache made her thighs tighten.

She'd never seen a naked man before, but how could she have behaved so wantonly as to openly stare at him as she had done? She understood the practicalities of how babies were created, but how something that size could possibly fit where it was intended to seemed to her mind incredible. Perhaps he was not human after all, because what human could be shaped with such a body part?

The fluttering inside her grew stronger, spreading out in every direction like ripples on water after a stone broke the surface. Something was inside her; it felt as though a living creature that she could not identify was struggling to escape.

She was aware of Sigrun's arms slipping about her waist and that she had been lost in a reverie for too long.

'Poor Aelfhild, you must have nearly died with terror. I know I would have done in your place.'

Sigrun's blue eyes were full of distress. She, no doubt, would have fainted and drowned.

Aelfhild shook her head thoughtfully. She had been scared at first but that had given way to fury as he had laughed at her. She'd wanted to fight him, not run, to be one of the women of legend who drove attackers from her home, a shieldmaiden like the traders who came to York laughed about as they boasted how they would best and bed such women.

If Aelfhild were such a woman no one would easily bed her without her consent! She remembered the flush of satisfaction as the Norman had wiped away the blood she had drawn, but that thought turned to sorrow. She twisted to look at Sigrun. Tears filled her eyes as she admitted what she had done.

'I lost the brooch Torwald gave me before he left to join the rebellion in York.'

Sigrun's mouth twisted and she pulled Aelfhild closer. The two women embraced silently. They both grieved for Sigrun's brother, but for different reasons: Sigrun with the natural sorrow anyone would feel at her brother's death and Aelfhild for the additional loss of the first man who had touched her heart. The difference in their status meant he would never have married her, she was realistic enough to understand that, but she had treasured the hours they spent together.

'I'll go back for it.'

Sigrun shook her head with a violence she rarely exhibited.

'No! You mustn't leave the priory again. You could have been killed, or worse! We're safe here as my mother wanted. No one can touch us within these walls. No man.'

Sigrun's voice was full of terror and her body convulsed. She had been in York itself when William's army retaliated and had narrowly escaped rape. To her, sex was a thing of horror to be endured.

Aelfhild looked on with mingling pity and interest that something she craved could cause such a reaction in her friend. 'I won't, I promise.'

And there was the difference between them, Aelfhild mused as Sigrun continued the heroic task of de-knotting Aelfhild's hair. Sigrun shrank from the idea of ever leaving the priory, whereas Aelfhild burned to escape even if it meant facing dangers such as she had encountered today.

If she ever left the safety of the priory she would have to learn to fight. She had been victorious today, but a scratch on the arm would not stop most men. She also suspected, from the way he pinned her to his body and lifted her from beneath the water with such ease, that if the man in the river had wanted to take her, she would have been powerless to prevent it.

She ground her teeth, hating the small flame between her legs that flickered disloyally into life at the memory of his hands on her. No man would take her in the manner the men of York had joked about heroes taking the warrior women of legend. The Normans had taken England, but no one would conquer her.

By the time the women made their way to the refectory for the early evening meal, Sigrun had recovered her composure and Aelfhild showed no signs that she had spent the day doing anything out of the ordinary.

They crossed the cloister side by side in a silent procession with the other inmates. The women ranged in age from their teens to their mid-forties. Some had chosen the life of the veil either through a sincere devotion or in preference to what life intended for them otherwise. Others like Aelfhild and Sigrun had been placed there by guardians to safeguard them. At least one to Aelfhild's knowledge had arrived with a swelling belly and now wandered the cloisters red eyed, grieving for the child she had given up. No spoke of how they viewed their home.

Only Sigrun knew that to Aelfhild the place was a prison rather than a sanctuary.

The bell tolled for the second time. The women quickened their pace. Hilde, the prioress, disliked lateness. She ran her establishment with an iron hand, perhaps hoping one day to be spoken of with the same reverence as her namesake at Whitby was.

Midreth, leading the procession, reached the heavy wooden door to the refectory and pushed it open. Instead of the oppressive silence that usually greeted them a male voice boomed out.

'I have not travelled all this way to be thwarted at the last! I respectfully ask, *again*, that you bring her to my presence at once!'

Aelfhild reeled. Her limbs became water. The voice was unmistakable, the tone of exasperation equally familiar, the demand for *her* to be brought more dreadful than any other utterance she had heard. The Norman was here and he was looking for her.

How had he discovered where she was? More than that, why? The small injury she had caused him with her pin could not have been enough to warrant seeking her out to demand vengeance. Vomit rose in her throat. She should run. Leave the priory and hide somewhere where he could not mete out a punishment. Possible places to shelter filled her thoughts, but she knew as she thought it that such an idea was impossible.

Midreth turned and looked back at her companions in alarm. 'What should we do?'

Seeing that she was not the only one startled by the unexpected male invasion of their female domain gave Aelfhild the courage she had briefly lacked, and her legs regained some of their solidity. Now she was furious that her first impulse had been to escape rather than to confront her adversary. She had been tested and found wanting.

Straightening her back, she slid a glance to Sigrun to see if she had noticed Aelfhild's reaction, but she was whispering with the two novices and had seemingly not seen anything untoward in Aelfhild's behaviour. No one had.

The prioress was replying to the visitor's unsettling demand in her low, firm voice. Aelfhild couldn't make out her words, but her tone was decisive.

'We should go in,' the woman standing behind Aelfhild whispered.

There were murmurs of agreement. Everyone apart from Aelfhild was curious to discover the owner of the voice.

'Why hasn't the message arrived? A letter bearing news of my arrival should have been sent a week ago!' the Norman replied angrily. 'Why are you not expecting me?'

Aelfhild's shoulders sagged with relief and she almost laughed aloud. When they had met, he had mentioned that he was travelling. He was not here for her and their meeting had been coincidental. She would slip away and he would never know she was here at all. She turned to go, but Sigrun seized her arm and pulled her towards the doorway. Reluctantly Aelfhild followed.

The women crept into the refectory and made their way on silent feet to the back of the long, high-ceilinged room. The Norman was standing in front of the fire with Hilde. That he had succeeded in gaining entry this far into the building was notable in itself. Most visitors were admitted no further than the porch. Hilde protected her domain fiercely—an elderly, tiny woman whose size belied her strength of will and strength of arm. She came barely up to the Norman's chest. Her head was tilted back, his forward as they stood face to face in a manner that reminded Aelfhild of pieces on a *hnefatafl* board. Which player would withdraw first was anyone's guess.

Aelfhild bowed her head in what she hoped would pass as modesty and peeked out at him from under her veil. Three more novices whose turn it was that day to prepare the meals had been carrying food to the tables, but now gave up all pretence that they were ignoring the spectacle and joined Aelfhild's group. Aelfhild followed the cluster and stood in the corner of the room behind the others, hoping to remain unnoticed.

'I receive many messages. Until I know who you claim to be from, how should I know if you speak the truth?' the prioress said calmly. 'I most certainly will not release any woman from my care other than to the designated person.'

The Norman gave a cold laugh. He delved inside his cloak and brought out a leather pouch on a long cord. He tipped the contents into his left hand, then held up a large ring. It glinted gold in the shaft of late afternoon light that streamed through the high window.

'I may have no letter to prove my legitimacy, but perhaps this will secure your co-operation. The seal of Gilbert du Rospez, knight of King William.'

A soft murmur rippled through the women, this time with a hint of warmth. A Norman, but a noble one. A rich one, perhaps. The ring had done nothing to melt Hilde's frostiness. She waved a hand at the gathered women to silence them.

'The name means nothing to me. Why should

I send away one of my charges on the sight of a seal?'

The Norman seemed to pause. Perhaps it took time to translate the meaning to his own tongue. He folded his arms. 'What if I was to tell you I was the owner as well as the bearer?'

'Is that what you claim?' Hilde stared at the Norman. 'Do you bear the name as well as the seal?'

'Would it make a difference?' the Norman asked sardonically.

'I am not foolish enough to bring the wrath of our King on my establishment. I have seen how you Normans deal with resistance. Are you Gilbert du Rospez,' Hilde snapped, 'or are you merely a rogue who has come by this seal by foul means?'

The Norman lapsed into silence. He seemed to be battling with some inner turmoil, then came to a decision. He folded his arms and jutted out his chin.

'I am du Rospez. Now, tell me, who is my bride?'

The word *bride* caused the women to burst out once more in a riot of talking. Even Hilde's curt demand for silence did nothing to quell the noise. Sigrun slipped a trembling hand into Aelfhild's, who pressed it tightly. Aelfhild glanced around in her scorn, wrinkling her nose in distaste that such news could excite the women.

Hadn't their fathers, brothers, lovers been cut down by men such as this? Were others so keen to be released from confinement here that such a possibility could excite them? She would rather live the span of her life as a solitary anchoress than marry such a hated enemy.

'Not tonight,' Hilde said firmly. 'As you can see we now have an audience and this is no longer the private matter I intended it to be. I shall not name the girl under these circumstances. Neither will you name her, or I shall have you turned out instantly.'

She looked into the Norman's face and a serene smile graced her lips. As much as Aelfhild resented the punishments Hilde had bestowed on her for various misdemeanours, at this moment she felt nothing but admiration for the prioress.

The Norman tossed his head back in annoyance. In profile the kink in his nose was obvious. His hair had dried to a lighter brown and was now pushed back behind his ears where it brushed around his collar. His bearded jaw masked his age, but he could have been anything from twenty-five to forty. He was imposingly tall and broad, but now he was dressed in a good cloak of dark-brown wool and his hair was dry, he did not look half as monstrous as he had in the river. Aelfhild could not help but smile at how foolish she had been. No wonder he had mocked her in such a demeaning way when she declared him to be a dwarf. She mocked herself inwardly now.

The Norman glanced around him and took notice of the women for the first time. He took three strides towards them, but stopped halfway across the room as a collective murmur of apprehension swelled.

His eyes roved over the huddle of women appraisingly, settling briefly on each one in turn. He paused longest on Godife, a handsome, dark-haired woman in her late twenties. His eyes crinkled at the corners in obvious appreciation before he moved on. His eyes slid over Sigrun without pausing to where Aelfhild stood behind her in the shadow.

Invisible claws tightened around Aelfhild's throat as their eyes met. She was unable to tear her gaze away as the tightness eased and the claws became fingers, caressing her neck in a manner that sent her stomach spinning. When the Norman had surprised her in the river his gaze had been unsettling enough. Now it caused her blood to turn hot in her belly.

The Norman's eyes widened in surprised recognition. A smile flickered across his lips, drawing the scar to one side in a crooked manner that did not diminish the appeal of it. He raised an eyebrow. Panic washed over Aelfhild, obliterating the shameful desire that had reared within her. He was going to reveal that they had already met. She shook her head ever so slightly, sending a desperate plea with her eyes for him not to give away her secret. He closed his lips and reached up with his left hand to brush a lock of hair awkwardly back from his cheek.

His eyes never left Aelfhild's. The dark-lashed depths that commanded her attention were the colour of burned oak and impossible to break free from even at the distance between them, to the extent that Aelfhild almost forgot his crooked nose and scarred lip. She twisted her skirt in clammy hands, wondering how someone who by rights should be disconcerting to behold could be at the same time so enticing. She decided his eyes were the source of the disconcerting effect he had on her. Currently, they were deeply thoughtful.

Please, don't, Aelfhild mouthed. She shook her head once more and took a small step backwards.

Slowly, deliberately, the Norman lowered one eyelid, then raised it. He was winking at her! He held her with one final penetrating look before he turned his eyes from her. Aelfhild felt a flush of alarm spread across her throat and chest that by entreating him to keep her secret she had placed herself in his debt.

'One of these women is the maiden I seek. Am I correct?' the Norman asked. 'Let me meet her at least.'

It was halfway between an entreaty and an order and Aelfhild's interest was piqued. He did not seem overly comfortable issuing commands.

The prioress was granite faced. 'You see the uproar you have caused. You shall cause no more on this day. I have no proof you are who you say you are or that what you tell me is true. Until I do, you will not remove any of the women who have been entrusted to my care.'

The Norman looked again at the ring in his hand. He closed his fist over it, squared his shoulders and set his feet. A soldier's stance. Aelfhild realised that she alone was looking at the man holding the ring and he was looking back at her once more. Unsettled to find his eyes on her again, she lowered her head and modestly pulled her long veil closer around her shoulders and face. The Norman slowly turned his head to face Hilde.

'Then I will wait. May I have a room here or will I have to spend the night in the open?'

Hilde pursed her lips. 'I am bound by laws of hospitality to offer you shelter for the night, but until the message arrives from the girl's home I shall not present her to you. I bind you, too, not to name the girl until that time.'

The Norman's rugged face twisted with irritation, but then he did something unexpected. He bowed deeply to Hilde, took her hand and lifted it to his lips briefly.

'In your house I shall abide by your wishes, lady prioress.'

Hilde's face softened and a hint of cream touched her milk-white cheeks. Oh, he was cunning, this Norman!

'I shall provide you with quarters in our guest rooms. You may bathe and I will have food sent across.'

'Thank you. I have bathed already, but a meal will be welcome.' Once more the Norman's eyes flickered to where Aelfhild stood. Unbidden, her lips began to curve into a smile and for a moment they felt like compatriots, their shared secret a private amusement. She pressed her lips together firmly.

Oblivious to this, Hilde continued. 'In the morning we shall talk again and see if we can come to some arrangement. Let me escort you there.'

Hilde folded her hands and walked serenely down the centre of the refectory, heading for the small door at the end that led to the outside court-yard. The Norman followed, taking long, easy strides and moving with a languorous grace. He slowed as he neared the women, passing so close to Aelfhild she could reach a hand out and touch him. Could stroke her fingers down his tunic where his broad frame tapered to a lean waist and feel the muscles concealed beneath the cloth. A shudder went through her.

His eyes slid rapidly sideways to land on her once more and he paused for a heartbeat. Had she inadvertently spoken her secret thoughts aloud or were they evident on her face? Shocked at the thought he could discern the unseemly acts she was imagining, she lowered her head and held her breath, only releasing it when he had left the room and disappeared from her presence.

Aelfhild leaned against the wall. Her legs were distressingly shaky and the cold stone did noth-ing to ease the heat that curled about her throat. She realised Sigrun was talking to her, pulling at her arm.

'You're white as ash!'

'That was the man from the river.' She was finding it hard to speak without her voice shaking.

Sigrun began to speak, but at that moment

Hilde returned. She stopped in front of the gathered women.

'Why are you not in your seats? Have you forgotten yourselves so much that you are happy to let the food you are graced with turn cold! Be along now, all of you.'

The women settled at their places. Aelfhild barely registered the customary prayers of thanks for the watery gruel. Meals were eaten in silence. Usually Aelfhild disliked this, missing the easy laughter and discussion that had filled Herik and Emma's house. Now she relished the silence because it meant she was safe from having to make conversation. The meal ended and the women rose to begin their final tasks of the night. Sigrun was the last to leave the table and Hilde drew her aside.

'Our guest needs serving. Take him bread and stew. He already has wine.'

Aelfhild lingered as she piled the bowls on to the table.

'Why me?' Sigrun whispered, voice sticking in her throat.

'I do not have to explain my reasons to you. Don't speak to him. If he tries to talk to you, ignore him.'

The prioress swept out. Sigrun looked close to tears. 'I can't do it. He looks too terrifying.'

The thought of being alone with him made Aelfhild's stomach churn with a mixture of trepidation and desire. She doubted Sigrun felt the desire, only the fear.

'I'll go instead. Keep out of sight in the courtyard so Hilde doesn't realise you disobeyed her.'

Aelfhild filled a bowl from the large pot on the table and balanced a hunk of bread on the rim. She paused outside the quarters outside the main building where the occasional guests were housed. She could pretend she was doing a favour to her mistress, but for once Sigrun's feelings took second place to her own. She wanted to see the Norman again.

Chapter Four

Guilherm sat at the low table, a goblet of weak wine in his right hand. He had removed his cloak and scraped the bristles from his face in warm water and now he was hungry. He was trying to keep his irritation in check by observing a hole in the corner of the room where a mouse had scuttled beneath the floorboards on his arrival. He was placing private bets whether the animal would appear before the prioress deigned to send a servant to provide him with food. He suspected from the expression on her face when she had left him in the sparsely furnished lodging that the mouse would win.

He did not mind eating alone. Solitude was preferable to watching people stare while they pretended they weren't. The light through the small window was fading rapidly and the single rush light that he had been given would leave him in darkness before long.

Gui cursed his luck. Until he found himself publicly claiming the false identity he had not been sure whether he would actually carry through with Gilbert's suggestion to impersonate him. If Lady Emma had written to forewarn of his arrival as she had been supposed to do he would have had no need, but clearly she had continued with her intention of making it as hard as possible for Gilbert to retrieve her daughter. Now Guilherm would have to continue the deception until the prioress decided he would be allowed to take the girl away with him.

He thought back to the huddle of women who had witnessed the scene and wondered which of them the girl was. He cast his mind's eye along the line of women, remembering the shock that had coursed through him when he saw the river sprite again. He should have guessed from the shapeless grey tunic that she had removed that she was an inhabitant of the priory.

He thought further back to the vision of her delicate figure sheathed in the clinging wet linen that had so exquisitely shown off all she had to offer. It had been years since a woman had woken any sense of excitement in Gui and the invisible hand that had pulled his guts out through his chest was alarming in its violence. He drained the goblet and closed his eyes, imagining he had met the girl under other circumstances when he was not so repulsive.

He became so lost in the fantasy that the sudden, demanding rap at the door made him jump. His food had arrived and the mouse had lost the bet after all.

'Come in.'

The door opened and let in a draught that whistled around his neck and midriff. He gave a slight shiver and spoke without turning.

'Come in and close the door behind you. The night is chillier than the day promised it would be.'

The door banged shut with surprising violence. Gui looked over his shoulder and found himself face to face with the girl from the river. She had appeared at the point when Gui's imagination had her on a bed in a state of arousal and a position that would make her blush to learn. A *frisson* rippled through him at the knowledge she had no idea what he was thinking.

Unlike the look of ecstatic abandon his imagination had conjured for her, however, the river girl's face bore the angry expression she had worn during that encounter. Her pale eyes bored into his. She held a wooden bowl in her outstretched hands and had moved no further from the door. Gui realised she was waiting for him to say something.

He gave a rueful grin as he realised his manners were sadly lacking now he was no longer in company, then forced it from his face as he realised it could look as though he was grimacing. He cleared his throat.

'Greetings again, little water sprite.'

She gave him another evil look. Any thoughts Gui had been harbouring that she had come to thank him for keeping her secret vanished.

'I preferred you when you were using your pretty eyes to beg me to deny our previous acquaintance,' he said wryly. 'Now you look as though you'd burn me on the spot if you could summon enough heat in them.'

The girl opened her mouth as if to retort, but closed it suddenly. She took a jerky step towards him. Gui indicated the bowl in her hand with a hunk of bread balanced precariously on the rim.

'For me?'

She stepped closer to the table and placed it in front of him, face still surly. Gui examined the greasy-looking stew and bread that was mostly crust without enthusiasm.

'Thank you. I'm sure I'll enjoy it.'

She snorted in a manner that implied she believed differently and for the first time her face lost some of the surliness. Gui broke a small morsel of the bread between his gloved fingers. Dipping it into the bowl caused unidentifiable chunks to rise and sink beneath the surface. The stew did little to soften the hard bread and the taste was as unpleasant as he had anticipated.

'I can see why you were trying for a fish with this waiting for you here.'

She didn't speak, but at his second reference to their previous meeting a hint of pink crept across her alabaster cheeks. The flush of colour suited her. She'd spent too much time inside. A couple of weeks in the Breton sunshine would give her the rosy glow that Gui remembered from the girls in his childhood.

She had been lingering by the table, close to Gui's side, but as he picked up the spoon she walked to the door, still without speaking. He had spoken more with her than he had to anyone since leaving York. Though he avoided company if possible he couldn't face another evening feeling homesick for Brittany and lonely.

'Wait!'

She twisted her head to look over her shoulder at Gui. Her spine curved in a sinuous line from neck to waist, emphasising her slender figure.

'You could keep me company while I eat.'

Her eyes shifted to the sheathed sword that Gui had left propped against the second stool when he had removed it. Stung by her obvious wariness he reached across and slung it on to the bed at the far wall.

'You're perfectly safe with me. I've been travelling alone for days and would appreciate some company.'

She turned to face him, halfway between the door and the table with her hands folded before her.

'I didn't realise this was a silent order.'

'It isn't.'

She blurted the words so quickly Gui half-thought he had imagined them. She lapsed into silence immediately, looking as surprised as Gui felt that she had spoken at all.

Gui beckoned her to the table and pushed the free stool out with his toe. She slid on to it, perching on the edge and looking as if she would fly away at any moment. Her head was bent, but Gui could see her eyes were fixed on his hands as they moved from the bowl to his mouth and back.

A normal man—one graced with manners and the noble heritage Gui was pretending to possess—would have removed his gloves to eat. Gui's left glove was sturdy enough that he could hold the bowl steady so he did not have the embarrassment of seeing it sliding across the table, but being watched with such scrutiny emphasised the self-consciousness that had plagued him since his hand had been taken. He had no intention of revealing his deformity to the truculent girl who seemed so lacking in the art of hospitality. Let her wonder at his lack of manners.

Her lips twitched and she curled them inwards, biting the bottom one at the left side in almost the exact place where Gui's own lips had split and been forced crookedly back together. Gui folded his arms across his chest. He leaned back against the wall. The girl continued to stare at the bowl. Presumably anything was better than looking at Gui's ruined face. He regretted now having asked her to stay. Solitude was better than silence and an unwilling companion.

'Why won't you talk to me? Did your soaking earlier cause you to lose your voice?'

She dragged her eyes away from his hands to finally meet his eyes. At least she was no longer glaring.

'We've all been told not to speak to you.'

'You're speaking to me now,' Gui pointed out triumphantly.

She gave him an evil look, furious at being tricked.

'Only because to not answer your questions

would be rude. I wouldn't do otherwise. I won't do again.'

'You heard me tell your prioress why I'm here.'

She nodded.

'Aren't you curious which of your companions I'm looking for? I suppose there is no way I can persuade you to help me identify the woman I am here for.'

She scowled. 'Why would I help you take a woman forcibly from her home?'

'I will find out anyway.'

'You'll do it without my help.'

Gui smiled. 'Do you know where I had travelled from when we met each other?'

Another shake of the head.

'I came from York.'

The girl drew a sharp breath. His words were significant to her. She knew the woman who came from there. She quickly rearranged the bowl and goblet on the table, eyes firmly on what she was doing. Gui gave a curt laugh, devoid of humour, and settled back on the stool, leaning against the wall and crossing his arms.

'Did you volunteer to serve me or were you sent?'

'I was sent,' she admitted cautiously. 'Why?'

'I thought you might have been coming here

to thank me for not revealing how we met. Is that why you came?'

'No, I did not!'

He licked his lips and grinned.

'Do many of the women here spend their time dancing around in fields and singing to themselves? It seems out of keeping with the devoutness of your choice of life.'

The girl paled and muttered something beneath her breath. Gui couldn't be certain, but thought he heard the word *choice*.

'I wonder if this frostbitten welcome is because of who I am,' he pondered aloud, 'or whether the same would be extended to any man who dared enter this female sanctuary.'

'Sanctuary!'

The word exploded from the girl with the violence of an arrow loosed from a bow. She pushed herself from the stool, knocking it over in the process, and spun away from the table. She faced the slit of window, eyes turned towards it. The window was large enough to admit light into the cell, but high enough to prevent the occupant viewing the world beyond. Her hands were by her side as she craned her neck, her fingers curling and uncurling at her skirts.

She wore the same shapeless grey garment she had removed by the river that hid the figure

Gui had so recently been enjoying remembering. The veil she wore masked her hair and acted as a frame for a pair of angular cheekbones and a shapely jaw, but was not as heavy or austere as that worn by the prioress or the nuns who had attended her. Her clothes were plain, but not the habit of a nun or sister so she had not yet taken holy orders, if she ever intended to. He imagined sliding his hand slowly beneath the unsightly garment, running his fingertips lightly up her slender body and easing it off her until she was clad only in the clinging shift she had worn in the river. He reeled. Blinked away the vision that had struck him so unexpectedly.

Careful to make no sound that might disturb her, but desperate to draw closer, Gui pushed himself from the stool and stood beside her. She flinched, shoulders tensing as she became aware of his presence, but did not shy away. Gui followed her gaze. He was taller than she, but even he was barely able to make out the courtyard beyond the window and nothing beyond the high wall.

He remembered the joy that had filled her voice as she sang and the carefree way she had danced along the riverbank. He stepped a little closer, turning so that he was standing opposite her. She faced him with the same obstinate manner that had been apparent when she had squared up to him in the river.

'If this is a sanctuary, it is from men like you,' the girl snarled. 'Normans who brutalised the countryside at your King's orders!'

Gui sighed. 'I told you before, I come from Brittany, further to the south and indescribably more beautiful than the flat north coast that our King hails from.'

'It's all the same to me,' she snapped. 'Men are the same wherever they are from and who can tell the difference between men from whichever part of France when they are raping and slaughtering the English?'

'I've never raped!' Gui whipped back. Slaughter in battle he would admit to, but he had never been guilty of defilement.

'I felt your—your body! In the river when you dragged me under the water.'

Despite his outrage at what amounted to an accusation of attempted violation, Gui felt a flicker of amusement. She was truly innocent if she thought that the slight swelling that had brushed against her was the sign of a man's arousal! If the water hadn't been so cold she'd have had a lot more to remark on. That was one part of his body he felt no shame over, at least.

He was not going to let her barefaced slander go unchallenged, however.

'What I was doing was bathing, as I've told you before, and I didn't drag you under to grope you. Besides, what you felt was a natural response. Don't flatter yourself that it has anything to do with your charms, child.' He was lying. He'd dwelled on her charms enough since the glimpse of what she possessed. He hoped she couldn't see that in his eyes.

'I'm not a child. I'm almost twenty.' She sounded indignant. 'If I told them what you were doing when we met, do you think you would be allowed to stay here?'

Gui exhaled loudly. Remembering the desperation in her eyes when she had feared he might reveal where she had been, he knew it was an empty threat. He hardened his voice as he towered over her. Her eyes widened, but she did not step away.

'Shall we go together and find the prioress? Tell her you were accosted by a naked man— Breton or Norman—as you were fishing dressed only in your shift and see what difference it would make. The outcome would be the same for you, I imagine.'

They watched each other, eyes locked in challenge. They were standing closer than they had been in the river. Much closer. He could smell the slight scent of lavender, which made him want to bury his face in the soft spot behind her ear to see if she was the source of it. The room seemed to grow hotter as the intensity of her gaze held him fast.

'What would happen to you if I told the prioress?' Gui asked. 'You really didn't want me to admit to having met you, did you? I think you weren't supposed to be there.'

It was not a threat, but her eyelids flickered. Long and pale, her lashes framed those almost colourless eyes of watery blue. He remembered how he had considered she might be a simpleton when he first saw her, but her eyes blazed with a fierce intelligence that made him draw a sharp breath. She licked her lips nervously. They were wide and soft, made for kissing. He'd bedded women since coming to England, but he never kissed them, too conscious of his scarred lip. He wanted to kiss this sprite more than he'd wanted anything for a long time. Perhaps he should do it and risk the consequences. Let Gilbert return and find his bride for himself.

'If you kiss me now, I won't tell anyone how we met,' he said daringly.

'Why would I do that?'

Gui was pleased to note it was surprise rather than disgust that sang in her voice.

'So you can say you kissed a *dweorgar* and lived to tell the tale.'

She covered her mouth to hide a smile, then quick as lightning lifted on to her tiptoes, put her hands on his shoulders and pecked at his cheek. He turned his head and their lips met. It did not last more than a couple of heartbeats, but their mouths melded together, her warm lips moving in unison with Gui's and slightly parting with an eagerness that hinted at the promise of what she could offer. He sighed with longing when she broke away.

'I have to go.' She ducked past Gui and headed for the door. Gui followed, reluctant to see her leave, and rested his hand on the frame, barring her way.

'Will you tell me your name before you leave?' he asked.

'And risk getting into trouble?'

Gui reached for her hand and held it, not tight enough to hurt, but firmly so that he commanded her full attention. He rested his thumb on the inside of her wrist. Without his glove on would he feel her pulse racing beneath the skin?

'Let me go!'

'I won't tell anyone you did. I'm good at keeping secrets.'

She looked down at his hand holding her captive. With a sudden jerk of her whole body she twisted her arm, pulling away from him. She stepped back. He held on, stepping with her as she went backwards so that they were just as close. They might have been dancing rather than arguing. Slowly he uncurled his fingers far enough for the girl to slip her hand free. She stalked to the door, pausing as she got there to turn back.

'That is the last time you'll touch me. If you try it again, it will go badly for you.'

Gui inclined his head in a graceful bow as the girl hurled herself out of the cell, slamming the door behind her.

It was probably for the best. As much as he craved a further, deeper taste of those lips, tempting a novice into his bed would see him damned for certain.

It was only as Gui settled on to the straw mattress in the wooden pallet that it occurred to him the girl herself was the age of the woman he was searching for. He fell into a troubled sleep, hoping fervently she was not the one.

Aelfhild pressed her forehead and palms against the wall beside the door. Her second encounter with the strange man had been just as unsettling as the first and her heart pounded with the intensity of an army marching through her body. Her wrist tingled where his fingers had touched her, though it had not been painful at the time. The memory of his hand on hers caused her chest to tighten as though the breath was being squeezed from her ribcage. The sensation was disturbing, as much for the lack of distress it had caused her as the act itself.

She glanced to the high window, seeing light flicker as the occupant paced around the room obscuring the lamp. She half-expected him to follow and continue to wheedle information out of her about the identity of his bride. A small part of her hoped he would follow and demand another kiss, despite her insistence he should not do so. Relief fought with disappointment. Before either could win she stepped hastily away from the door, determined not to be found lingering.

She did not return to her room immediately, but instead walked to the gate and looked out at the darkened countryside beyond, wishing she could slip through the wooden bars, and considered what she had learned.

She knew the Breton was here to claim a bride, but Aelfhild had not spared any thought for who it might be beyond dismissing herself as a candidate. There were five women in the priory who had not yet taken vows and who had not come to the priory through their own choice, but the mention of York convinced her she knew whom the unlucky woman was. This nobleman must have considerable influence to be able to demand Sigrun's removal from the confines of the cloister!

Aelfhild returned to her cell in two minds whether or not to share the new information with Sigrun. By the time she pushed the door open she had decided not to. Just because the man had come from York did not mean the woman he sought also came from near the city. There was no purpose in disturbing Sigrun's peace of mind unnecessarily. All her considerations proved to be redundant because she had barely closed the door when Sigrun's arms were about her waist and her tear-wet face was pressed against Aelf-hild's neck.

'He's here for me,' Sigrun gasped through breathy sobs.

Aelfhild disentangled herself. 'You don't know that.'

Sigrun was shaking visibly. She looked as if she was about to cry once more. Aelfhild felt the same urge well up inside her.

'I do know! Hilde summoned me after I went back inside. She told me he named my mother when he arrived.'

'That devious old hag! She sent you to him on purpose!'

Sigrun looked horrified at the language, but Aelfhild hushed her attempts to remonstrate. The deference owed to the prioress was the least of her concerns at the moment. She grasped at the first comforting thought that came into her head.

'She must be mistaken. Your mother would never have consented to you marrying a man such as that.'

'Such as that!' Sigrun moaned, clutching again at Aelfhild's dress. 'He's so ugly. I would have died if Hilde had sent me to him. Is he the monster he looks? Did he hurt you at all?'

Aelfhild led her mistress to the bed and gently made her sit. She had meant the Breton's surly manner rather than the way he looked. The pulse in her wrist throbbed and she imagined she felt his leather-clad fingers encircling her wrist once more.

'He didn't hurt me,' she replied thoughtfully. 'He was—'

She struggled for the words that would capture the Breton. 'He's a man not a monster, but he's strange. He kept his gloves on even while he ate and wanted me to stay while he did. I think he was trying to discover who he was looking for. He was angry that Hilde wouldn't identify you.'

'He doesn't know who I am!' Sigrun brightened a little. 'Perhaps someone else can take my place.'

Aelfhild snorted. 'He'd know soon enough when your mother did not recognise the bride!' Besides, she thought, why should anyone else be forced to endure the path that had been set for Sigrun to follow? Sometimes she wondered how her mistress viewed the world through such eyes when Herik had been so straightforward and Lady Emma such a sensible woman.

The memory of the naked man bursting from beneath the water rose again in her memory. Aelfhild's first inkling of the possibilities of pleasure had been when she had shared covert kisses with Torwald before he had gone to his death in York's uprising. No sooner had those feelings been awoken than Aelfhild was sent to the priory with Sigrun, far from the company of any men beyond the invalids and elderly in the villages. Since then the feelings had been dormant. Remembering the way the Breton's dark eyes had pierced her, she was astonished at the fluttering tightness in her belly at the touch of this man of all people.

'Perhaps it will not be so bad once you became accustomed to him,' she ventured.

She pressed her fingertips to her lips where

they had brushed against his. They felt more sensitive to the touch, more real, more aware of the sensation than ever before, as if she had sprung awake after years of sleeping. She had kissed the *dweorgar* and survived. What impulse had caused her to carry out his suggestion, she did not fully understand, but once he had suggested it she could not have left the room without obeying.

Sigrun flung herself face down, her body trembling. 'I'd rather die than marry an enemy of our people. My mother must know that. She would not consent to this.'

Aelfhild writhed inwardly. Torwald had gone to his death trying to fend off men such as the Breton. How could Aelfhild have kissed him, much less contemplated what it would be like to repeat the act? Shame flooded her that she could entertain such thoughts about a man who had taken part in the ravishing of her country. She pushed the feelings down, despising herself as a traitor for what she had done.

Sigrun sat up again. 'Give me your knife. I know you have one. I'll slit my wrists now. I mean it!'

Aelfhild clutched her arm, aghast at what she was hearing. 'You of all people wouldn't commit such a sin!'

Sigrun sobbed louder. 'No. I couldn't. But what can I do?'

Aelfhild paced around the room, desperately seeking the words that would offer solace, but finding none. A cloud passed across the moon, momentarily darkening the sky and the river encounter once more flickered in her memory. An idea struck her that was so outrageous she wondered where it came from, but once in her brain it would not be dismissed.

'Perhaps you're right about your mother. The man said there should have been a letter, but perhaps Lady Emma never wrote one. Without a letter he has no claim.' She flung back the lid of the chest at the end of the bed and pulled out a bag.

'Start packing. We're leaving.'

Sigrun looked at her in amazement.

'We're going to York. We'll plead with your mother to intervene. If we leave before dawn, they won't discover until morning and we'll be miles away by then.' Without bothering to see Sigrun's reaction Aelfhild pulled off her voluminous tunic, slipped on a dress she had not worn since arriving and put the tunic on over the top. Sigrun gave the first weak smile Aelfhild had seen and did the same.

Aelfhild continued to pack her belongings into the bag, wrapping her jars of ointments and bundles of herbs carefully. She threw Sigrun's spare linens in as well and stripped the thin blankets from each bed, promising herself she would return what she had taken, and rolled them neatly before securing them with a length of tablet-woven braid Sigrun had brought from home.

She twisted her hair up and pinned her veil firmly in place with a long pin. Sigrun had fetched both their travelling cloaks from the peg. They faced each other for a moment. Fear brimmed in Sigrun's eyes. Hope stirred in Aelfhild's heart. They waited until they had heard no sound in the building, then a little longer just to be certain before they left the room.

The night was so late it could almost be called morning and the priory was in silence as the two women crept through the building, stopping briefly in the pantry to help themselves to a few apples and the hunks of bread intended for the pig. Cold air hit Aelfhild as she eased the door open and slipped out to the courtyard. They edged along the walls, keeping to the shadows, but there was no one around.

An angry bellow pierced the night. Aelfhild flung herself back against the wall, but no one appeared to intercept them. The cry came again. The source was the visitor's room. The Breton's voice came to them, speaking urgently in a language she could not understand. Aelfhild wondered who was with him. He gave another furious roar like a beast.

'Dweorgar,' she whispered in horror.

Aelfhild clutched Sigrun's hand and pulled her along until they reached the tree at the rear of the building and scrambled over the wall to freedom.

They ran as long as they could towards the river, then slowed to a walk that became harder. They passed buildings that had been burned in the raids by William's soldiers the previous winter. The surviving villagers—the old and the ill—had not bothered to rebuild them. Weariness threatened to overwhelm Aelfhild and she knew they couldn't go much further. It would be dawn soon and they had not slept at all. When they came across a half-collapsed hut in a field beside the river, Aelfhild pulled Sigrun inside. They dropped to the ground, wrapped themselves in blankets and assured each other they would wake at first light and be on their way.

Aelfhild had no idea what filled Sigrun's dreams, but her own were filled with a half-human beast who roared with the Breton's voice and whose mouth roved across her flesh, stealing kisses that left her powerless to resist.

Chapter Five

Guilherm awoke to the news that his bride had fled in the night.

He had slept as badly as always, waking in a tangle of sheets from horror-filled dreams in which he was lying amid the dying and dead on the battlefield. He was never sure which he was, but when he roared for help in his dreams his voice was silent. When the cautious knocking on the door woke him his first thought was that the girl from the river had returned to bring him breakfast. Her knocking had an angrier rhythm to it though. He pulled his tunic on and opened the door to discover the prioress herself standing there. Blinking in the half-light, he stood mutely as Hilde explained that his intended bride—and it took him a moment to remember that he had claimed to be Gilbert—was no longer to be found within the priory.

He cursed, then apologised, remembering where he was. The prioress acknowledged his apologies with a face of stone. She left the small room and walked to the centre of the courtyard. Gui followed, arranging his clothes and ensuring his glove was securely bound over his wrist. The sun was beginning to rise, a sight that Gui tried not to be awake for as often as possible.

'The message you spoke of arrived at first light and I sent for the girl to inform her. We discovered her absence then. I will organise a search party and have the woman returned here,' Hilde said. 'If you would be prepared to join the hunt, she may be found sooner.'

'I would gladly help, except that thanks to your refusal to introduce us last night I have no idea who I am searching for,' Gui snapped.

Hilde's eyes flicked to the floor and her face took on a strange expression. 'You have met the woman in question, though you did not realise it at the time.'

'The girl you sent with my meal last night?'

The answer showed in her eyes. Gui's heart sunk. His sprite was meant for Gilbert as he had feared.

'I spoke to her after she had returned from serving you and told her she was the woman you were seeking.'

Gui's fist clenched. 'Why did you do that?'

Hilde looked unperturbed by his anger. 'Lady Sigrun is modest and retiring. To present you tomorrow without warning would unsettle her sensibilities. I thought perhaps that if she had seen you as a courteous guest she may not be so distraught at the thought of your marriage.'

Gui pursed his lips at the term Hilde had used. He would not have described the girl using either of them, but Hilde would not be the first guardian to have been deceived as to the true nature of her ward. The girl—Lady Sigrun, as he must now think of her—had been eager for her whereabouts on the afternoon he arrived to remain a secret. Perhaps the face she presented to the world at large was indeed compliant and meek.

But anyway, he hadn't treated her with courtesy, had he? He had teased and wrangled, and threatened to reveal her secrets and wheedled a kiss out of her, until the thought of him as a husband had caused her to run. He bit back his recriminations. Even if Hilde had not warned her, Gui had attempted to hint the identity of his quarry. He was as much at fault as the prioress. Gilbert would not have failed by such a blunder. Gilbert might not have appeared such an unappealing prospect of a husband either!

'Perhaps you should have warned me what your intentions were. I might have taken the time to pay more attention to her and less to my soup.'

'She would not have welcomed your attention. I forbade her from speaking to you. I trust she obeyed me.'

'She was as compliant as I am sure anyone who knows her would expect her to be,' he said cautiously.

He felt a stirring of interest at the notion that he was privy to this secret, carefree side of her, crushed immediately beneath the knowledge that she was destined to marry his friend. She had looked on him with anger but not fear or revulsion, as few were able to do. The novelty had been refreshing, but apparently it had not been enough to prevent her fleeing from the ordeal of marriage to him. Even after she had kissed him. Perhaps because of that.

'I'll gladly join the search. Do you have any idea where she might have gone?'

'At present, no. The sisters take alms and minister to the old and sick who were lucky enough to survive William's destruction of their homes. We'll start by searching those villages.'

Gui looked towards the heavy gate, guarded by a stout, fierce-faced portress. He had difficulty imagining how the slightly built girl had heaved it open. Hilde followed his look.

'That's not how she left. That gate is never opened after dark. We have no idea how she escaped.'

Escaped! The prioress's description reminded him of the way the girl had retorted with scorn at his description of the priory as a sanctuary.

'You're certain she has left?' Gui asked. 'She isn't merely hiding?'

'Yours was the last room that had not been searched.' Her eyes bored into him accusingly. Gui wondered if she had expected his bride to be found in his bed. The unfairness of the suspicion struck him, mingled with regret that he had not managed to tempt the girl to stay with him and relief that he had not bedded his friend's betrothed.

'If you spoke to her, you know she left me last night,' he said.

'Then she is no longer anywhere in the priory,' Hilde agreed.

Gui stalked round the perimeter of the courtyard and behind the main building until he came to a gnarled tree that leaned over from outside the wall. The branches were low enough for a determined woman to jump for. He ran his fingers over the rocks that had been piled and fit-

ted methodically to create a wall. There were few
gaps, but a small shoe could dig into the cracks
and gain a foothold. He pictured the girl hauling
her lithe frame upwards, feet scrabbling against
the rough stone wall, hands clinging on as she
disappeared to freedom, and a touch of admiration crept over him.

Gui's arms were strong, even if he had no hand
at the end of one. He took a jump and heaved
himself up with the branch in the crook of his
elbows until he was high enough to peer over
the wall. From the direction he faced this was
how the girl had returned from their encounter
yesterday.

'Those branches will be gone before the day
is out. No other girl will follow her lead, I can
assure you!' Hilde said grimly.

'What would I find if I took the path of the
river in that direction?' Gui asked, still looking
out to where the river glinted in the distance. He
lowered himself. 'Is there a village?'

Hilde agreed there was. Gui's scalp prickled.
'Then that's the direction I'll search.'

He might be entirely wrong but if there was
a chance the girl had retraced her steps past the
scene of their encounter he wanted to be the one
to find her.

'They'll be brought back and I'll make sure

they're both sorry they dared to act with such contempt.' Hilde turned to him with a gleam in her eyes. 'You'll have your bride, but she'll be missing the skin of her backside!'

Gui gave her a cold smile, disliking her intensely.

'Have my horse readied. I'll leave immediately.'

He rode fast, outstripping the searchers who were on foot or rode mules. Every hut or makeshift shelter he encountered was empty, or occupied by vagrants who did not welcome his intrusion. There was no sign of the girl by the river where they had first met, or in the hamlet where she must have visited. The only inhabitants were old men and a couple of women who eyed him with open hostility. All denied knowing Lady Sigrun or having seen her passing by.

Guilherm determined that he would ride in his present direction alongside the river until midday, then cut back and start searching the woods. He was starting to give up hope when he spied two cloaked and hooded figures walking side by side carrying rolls of baggage in the distance. He could no longer fire a bow, but his archer's keen eyesight had not diminished. He slowed to a trot and dismounted to follow them from a distance. His patience was rewarded when the shorter figure lowered her hood to reveal the familiar blonde head.

Gui stopped himself from crying out and pulled his horse's head sharply, taking cover in the sparse clump of trees. He looked again to confirm he was not seeing things, but sure enough, there was the girl who he now knew to be Gilbert's bride.

Lady Sigrun. Jealousy prickled him and he could hardly bear to form her name silently. He had never entertained the thought that she might be his, but knowing she belonged to his friend was a harder blow than he had expected it to be. He stifled his regret. The other figure must be the companion the prioress had mentioned. Gui watched with interest, getting the measure of the women.

His woman—no, not his, he cautioned himself regretfully—*Gilbert's woman* yawned and stretched her arms high and wide, throwing her head back. She spoke to her friend, then scurried to the river, hoisted up her skirts and squatted down in the reeds. Gui turned his head rapidly, caught by surprise at seeing her in such a private act.

He looped his reins over a tree branch, chose a different tree and dealt with the same need Lady

Sigrun was dealing with. A surreptitious glance over his shoulder assured him Lady Sigrun had finished her business. She stood and adjusted her skirts. Gui walked slowly towards her, keeping into the treeline where he hoped she would not notice him. She knelt and rinsed her hands in the stream, then splashed her face and removed a long pin from her veil, letting her hair fall free. Still kneeling, she took a comb from the pouch at her waist and began to run it through her hair until it gleamed and tumbled down her back, before pinning her veil on and turning her comb on her companion's deeper-blonde tresses.

Gui's stomach curled with longing to bury his face deep into the pale mass and drink in the scent of her. He wiped the smile from his lips. There was no time to admire the scene and the women would not be so calm for long once he made his presence known and captured her. He ground his teeth in irritation at being placed in this position. He had half a mind to let them go and give the lady the freedom she so clearly wanted.

He might have done so, but realised at that moment he was not alone in watching them. As he crouched in hiding another man appeared through the trees a little closer, a rough-looking man with grizzled grey hair on his cheeks and head, and tattered clothes. The man drew to a stop almost parallel with Gui and scanned the river. When he noticed the women he gave a low whistle of appreciation followed by a cackle. He fiddled at his belt and Gui saw a dull-bladed dagger appear in his hand. Gui didn't know whether the man had rape or theft in mind and did not intend to wait to discover which. The man began to move stealthily towards his prey. Gui moved, too, and intercepted the would-be attacker. He seized the man around the neck from behind with his right arm and pulled him backwards off balance, dropped him, then brought his right fist around to box the man about the forehead. The man struggled, but a series of swift sharp blows had him slumping to the floor unconscious. Gui released him and prodded his victim with the toe of his boot. The man groaned. Satisfied he would live, Gui took the knife and slipped it into his belt. He stood, looked towards the river and straight into the face of Lady Sigrun.

She stood frozen, an expression of horror on her face. Gui took a step towards her and she cried out, 'Run!'

The other girl lost no time in picking up her skirts and running towards the remains of a hut a little distance from the riverbank. Gui's quarry ran instead towards him, fists raised.

'Leave us alone!'

As he had done to the would-be attacker, Gui ducked, slipped behind her and wrapped his arm around her torso, pinioning her to him. The girl cried out, more in anger at being restrained than from fear. Her body went limp and she dropped to her knees, slithering down and out of his grasp like a fish sliding sinuously from a net. Surprised, Gui dropped with her and managed to tighten his hold enough to prevent her escaping this time with both arms coming firmly around her waist. He rarely used his disfigured arm. She tried to wrench herself free from his grip, but he held tight, spreading his legs to straddle her.

'I told you never to touch me again,' she cried. 'Take your hands off me, you *waggot*! You cur! You torturer of innocent women!'

She bucked and squirmed in his arms, back arching and pressing against his chest, head grinding into the curve of his shoulder. Her hair smelled of rosemary and his breath caught in his throat as he drank it in. To be so close to her for the second time in as many days set Gui's senses aflame.

'I'm not going to hurt you,' he whispered urgently into her ear, his lips close enough to feel the softness of her skin. It was all he could do not to skim his tongue from the delicate lobe down her neck.

'I'll hurt *you* if you don't let me go!'

The fire was high in her cheeks. She was more fully alive now than when she had been meekly waiting on him. Gui felt a prickle of excitement grow inside him that had long lain dormant. This was a woman to be reckoned with! He didn't know whether he wanted to drop fully to his knees in worship or quench the flames of her anger into submission with kisses.

She tugged fruitlessly at his arms, but was unable to part them. His left hand was above his right so she concentrated on that and clawed at the glove. The leather was thick and even had it not been filled with wool, it would have had no effect as she dug her nails in. Gui laughed.

'Don't laugh at me! I told you if you touched me again you'd regret it.'

In furious desperation the girl wrenched the pin from her veil and drove it into Gui's left glove with enough force that it went right through from back to palm. Such an action would have caused excruciating pain if he had possessed the limb she believed him to have.

Gui loosed his grip on her and twisted her round to face him. She fell forward on to her hands and knees, the veil fell and her hair spilled down. Gui lifted his hands before him so the glove that was skewered was at eye level and slowly drew the pin out, enjoying the moment of drama. He dropped it at his feet.

The girl paled, looking sick.

'What are you?'

'I'm the man who has come to take you to York,' Gui growled. 'Did you think you could evade me for ever, Lady Sigrun?'

Aelfhild gasped. No words that might come out of his mouth could have surprised her more. She tore her eyes from the monstrous hand that seemed to have mended itself by some sort of magic and looked into his eyes.

'What did you call me?'

'I called you Lady Sigrun,' the Breton said. He gave a mocking bow. 'My lady.'

'You're mistaken,' Aelfhild laughed. 'I'm not Lady Sigrun.'

'Do you think I'm stupid?' the man growled. 'I'm not going to let you go just because you deny who you are. How many women do you think escaped from the priory and are running around the countryside this morning? Besides, your prioress told me who you are.'

'That's what she told you?'

The man ground his teeth. 'Yes. She told me she purposefully sent my bride to me last night and when I mentioned York last night I saw how you reacted. So, you will excuse me if I choose to disbelieve your denials, *Lady Sigrun*.'

'But I'm—' She stopped abruptly. The reason for his error struck Aelfhild in a flash. Hilde had sent Sigrun to him, but Aelfhild had gone in her mistress's place. What else was the man supposed to think?

'With such evidence as you have laid out, who else could I be?' she agreed.

His full lips twisted into a smile.

'Now, are you going to be sensible and come with me willingly or do I have to take you by force?' He gave her a stern look. 'I'll bundle you over my shoulder and take you like that if I have to.'

He could do it, she knew. He had strength that she was unable to match. Aelfhild sat back on to her heels, ready to spring to her feet and run if the opportunity presented itself. She glanced towards the hut where Sigrun had taken refuge. A quick glimpse of blonde told her Sigrun had been watching, but now ducked back inside. She climbed to her feet and noticed the way the Breton's eyes skimmed over her as she smoothed her skirts down. He found her attractive. Perhaps that could be a better weapon than strength. If Aelfhild could lead her captor back to the priory it would give Sigrun time to keep running, though she expected Sigrun would stay there rather than taking the time to escape.

'What do you intend to do now you have found me? Am I to be taken back to Byland to receive my punishment and suffer Hilde's disapproval?' She allowed her lips to tremble plaintively.

'I'd rather not,' he said, 'and I doubt you're really eager to return to face a whipping.'

'So you'll let us leave?' Aelfhild asked hopefully. Their eyes met. She reached a hand out in supplication and laid it on his broad chest. She had intended the gesture to stir *his* heart, so was unprepared for the jolt of desire that raced through her body at the feel of his firm muscles beneath her palm. His eyes widened in surprise, then he blinked and shook his head as if waking from a sleep.

'Absolutely not! I'm certainly not going to let you out of my sight now I've found you!' His expression hardened. 'And while we're on that matter, how stupid are *you* to be running in the middle of the night with no one to protect you! You're lucky it was me who found you rather than someone intent on causing you ill.'

A scolding about her well-being was the last thing Aelfhild had expected. Anger simmered in his voice. Her heart ceased to beat, then raced at double speed to make up for it. She forced her face to show nothing, but wanted to run. His brown eyes now looked as though they belonged in the face of a wolf about to devour a lamb. She would not be the lamb he slaughtered. His concern was motivated by his wish to see his bride safe after all. She gazed back unblinking, determined to appear unaffected by his attempt to intimidate her or the intimacy they had unexpectedly shared.

'No one is causing me ill except you by trying to take me back against my will.'

He laughed, then his expression darkened. 'Is that what you think? Shall I show you otherwise?'

He seized her by the upper arm and tried to pull her after him. When she resisted he bent and lifted her off her feet, hefting her over his broad shoulder with ease. He marched back along the riverbank, ignoring her protests, and set her on her feet.

'See for yourself, my lady,' he commanded. He spun her around so that she had her back against his chest, his voice rasping in her ear. 'You thought you were alone, but you were far from it.'

A man lay twisted in the grass. At first Aelfhild feared he was dead, but he gave a rasping breath and she realised he was merely unconscious.

'Who is he?' she asked.

The Breton released her. He gave the prone man a kick in the stomach. 'His name? I don't know. He was watching you, too, and his intentions did not appear as honourable as mine. I saw to it he had no chance to try them and took this from him.'

Aelfhild hugged herself. She had not been aware that anyone was watching them at all. The Breton pulled a *seax* from his belt, the blade rusted and the handle wound round with twine, and held it in front of her eyes. 'I'll leave it to you to decide how he might have used this on you.'

Aelfhild recoiled instinctively then reached out and took hold of the weapon. She was annoyed to see how her hand trembled, causing the weapon to quiver. She tightened her fist around it and slipped it into her belt.

'What are you doing?' The Breton's voice was sharp. 'I didn't mean for you to keep it.'

'I need something in case I need to defend myself.'

The Breton reached out and deftly removed it from her belt before she could prevent his theft. His hand brushed against her waist, causing her stomach to contract where his glove skimmed across her belly. His eyes never left hers. He stowed the *seax* downwards in his belt like a dagger rather than across as it should be worn. He gave the man a final kick.

'If you have a weapon it can be used against you, especially one so easy to steal. If you need defending, I'll be the one to do it.'

A shiver ran down Aelfhild's spine as the intensity in his voice burned into her, reaching deep down as if the words were an embrace, not an admonishment.

'I owe you thanks for what you did, but it doesn't mean I have to submit to you now.'

He gave an exaggerated sigh. 'What will you do? Run again? Spend your life fleeing from marriage? Lose your virtue and get your throat cut by the next rogue who takes a fancy to you? You should let me take you back to the priory.'

'If you would leave me there I might, but you'll take me to York, won't you.'

'Yes.' The Breton scowled. 'You've caused me trouble indeed. If we have to go back and forth to the priory we'll be delayed another day in getting to Haxby.'

Aelfhild glared at Sigrun's bridegroom. She could go with him back to the priory and give Sigrun chance to escape, but suspected Sigrun would stay exactly where she was. In the unlikely event she did decide to continue the journey alone she would most likely suffer the fate he had described. A home this man was intent on taking her to anyway. A daring thought began to take root in Aelfhild's mind. She forced a smile.

'We're already close to the road to York. If I consent to come with you willingly, will you send a message to the priory and not take me back there? We set off for York from here?'

'Why?'

He was watching her closely. Now she had time to study him close up, Aelfhild saw the shrewd intelligence in his eyes. She felt a little of the fight go out of her. Disconcertingly it was replaced by a sensation that was far from expected or welcome.

A bitter taste filled her mouth. This man had conquered her country and intended to take her as his wife, yet she could not ignore the desire that surged inside her at his touch. Yes, he was alarming with his crooked nose and scarred mouth, but eyes that meltingly brown could make a woman forget the faults. She was still not entirely convinced he was human, with his unnatural hand that she could stab without causing him pain, but if he was determined to take Sigrun to York he could act as escort and guardian to the women. They would use him as he would no doubt use them in return.

Aelfhild dropped her smile. It would not do to appear too eager. She stuck out her lip and pouted. It came more naturally than the smile did anyway.

'I can't escape from you, you're too strong, too fast and too cunning. I'm just a poor maiden with no protector.'

The Breton raised his eyes and gave her a sceptical look. Aelfhild wondered if she had gone too far. She gave an angry sigh. 'I don't like it, but if my fate lies in Haxby then that is where I must go.'

The Breton pursed his lips. 'If you're trying to trick me...'

'No tricks, I promise,' Aelfhild said earnestly. 'It seems stupid to double back, and besides, I'd rather escape whatever punishment Hilde metes out.'

He narrowed his eyes. 'I might not want to take you back there, but I should. You've agreed more easily than I expected. There will be no more attempts to abscond?'

'None.' Her eyes strayed to the groaning man on the ground and a genuine chill ran over her body. She stepped back and in the process moved a little closer to the Breton. She looked into his face and saw concern flit across his eyes. She couldn't tell what emotion he read in hers, but he moved closer to her and let his hand linger on her shoulder before withdrawing it slowly.

'I give you my word. We shall travel together. All three of us.'

'Three?'

'My companion has to come, too.' She walked hastily past him, raising her voice as she headed to the hut so that Sigrun might hear what she had to say. 'I can't send her back and I won't leave her here. You would not expect a noble lady such as myself to travel unaccompanied and unchaperoned, even with the man who is to be my husband. *Especially* not with the man who I am to marry. A lord such as yourself should understand that, unless you think we are savages up north?'

'Aelfhild! Where are you, girl?' she called. Remembering she was the noblewoman now, she added an edge to her voice that Lady Emma used. It seemed unjust to use it on Sigrun, who in fairness had never demanded anything of Aelfhild beyond companionship, but she felt it vital enough that Sigrun understood her plan. 'Come out and attend to me at once!'

Sigrun's head appeared from the doorway. She looked at Aelfhild in confusion at hearing the strange cries.

Do as I say, Aelfhild mouthed.

Sigrun glanced over Aelfhild's shoulder. Fear crossed her face.

'Don't be frightened,' Aelfhild said. 'I'm afraid my attempt to run was futile. My husband-to-be has found me. He's taking me—us—back to my mother's house.'

Sigrun's mouth became a circle of astonishment. Her head ducked back inside, then reappeared, closely followed by her body.

Aelfhild heard a sharp intake of breath from behind her. Aelfhild knew without turning what expression she would see on the face of the man behind her. Aelfhild's hair was flax. Sigrun's was summer wheat. Her eyes were the blue of a summer sky, not a winter stream. She had a womanly figure and her father's height. Aelfhild almost changed her plan.

'Here is your true bride,' she should say. *'See what a beauty you have really won.'*

She couldn't do that to Sigrun, though. It was not her fault she was beautiful and, in truth, it had never before this moment bothered Aelfhild to consider herself less so.

'This is the Lady Aelfhild, my companion.' She turned to the Breton who was, as she had predicted, gazing at Sigrun. She realised at that point that she could not remember his name, though he had given it to Hilde in front of the women. Embarrassed, she looked at him questioningly. 'And you are?'

The Breton tore his eyes from Sigrun's form.

'Gui,' he murmured, as if waking from a dream.

Aelfhild wrinkled her forehead. That did not sound quite right. The Breton blinked and took a step towards her.

'Gui—Guil—Sir Gilbert du Rospez.' He bowed deeply to both women. 'Pardon me, I was not thinking, merely remembering a childhood diminutive. I am Gilbert du Rospez.'

Remembering nothing! Busy ogling Sigrun, Aelfhild thought with unaccustomed envy.

'Well then, Sir Gilbert du Rospez.' She rolled the unfamiliar words around her mouth, trying out his pronunciation: *Geelberr du Rhopey.*

He said nothing for a long time. Perhaps she was mangling his tongue too badly. He gave her a smile, his misshapen lips twisting and his eyes glinting. 'It might be easier for you to call me Gui, Lady Sigrun, Lady Aelfhild.'

He inclined his head towards each woman as he spoke. Aelfhild and Sigrun exchanged a glance. Remembering to answer to the correct name was going to be a challenge!

Ghee. A little easier to say. She tried it and he smiled.

'Wait here,' Aelfhild instructed him. 'We need to gather our belongings.'

She swept past him and pulled Sigrun into the darkness of the pig shelter with her. Rapidly she began to pack their blankets while she outlined her plan in a hushed voice.

'Why did you say that you were me?' Sigrun hissed.

'I tried to tell him I wasn't, but he wouldn't believe me. He told me that Hilde had sent you to him and kept insisting I was trying to trick him. It seemed easier to agree.' Aelfhild peered outside where she could see Sir Gui pacing back and forth, guarding the entrance.

'It won't work!' Sigrun whispered. 'He'll be furious when he discovers what we've done.'

'It will. He has no reason to suspect otherwise.' She folded her arms and gave Sigrun a stern look. 'Unless you'd prefer to tell him the truth now and travel back home as his bride.'

Sigrun shook her head. Aelfhild drew her into an embrace.

'Then I'll be you and you'll be me. When we're back in Haxby who cares if he is angry at being deceived. Your mother will stop him marrying you and we'll both be safe. We have to get back there and he will keep us safe on the journey. He won't let anything happen to his bride.'

'What if he expects you to kiss him, or to lie with him?' Sigrun asked.

'I won't let him, of course! He doesn't scare me and I'll make sure he doesn't think of laying a finger on me.'

Aelfhild glanced to the door again. Sir Gui had stopped pacing and stood with his back to the doorway, arms folded and legs planted apart like a sentry. His broad frame and height blocked what little light there was. In truth, the idea of him placing his hands on her caused those unsettling emotions to rise again in her belly. She swallowed down disgust at herself. Breton or Norman, he was one of them, an enemy who was the cause of her country's plight and she had more self-respect and loyalty to England than to spend her time daydreaming what it would be like to be kissed by him for longer than a brief touch of the lips.

'He won't touch me,' she repeated, wondering whom she was trying to convince. She delved into Sigrun's bag and took the finely embroidered *fillet* that was more fitting to a noblewoman's status. She tied the band around her forehead, catching the hair back. Sigrun did the same with Aelfhild's plainer strip of cloth. A couple of finger rings passed from one woman to the other, a fine woven girdle was exchanged for the plaited one and Aelfhild looked the part of a lady. The women grinned conspiratorially.

'Let's go. We have a long journey ahead of us.'

Chapter Six

Gui had time to retrieve his horse and return to the hut in the time it took the two women to pack. He strode back and forth in front of the doorway, trying to make sense of their whispered discussion, but they spoke too quietly and rapidly for him to catch their words in the language he was still learning. They sounded as if they were at odds from the tone. He wondered if they had quarrelled over Lady Sigrun's decision to accompany him, but when the two women emerged blinking into the sunlight bearing bags and blankets after what felt like hours they held hands tightly. They had wasted time adorning themselves with belts and rings!

He had begun to grow suspicious of how long it had taken them to pack their belongings and the sight of their sparse luggage did not lessen this. He admitted to slight relief that they had not brought too much with them, which was met by expressions of stone.

'We were running away. We didn't stop to pack our embroidery.' Lady Sigrun arched an eyebrow.

Gui stifled a smile. He couldn't imagine her possessing the patience to sit still long enough to complete work. Her companion, perhaps, but not this lively woman who seemed more inclined to hurl herself about the countryside.

'Or your fishing hook?' Gui muttered as she walked past him, in a voice low enough that only she would hear. The glare he received as she whipped round to face him transformed her face, lighting her from the inside with a fury that was stunning to witness. A ripple of excitement coursed through him. She was one of those women who became more attractive and vital the more irate she was, while her companion's beauty shone at all times, whatever her expression. Gui was lost in a reverie of remembrance of their first meeting so missed her addressing him until Lady Sigrun raised her voice sharply.

'Sir Gilbert! Are you listening to me?'

He gave a start, recalling that the name temporarily belonged to him and resolved to pay more attention in future.

'I'm sorry, my mind was elsewhere. What were you saying, my lady?'

'I asked how we are to travel.'

Gui waved his hand towards the horse. The two women, now standing side by side, stared at him as if he had suggested they fly home. The servant who Lady Sigrun had called Aelfhild stood close to her mistress, her expression sweet and slightly worried. Lady Sigrun's hands were now on her slender hips and her expression was bullish. She pursed her lips and turned to Gui.

'You expect us to ride this horse?'

'It isn't as hard as it looks,' Gui said reassuringly. Knowing he would have to control the horse with one hand, Gilbert had chosen a well-broken animal for his friend.

'You expect *all of us* to ride him,' she clarified.

'She, not him, and, no, not all at once. The poor beast would expire within a day.' Gui ran his open palm down the mare's neck, giving her a stroke and a good scratch. She tossed her head and snickered in enjoyment.

'Her, not she,' Lady Sigrun corrected. 'If you're going to stay in my country, you should speak my language properly.'

'You can teach me as we travel,' he answered, determined not to rise to the cheap jibe. He'd heard worse since arriving in England and would no doubt hear more still if he didn't return to France and try to build a life there instead.

She crossed her arms, then uncrossed them and twisted the end of her belt round her hands. She seemed incapable of keeping them still and a picture flashed through Gui's mind of her laying them on him as she had briefly done in supplication, but letting them move over his body in exploration. He shivered and forced the image from his mind. She had only touched him to beseech him to let her go free.

'I would have expected a lord such as yourself to have provided more fitting transport for his bride,' the lady sneered.

In truth, Gui hadn't given any thought to how they were going to travel from this point on. Her scornful words made him wonder if she had guessed he was not who he said he was. Now he had the women in his possession he had half a mind to admit his true identity and rank, but suspected if he did the noblewoman would see this as the opportunity to create further trouble for him. She might even attempt to run if she knew she was in the company of a man so far below her own station.

'I intended to commandeer a cart of some sort from the priory when we left so you could have travelled in comfort. Obviously, that is now out

of the question as you decided to run,' he said
scathingly. Let her take some of the blame for
their situation. 'I don't want the journey to take
weeks so to save your energy you'll take turns
to ride. I'll lead the rein and walk. I'm used to
travelling on foot.'

'Perhaps we can hire a second horse in one
of the towns.'

The companion, Lady Aelfhild, spoke in an
accent that made Gui instinctively want to bend
his knee in obedience.

'What towns would those be?' he laughed in
surprise. 'Where has horses left now other than
in the cooking pot?'

Almost before the words had left his mouth
Lady Sigrun had swept towards him, seized his
arm and tugged hard.

'Come with me. Now, if you please.'

If he'd wanted to Gui could have stood firm
and she would no more have been able to move
him than she would a tree, but her action was so
bold it raised his curiosity. He permitted himself
to be led inside the hut. Once inside she dropped
his arm and rounded on him with a ferocity that
left his heart racing.

'What do you think you are doing, telling her
such things as that?' she demanded in a harsh
whisper, reaching up on to her toes and pushing

her face close to his so that her breath tickled his cheek in a most distracting manner.

If a man had behaved towards Gui in such a confrontational manner he would have earned the crack of Gui's forehead across his nose, but it was not within Gui's nature to strike a woman, however rudely she spoke to him.

'I was telling her the truth.' He folded his arms and returned Lady Sigrun's belligerent scowl. 'Yorkshire is starving. Any town that had horses left will have eaten them over the winter, not kept them for ladies to ride!'

She bit her lip, but not before Gui had seen the way it trembled. Her lips were full and soft and the memory of them on his cheek and mouth sent a gentle shiver over his skin.

'Should I have lied and let her believe we'll be heading into civilisation or is it better to prepare her for the truth?'

'You didn't have to lie, but you could have been kinder,' she muttered.

Gui's eyes were growing accustomed to the darkness and he could see the troubled expression in the lady's pale eyes, ringed with shadows that hinted at how badly she must have slept the night before. He cursed himself for his lack of tact and shook his head, remembering how long Lady Emma said the two women had been cloistered away from the world. He softened his expression, uncrossing his arms to appear less threatening and dropping them to his side. Lady Sigrun stepped back, moving partly into a shaft of light that broke through a gap between the slats of the roof. Her hair almost glowed in the light as strands drifted around her angular face, and now the heat had died in her cheeks a little she looked pale and otherworldly.

'You're right. I didn't think,' Gui admitted. 'It's been a long while since I had to consider anyone's feelings. Things are different now to when you entered the priory. Do you know what has taken place this last year? How William ordered his army to wreak revenge on Yorkshire for the uprising in York?'

'I do. I've seen what has happened to the villages nearby. I'd been visiting one before we met yesterday.' She gazed at him solemnly. 'Is it really true that all Yorkshire is desolate? There is nothing left of the towns or villages?'

Gui thought back to the journey he had made and the destruction he had seen. He remembered nights in York listening to the soldiers bragging about the homes they had burned and the livestock they had stolen or slaughtered. He filled with shame at his countrymen and King.

'I'm afraid not,' he replied softly.

Her whole body sagged and she dropped her eyes. Gui reached out his hand and took hold of hers, drawing it to him and giving it a gentle squeeze. 'I'm sorry to have to break such news to you. Does your servant not know any of this?'

'She never leaves the grounds of the priory. Not many of the sisters do, but I take medicines and ointments to try to ease the suffering of the old who are still alive. I've seen what has happened to the village and I've heard tales of what happened. They say it is worse closer to York.'

She turned her eyes on him again, now suddenly brimming with fear and entreaty. 'Where will we get food? Where shall we sleep on the journey? That man you showed me in the grass— there will be others like him, won't there?'

Gui thought long and hard before answering. The journey would be hazardous and lacking in the comforts a woman of her status would expect. She was so slightly built that he feared the gruelling trip might prove to be too much for her. Still stinging from the accusation of insensitivity, he was reluctant to answer truthfully.

'Shall I be kind and soften the blow?' he asked drily.

'Not to me.' She narrowed her eyes and lifted her jaw. He remembered the ferocity with which she had fought him off on two occasions now and the fact that she had run in the night. She was looking at him with such determination he found himself unwilling to lie to her or spare her the truth. He suspected, too, that Lady Emma had been wrong about her daughter: she had more resilience than the mother gave her credit for.

'I don't know the answer to any of your questions, I'm afraid,' he admitted. 'We're on the wrong side of the river at the moment so I don't know who or what we'll find until we cross back over. These are unsettled times and there may be danger, though I hope William's army has seen to most threats.'

Her face became grave as he spoke. She looked as though she was about to cry, though Gui did not know whether this was from the thought of the dangers facing them on the journey or because of what waited for her at the end of it.

'Thank you for being honest with me.'

Despite her previous insistence that he should never lay hands on her again, she hadn't resisted his touch when he took her hand. Emboldened by this and feeling the urge to offer comfort and reassurance, Gui drew closer and cautiously patted her on the shoulder. She stiffened beneath his touch, but did not pull back. Gui put his other gloved arm on her other shoulder. Her eyes slid to it and he realised with a sinking feeling he would have to tell her at some point why he had felt no pain when she drove a pin through his glove, but that could wait.

She gave him a slight smile and Gui's heart fluttered into life. Dust prickled his nose and eyes and it was this, he told himself, which caused his chest and throat to tighten. The hut was cramped and stuffy. Being so unexpectedly in close confinement with the woman whose touch he coveted sent a tremor the length of Gui's spine. The trace of rosemary on her skin or hair mingled with her own scent that reached inside Gui, inflaming the craving that had laid dormant for so long. His pulse sped until it was hammering in his ears. His mouth felt dry and he swallowed, feeling his tongue scraping across the roof of his mouth.

'On my honour, I won't let either of you come to any harm,' he breathed, letting his hand glide deliberately down the length of her arm.

'Either of us!' Lady Sigrun clapped her hands to her cheeks, pulling back from Gui in the process and breaking the enchantment she had woven around him. 'We've left her alone!'

She slipped past him, close enough that her skirts brushed against his legs as she headed for the doorway. She paused and looked back over her shoulder.

'Don't tell her what you told me. She doesn't need to know what we might encounter.'

Gui spread his arms and bowed his head in assent. She gave him a serious nod. For a brief moment, they were allies, equals, which oddly pleased him more than a smile might have. He lingered a moment in the dark, leaning his head against the wall. He realised now that, before he had uttered the words that had allowed the outside world to invade the hut, he had been preparing to kiss her for a second time and to do it with more thoroughness than the brief meeting of their lips the previous night.

That he now knew she was Gilbert's bride had not even entered his mind. Gilbert might as well not have existed. Gui's stomach writhed at the unconscious betrayal of his closest friend and his conscience demanded to be obeyed. There would—could—not be any more such occurrences. The thoughts he had entertained were forbidden. *She* was forbidden to him. Anything else would be such a gross betrayal of the trust his friend had placed in him.

He exhaled deeply, acutely aware of the perspiration which made his tunic cling to his back and chest. He'd cajoled one kiss from her and that would have to suffice. Once more in command of his emotions and body, he followed Lady Sigrun back outside.

Lady Aelfhild was standing by the horse where they had abandoned her. She was stroking the mare's nose and whispering into her ear, showing the first sign of pleasure Gui had seen. Lady Sigrun was standing halfway between the hut and the horse, watching. She glanced back at Gui when he joined her silently.

'You need to understand that my companion is easily disturbed. I won't have you upsetting her. She'll need you to be kind. Can you be kind?'

Her voice was urgent and Gui was stung by the accusation that he would be cruel. Thoughtless, perhaps, but not intentionally so.

'Let's get moving.' He took her by the elbow and escorted her to the horse and waiting woman.

He nodded at Lady Aelfhild, who lowered her head as he took the reins, looping them over his glove. Gui steadied the horse, then held his hand out for Lady Sigrun to put her foot in.

'Mount up, my lady, and let's be on our way.'

Instead of obeying, she stepped to one side and Lady Aelfhild stepped forward to take her place. Gui looked at them in surprise that the lady would give way to her companion, even if they were as close as sisters. His expression must have told, as the women exchanged a quick glance and Lady Aelfhild hesitated.

'Aelfhild is not used to walking as far as I am,' Lady Sigrun said in decisive tones. 'She should ride first.'

Gui cast his eyes over the two women. They had removed their shapeless habits and now stood clad in dresses that emphasised their figures much more enticingly. Lady Aelfhild did not look particularly frail, being taller and with a figure that displayed captivatingly curving hips and high, full breasts. She towered over the more slightly built Lady Sigrun in a manner that made that woman's slight figure look more delicate than usual. The expression on her face was anything but fragile and he cautioned himself to remember her size belied the ferocity that he had already borne the brunt of.

'As you wish. As long as you can keep up. I walk fast.'

Lady Aelfhild settled into the saddle without help and proved to have a good seat. Gui took the reins. Lady Sigrun picked up both their bags and heaved them across her shoulders so one fell on each hip. To Gui's slight irritation she set herself at the other side of the horse to him so he was unable to engage her in conversation.

It was going to be a long journey if it was to be conducted in silence.

The weather was warm, the ground rocky or tangled with weeds and the going was hard. Feeling thwarted by the lack of conversation, Gui set a rapid pace closer to a march than a stroll and kept his eyes alert for any signs of danger. He kept to open ground and followed the path of the river so at least an attack, if it did come, could only come from one side. His encounter with the vagrant had shaken him more than he cared to think about and he could not forget the look of horror on Lady Sigrun's face when he had showed her the man. He hoped he would not have too many instances where he needed to fight. One unsuspecting rogue who gave no struggle was one matter, but Gui was less certain if he would be able to keep the women safe, despite his assurances. Determined to put as much ground as possible beneath their feet before dark, he increased his speed, but a cry of protest from the other side of the horse stopped him in his tracks.

He peered round at Lady Sigrun, who was breathing hard.

'We've been walking for ages. I need to rest for a while,' she gasped. Without waiting to see if he agreed she dropped the bags to the ground and sat beside them, legs spread out before her.

She rolled her feet in small circles and looked at him accusingly.

'You deliberately went quickly.'

'Yes, I did.' He felt ashamed at the sight of her now sprawled on the ground. 'I did not intentionally go fast to make you suffer, but because I want to get as far as possible before dark.'

He offered his hand to the companion, who put her foot in it and dismounted gracefully, consenting to rest her hands on his shoulders briefly to steady herself. Lady Sigrun was watching closely, her eyes narrow with interest. Perhaps she did not take kindly to the sight of her companion in the arms of her future husband.

Lady Sigrun gathered her hair between her hands, twisting it off the back of her slender neck into a bundle on top of her head. With one hand she flapped at her throat. Wisps of damp hair stuck temptingly to her neck, lifting in the breeze she created and practically inviting him to help peel them off.

'I'm hot and so thirsty.'

'We all are,' Gui agreed. He rummaged in the horse's pannier and unearthed a leather bottle. It was empty, but they were close to the river so he filled it, then sat back on his heels. The scratch on his arm was red and itchy. He rolled his sleeve and bathed it, cupping water in his hand and letting it spill over the wound. Lady Sigrun joined him. She had the grace to look a little guilty when she saw what he was doing.

'Does that hurt?'

He pulled his sleeve over it, tucking the cuff back into his glove. 'Not enough to bother me.'

She knelt beside him and leaned over, dipping her fingers into the water. She trailed them languidly across her brow and throat, sighing with satisfaction in a manner that set Gui's heart racing. She sat upright and rivulets trickled down her neck, disappearing beneath her dress. She could not be aware of what effect her actions had on him. He took a long drink, passed her the water bottle.

'You don't have any food, do you?' she asked hopefully.

Gui thought of the bread and cheese Hilde had given him before he left. It might be all they had for the next day or two. Best not eat it straight away.

'Sadly not,' he lied. 'We'll have empty bellies for a while longer, but the water is getting shallow and the ground more rocky. I think we stand a good chance of crossing over soon without getting a complete soaking. Once we're on the correct side I'll stand a better chance of recognising somewhere and finding us a bed for the night.'

'*A* bed?' She blinked and flushed. 'Sir Gilbert, I have no intention of sharing a bed with you!'

She must have feared he intended to claim his rights as a husband before they married. Many men would take such an approach to their betrothed; some would be lucky enough to have a bride in agreement. Of course she had no idea he was not the husband she believed him to be and he had honestly meant separate beds for all of them. The slip had been unintentional, but his tongue had betrayed where his mind was straying.

She passed him the water bottle and twisted round so she was facing him.

'I think we should make something very clear before we travel any further, Sir Gilbert. I am travelling with you against my wishes and only because I have no choice. It was not my wish to become betrothed, to you or anyone, and there is some uncertainty whether there is a betrothal or not. Until that matter is settled beyond all question of doubt, I suggest you stop entertaining thoughts of sharing my bed, or anything else. I think in the hut you had a notion I would permit you to kiss me, but you were wrong.'

She licked her lips, which only made Gui want to try again. 'I kissed you last night and I should not have done, but you shouldn't have

asked me to. Do not attempt to touch me or provoke me into touching you again. Do I make
myself clear?'

He translated to his own language, which took
some time, such was her tangle of words. A notion indeed, and one that had not seemed entirely unreciprocated despite her declarations. For
the sake of his honour and his friendship with
Gilbert, an agreement between them that there
would be no intimacy was the best outcome he
could hope for.

'Yes, I understand and I agree. We shall be no
more than travelling companions, I promise, and
please call me Gui as I asked you before.'

Relief crossed her face. Unexpectedly she held
out a hand, presumably for him to kiss. After
insisting he should not touch her this seemed a
contradiction and Gui hesitated before taking
it. Instead of allowing him to bring it to his lips
Lady Sigrun shook it firmly, in the customary
manner of men he had seen in the north. She
was of that blood rather than Saxon stock, he reminded himself. He gripped her hand, which was
swallowed in his giant gloved palm, and shook it
again. Her eyes shone with approval as if he had
passed some unsuspected test. She slipped her
hand free and pointed into the distance.

'There's a ford about half a league further

downriver where it curves around the hill,' she said. 'I came this far once.'

'You know the river? Why didn't you tell me before?'

She gave him a triumphant smile. 'You're taking me back, but I don't have to help you.'

Gui ground his teeth, stung by her deceit. 'You sound remarkably like your mother!'

Her step faltered. 'My—mother?'

'When she told me I'd have to claim you from the priory myself.' He strolled to her side, enjoying the look of astonishment—a small revenge for her smugness. 'Oh, whatever you might hope, Lady Sigrun, your marriage *has* been arranged and Lady Emma has agreed to it.'

He watched dismay fill her eyes and a flicker of pity replaced the triumph. He could say nothing that would comfort her, beyond telling her that her real husband was handsome and kind, not a bad-tempered beast, and he had no intention of revealing the truth.

'Let's carry on before the night falls and we have no bed of any sort.' Gui pushed his cloak back over his shoulder and Lady Sigrun started forward, her hand outstretched towards him.

'That's my brooch!'

Gui looked down at his shoulder where it

glinted in the sunlight. He'd completely forgotten about it.

'Yes.' Gui smiled, remembering where he found it and the circumstances. 'It seemed a shame to let it stay at the bottom of the river.'

'Give it back.' Her cheeks reddened and she reached out once more as if she intended to rip it from his body, an idea which caused him no end of excitement.

If she had asked in politer terms he might have done as she said, but her tone rankled. He considered her demand and pulled the fold of his cloak back over it.

'You can't have it. Not now.'

'But it's mine.' Her eyes glinted as they fixed on the spot beneath his cloak where he had concealed her brooch. Gui realised with a start that tears were filling them. He didn't think she was the kind of woman to care so much about a trinket and her reaction intrigued him. He resolved to discover what significance it held.

'Perhaps when you're a little politer to me I'll give it back.'

'Why should I be polite to have my own property returned?' she exclaimed.

'Why shouldn't you be? I've treated you with nothing but courtesy and you've been continually hostile. I'm not your enemy.'

'Yes, you are,' she snarled. She tossed her head back, sending her hair flying. The fine white mass momentarily made Gui think of a spirited horse that needed breaking in. He wished he could be the one to do it, not Gilbert.

'That's exactly what you are! You invaded my country, you killed our King and slaughtered my people, and now you've dragged me from my home against my will.'

'If Godwinson had supported William's right to the throne as Edward had promised him, we would have come in peace to claim the title. He broke his oath of fealty,' Gui snapped.

'An oath not freely given and gained through trickery,' Lady Sigrun retorted. Her eyes blazed with fury. 'Everyone knows that. He didn't know he was swearing over the most holy relics.'

'So some say! You weren't there to see it happen.'

'Were you there to see it didn't?'

'Of course not!'

He'd been in Brittany, living in his father's house, but itching to leave and see more of the world. When the opportunity had arisen to follow Gilbert to England he'd clutched it with both hands, an irony not lost on him now. He reminded himself he was now escorting this cantankerous woman in order to receive the land

Gilbert had promised so he could return to the kind of life he had so eagerly given up.

'This is a matter we could debate for ever!' He gave a sudden laugh. 'I've had this argument so many times, but I didn't expect to be discussing politics with a woman.'

'I don't see why not. We're perfectly capable of thinking.' She sounded deeply offended.

'I don't doubt it. It's still unusual to be doing it.'

'I suppose there are other things you'd prefer to be doing with women,' she sneered.

Her face flushed red, the glow spreading beneath the neck of her tunic before Gui's eyes. She was one of those very pale women who coloured easily when embarrassed. Gui found it charming and wondered if her body would react with such speed when she was aroused. He ran his eyes up and down her body before looking back at her face. She wrapped her arms around herself, drawing back slightly, but meeting his eyes with a challenge that excited Gui beyond reason.

Gui blinked first.

'It's been a long time since I've done what you're thinking of,' he admitted. 'Also, I didn't personally kill your King. But we are here now and William is King, whether oaths were made or broken, and whether you like it or not.'

She looked at him coldly. 'Sir Gilbert, let me ask you, what value would a marriage oath be if it was made under such circumstances? Think about that when you take your unwilling bride.'

He had no words to answer her so simply stalked past her and back to the horse and the other waiting woman without bothering to see if she was following.

Chapter Seven

More refreshed, they pressed on. Despite her protests, and much to her annoyance, Sir Gui had insisted Aelfhild took her turn to ride, threatening to lift her bodily over the saddle himself if necessary. She was not as happy on horseback as Sigrun had been and sat rigidly, gripping the mare's belly with her legs until her thigh muscles burned and she could stand it no longer.

'I don't care what you say, I have to get down,' she told him as they reached the brow of the hill.

He'd been walking silently at her side, leading the mare. He frowned, which gave his already rugged face a craggy expression, but made no objection. Aelfhild drew up her knee and began to swing her leg over the mare's back. Halfway over she felt his hand settle in the small of her back. She froze, looking over her shoulder at him.

'Be careful,' he grunted.

She half-slid, half-tumbled from the saddle. Her dismount was far from the dignified and elegant one Sigrun had executed and if Sir Gui had not been standing close she would have landed in a heap. He spread his legs to brace himself as he steadied her, one arm encircling her waist. Her spine curved against his broad chest and her buttocks ground against his crotch. An image filled her mind of his standing naked in the water and she became acutely aware of what part of him she was crushing against. Her thighs gave a spasm from the effort of gripping the saddle and she staggered backwards a little. He shook his head vigorously to rid himself of the resulting faceful of hair and his body ground against her once again.

'Careful,' he repeated, this time in a low voice. 'If you twist your ankle, you'll have no choice but to ride.'

His mouth was close enough to her ear that his breath tickled. She pushed herself from his arms; disconcerted at how his closeness made the skin of her neck flutter.

They agreed that they would all walk and loaded the bags on to the horse. They travelled on in silence, Sir Gui leading the horse and the two women arm in arm. Aelfhild's mind kept returning to his revelation by the river.

Lady Emma knew about the betrothal. Lady Emma had agreed to it.

He could have been lying to annoy her in retaliation for not telling him about the ford, but he had said as much to Hilde and had seemed genuinely annoyed that the letter had not arrived. If that was the case, then Sigrun's cause was lost and there was no point carrying on the deception any longer. Aelfhild had made it clear that he would not be permitted any indiscretions, and he had agreed readily and would doubtless keep the same vow when he learned Sigrun was his true bride. She would break the news as soon as possible and suggest they told him the truth.

She glanced across at the knight. He walked with an easy gait, his stocky frame held alert, and his head roved continually from side to side as he walked, keeping an eye out for any dangers. They hadn't encountered anyone else as they had travelled, but knowing he was vigilant did make her feel safer. If only he had let her keep the *seax* so she could defend Sigrun if she had to.

She continued to observe him. He had a dark complexion that was strange to eyes that had grown up with blonder men from the north and she could not tear her eyes from him. In profile his broken nose did not look as crooked and from this side the scar that pulled his full, sen-

suous lips to one side was not visible. His jaw
was prickled with a light growth of stubble and
jutted out below the tangle of dark hair that fell
to his ears. He was remarkably handsome really,
despite these slight imperfections.

He must have felt her eyes on him because he
turned his head suddenly towards her. Embarrassed at being caught staring, Aelfhild's instinct
was to glance away and deny she had been looking, but she fought it down and held his gaze.
He broke eye contact first, glancing past her to
look briefly at Sigrun. His eyes widened and
the thick lashes flickered before he looked back
to Aelfhild. He raised his left hand to his chin,
then pushed his hair back behind his ear in a
strangely clumsy gesture. An expression crossed
his face that she could not interpret and her stomach twisted.

Sigrun was walking with her head down and
had not noticed his interest. Aelfhild moved
closer to her mistress, blocking his view. She
was not entirely sure if she had moved to shield
Sigrun in order to protect her or to prevent Sir
Gui looking with any further interest at her. It
took her aback to realise jealousy was mingling
with her sense of protectiveness. Either way it
would not do. They belonged to each other even
if they did not know it yet.

She wondered what he had done for the King

to be rewarded with a wealthy bride and all the land that came with her. She determined to find out before they arrived in York, reminding herself that for all his allure, he was one of the men who had sacked the city. Any feelings towards him marked her out as a traitor to her people. Sigrun, with her determination never to marry him, was a better woman than she was.

'We're nearly at the ford.'

She slipped her hand from beneath Sigrun's arm and strode ahead, keeping her eyes focused on the river so she did not have to see if they had started to speak to each other.

The water was knee deep at the ford. Without waiting for the others, Aelfhild sat down and began to remove her shoes and stockings. She had gathered her skirts to her knees and was dipping her foot into the water when they arrived.

'You don't have to get wet. I could put you on the horse to take you across, or carry you.' Sir Gui looked her up and down appraisingly. 'You're slight enough.'

The idea of him lifting her into his arms was unsettlingly appealing. 'There's no need,' she said as severely as she could manage. 'It won't be the first time I've been wet.'

He gave her an unexpected grin that made his eyes gleam with amusement. It was the first time she had seen him show genuine amusement.

'Let's both try to stay drier this time and hope we don't encounter any unnatural creatures.'

Aelfhild curtsied and flourished a hand. Ignoring him was hard when he proved to be unexpectedly charming. 'You may lead the way, *dweorgar.*'

He gave a barking laugh and his eyes crinkled at the corners. Aelfhild grinned back at the shared joke. Out of the corner of her eye she saw Sigrun looking puzzled and felt a rush of guilt. She was dallying with Sigrun's betrothed before her eyes. The sooner they revealed the truth of their identities the better it would be.

Once across the river they began to see the occasional person and more signs of the destruction Sir Gui had warned of. The sun was dropping in the sky when they turned their attention to the matter of food and shelter. Occupied buildings were few and far between. At the first one they arrived at, a wrinkled-faced woman appeared. She held a stout stick out like a sword.

'We're travelling and mean you no harm,' Sigrun said, speaking for the first time.

'We need shelter,' Aelfhild added.

The woman looked at Sir Gui who stood with the horse. 'What do you want? There's nothing left you haven't already taken or destroyed!'

'He won't hurt you,' Aelfhild said. 'He's with us. He's—he's our friend.'

She heard Sir Gui's intake of breath. She slid her eyes to look at him. His face was unreadable.

'He's one of them,' the woman snarled. 'Destruction is all they know.'

She whistled and a man's face appeared. The light was fading rapidly, but Aelfhild could see milk-white eyes that proclaimed his blindness.

'I can't see, but I can still fight,' he growled.

'There will be no fighting.' Gui sheathed his sword and held both hands before him to show they were empty. 'Please, take my companions in for the night. I'll find my own shelter. I have food you can share if you give them sanctuary and keep them safe.'

'They can stay. You can take your chance with the vagrants and brigands in the forest.'

The woman lowered her stick. She licked her lips, leaving Aelfhild in no doubt what caused her to agree. Sir Gui made no protest. He began to root in the pannier on the saddle. Aelfhild ran and caught him by the arm. He flinched and whipped his head round, looking suspicious.

'You should stay with us.'

She felt the muscles in his arm tense as he clenched his fist. 'I'm not welcome here. Nor should I be. I don't crave company anyway. I'll return in the morning.'

He sounded resigned to his fate. It wasn't fair. He had done nothing to these people so shouldn't suffer.

'But where will you sleep? Will you be safe?'

'I slept outdoors when I travelled to Byland and I've been a soldier for long enough. It isn't raining or cold so I'll survive the night.' He smiled warmly and touched her cheek, dropping his head close to hers. 'You care about the well-being of your "friend" though, do you?' he asked softly.

More than she should care about the well-being of her enemy, she realised. She forced her expression into a scowl.

'I care that my companion and I won't wake to find ourselves abandoned in the wild with no one to defend us. If you get killed, who will keep us safe?'

He laughed, then his eyes changed, filling with a solemn and earnest expression that stole Aelfhild's breath from her chest.

'I will not leave you in danger, but there is only one bed offered here.'

Aelfhild jutted out her jaw. 'Then we'll carry on.'

She turned her back on the woman and strode on.

'Fine principles, my lady,' Sir Gui muttered

as he came alongside her. 'But principles won't find a place to lay your head.'

Instead of staying by the river road Sir Gui began leading them deeper into the woods. The women exchanged an anxious glance.

'There is no shelter on the road. At least we'll be able to cobble together some sort of a tent with our cloaks.'

By unspoken agreement they walked closer to each other. Sir Gui's hand strayed occasionally to the short sword he wore at his side.

'I hope I don't need to use it,' he said when he caught Aelfhild looking. 'It's better to be prepared. We need to be careful, we don't know who might be about and the country is a dangerous place now. The whole journey will be fraught with danger.'

'But they'll be English. They won't hurt me.'

He stared at her with incredulity. 'You're a woman, and a beautiful one at that. Do you think your countrymen would treat you any kinder than a Norman or Breton if they took the notion into their heads to have you?'

'I would fight them off.' His compliment echoed in her mind and she did her best to ignore it. What did it matter that this man thought her beautiful?

'You would lose.' He spoke with certainty. No

menace or malice in his words, but simply a prediction.

A chill ran down her spine as she remembered the man who had been spying on her. Something of her fear must have shown in her face because Sir Gui reached a hand to her shoulder. The gesture was comforting rather than affectionate, but even so her skin quivered at his touch, every nerve springing into life. She moved a little closer to him. His stern expression softened and his fingers spread a little wider as they moved to her upper arm. His touch felt more like a caress now and she was hit again by the same sensation that had made her squirm with longing when he had held her in the hut. He'd called her beautiful. The fluttering in her belly caused her head to spin.

'Don't fear. In all probability I'm exaggerating. Few of them will have survived the winter. When it grew colder and the forests thinned there was nowhere to hide without being seen. The troops defeated the remaining rebels without much trouble.'

He sounded so complacent as he spoke of English deaths. She made a rude noise in her throat and shook him off roughly.

'You call my people rebels. I call them resistance, defending themselves against invaders that seized their home and lands. Would you have done the same if it had been your country that was taken?' Tears stabbed her eyes and her throat tightened. 'Wouldn't you want to kill those who hurt the ones you loved?'

'Yes, I would.' His face was grave. 'I was trying to comfort you, but I didn't think. I hope we're past that now. It will be women like you who make the peace and build the future, not men like me.'

He meant her marriage, of course. A new England would be forged in the union of the conquerors with the vanquished, joining together to produce children who belonged to both.

She tossed her hair back from her face and stalked ahead. He strode to keep up. 'I was raised with tales of warrior women who fought; shield-maidens who took arms against invaders and fought alongside the heroes. I wish I had been one of them. If I had gone to York when they rose up...'

'You'd be dead with the rest.' He rounded on her furiously and caught her by the arm. He pulled her to face him and glowered down at her. He had turned ashen. 'You talk of fighting as if it is something to aspire to, but if you saw it you'd change your mind soon enough. War is not a game. It's a nightmare and once you've lived it you won't ever truly wake.'

'So we women must endure the fate thrust upon us while men play their games!'

He snorted. 'Oh, don't be such a child. It's been thus since the world began. Women are bartered and bought. You'd have been married off to someone in any case and this way will stop bloodshed. Are you willing to make that sacrifice?'

The idea of being a piece in a game repulsed her, but it made sense. If she could have spared Torwald's death by giving herself to a Norman, would she have done it? Would she give herself to Sir Gui in Sigrun's place to prevent further deaths? She couldn't answer that fairly, not when the Breton was capable of making her head spin with need just by mentioning the idea. There would be nothing noble or sacrificial about the act of surrendering her body to his touch. The knot of guilt that had twisted her guts whenever she thought of her attraction to him began to loosen slightly.

'It will be men like you, too, who play their part,' she replied.

'Of course.' He gave a curt laugh, devoid of humour. 'You think it is only women who are not in command of their destinies, but it can happen

that a man is ordered to marry, despite his wishes
or inclination.'

She blinked in surprise. That had never occurred to her. Perhaps he had a lover in France
who he would have preferred to marry. He adjusted the neck of his tunic. She caught a glimpse
of the strong throat and the dark hairs that covered his chest. Her fingers itched to touch them
and see if they were as soft as she imagined them
to be. He caught her staring and grimaced, presumably misinterpreting her interest for distaste
at his scarred lip.

'If your husband was handsome and rich, perhaps you would mind being the pawn less than
if he was ugly and poor.'

Aelfhild held his gaze, determined not to appear daunted.

'If he was kind and gentle and tried to do his
best by her, a woman would learn to love him
quicker, whatever he looked like or however poor
he was.'

She glanced at Sigrun, who was leading the
horse. She seemed to have developed an affin-
ity with the animal. 'You should go see how my
companion is faring.'

He raised his eyebrows in surprise at her sudden change of subject. 'Tell me about her. She's
so quiet I forget she's there sometimes.'

Now was the time to start extolling Sigrun's virtues and plant the ideas of her as a suitable bride in Sir Gui's head, but the words were a weight on her tongue and she found them too hard to speak. They had swapped identities so Sigrun could borrow Aelfhild's history, too.

'She was left on the threshold of Herik's house, a foundling who no one claimed, despite all attempts to discover her parents. We were brought up together. She's very beautiful, isn't she?'

Sir Gui's gaze settled on Sigrun for longer than Aelfhild liked. 'Yes, she is. How lucky. To be impoverished but plain rather than handsome would be a great misfortune. What future would such a person have?'

His voice was abrupt. Aelfhild felt sick. He was describing her situation, though he did not know it. What future did she have?

'Go walk with her, please, I want to think in peace.'

He wrinkled his brow, but obeyed, striding to join Sigrun. His attempts to speak were rebuffed, which did not seem to concern him as he shrugged and left her be, walking silently at her side. Aelfhild had worried about how he would react when he finally learned the truth, but how could he be anything other than happy to discover the beautiful woman was rich and well connected after all?

* * *

Sigrun spotted the makeshift shelter first. Someone had arranged smaller branches at angles between two solid tree trunks and covered the structure with a rag-tag selection of skins and oiled wool. Aelfhild stepped towards it.

'Careful,' Sir Gui warned. 'There might be someone here.'

Sir Gui put his arm out behind him to prevent her stepping closer. Aelfhild's breath caught. His left hand had come to rest on her right breast. The gesture had been unconscious and she doubted he would feel much to excite him beneath the layers she wore. She could barely feel his touch herself, but she was conscious of the way her heart began to thump and the pressure on a part of her body that no man had explored before.

'Sir Gui, please remove your hand,' she said tightly.

He whipped his head round, glaring as though she had said the worst insult imaginable.

'What did you say?'

'Your hand—it's on my—'

She bit her lip and flicked her eyes downwards. He looked down and his face relaxed.

'My pardon, Lady Sigrun. I misunderstood you.'

He removed his hand and drew his sword slowly. The blade whispered in the silence as it left the scabbard and Aelfhild shivered. She edged closer to him, slipping her hand beneath her cloak and pressing it where his had so recently been.

'Is anyone there?' Sir Gui asked. No one answered. He edged closer and pushed the skins aside with the tip of his sword.

'It's empty. We'll sleep here.'

He walked to the horse and began unstrapping Sigrun's bag. Aelfhild rushed to get her own and as she unhitched the strap it caught on something wooden and pointed strapped to one of the panniers. She lifted it out.

'A bow!'

It was fine, dark wood, the grip polished smooth and glossy from use. The bowstring had been looped around the top notch and wound around the length of the weapon until it the time came to string it.

It was pulled from her hands before she had finished examining it.

'That isn't yours to touch.' Gui's face was thunderous once more.

'Are you an archer?' she asked.

'I was.'

'Why have you hidden it away?' Glancing at the pannier, she noticed a leather quiver with half-a-dozen arrows peeking out. 'Why do you carry your sword but not this?'

'I don't use it any more.' Sir Gui held the weapon protectively to his chest as if it was a lover.

'You could hunt something for us to eat,' Aelfhild suggested. 'There must be rabbits, or rats if need be.'

'I'm hunting nothing!' he snarled. He stowed the bow back in the pannier and pulled the leather back over it. 'Don't touch that again. I'm going to do a quick patrol. There's food in the bag. Help yourself.'

He stalked off and was swallowed by the trees. Aelfhild watched until he was out of sight, then followed Sigrun into the makeshift shelter.

There was barely room to stand and no furniture beyond a straw-filled sack that had once served as a bed. They left that for Sir Gui and spread their blankets and cloaks at the far end. The situation suited Aelfhild. Twice now his temper had flared with little provocation and subsided as quickly. She had upset him, but nothing she had said seemed to warrant such an outburst of emotion. She investigated the bag of food.

'There isn't much,' she said, picking out a round of cheese and biting into it. 'Not enough to satisfy a man as large as Sir Gui.'

'I don't care,' Sigrun said. 'Perhaps he'll give up hope and we won't see him again.'

'And if we didn't we'd be in more trouble. I don't know where to go from here.' Aelfhild divided the food into three, put a portion beside the pallet allotted to their companion and sat beside Sigrun.

'I'm sorry I made you leave the priory. We'd have been safer letting him bring you back properly.'

'I didn't want to stay and wait,' Sigrun said. 'I'm trying to pretend he isn't even with us, but it's hard. At least he doesn't know who I am.'

'He will soon enough.' Aelfhild gave her a stern look. 'You'll have to tell him sooner or later. You're going to marry him.'

'No, I'm not. That's why we're going to Haxby with him, isn't it? So my mother can refuse to grant his demand.'

Aelfhild stifled a sigh at Sigrun's naivety, which seemed doubly foolish after Sir Gui's earlier words. Did the noblewoman really think her fate would be so different to that of any other woman, or was she telling herself this to make it more bearable? She drew her knees up and hugged them, feeling troubled. Sir Gui had told her the matter was settled and Lady Emma had agreed to the betrothal. If he spoke the truth, then the sooner Sigrun and her future husband recognised each other as such, the sooner they would be able to start getting to know each other.

'I think we should tell him the truth anyway.'

'No! You promised me. You won't break that vow. If you do, I'll run alone.'

Aelfhild was almost tempted to test her mistress's words. She doubted Sigrun would have the courage to do any such thing. Sigrun drew her shoulders back and lifted her head. A light filled her eyes that Aelfhild had rarely seen and for a moment it was Lady Emma who sat in the cramped space beside her.

'Aelfhild, I command you to keep my secret. You owe my family a debt for taking you in and you will do as I say.'

Aelfhild gasped. Though Lady Emma had occasionally reminded Aelfhild of her birth and how fortunate she was to have been given a life in Herik's household, Sigrun had never held this over her.

Sigrun faltered at the sound of Aelfhild's dismay and the familiar, meek girl was back. She clutched Aelfhild's hands. 'I'm sorry, I didn't mean it. I won't force you. I've never asked anything of you in all the time we've lived together, but I'm asking now. Don't tell him. Not a word or a hint. Not until we get to Haxby.'

A tiny voice murmured in her ear that this outcome was satisfactory for her, too. If they continued to deceive him, Sir Gui would continue to treat her with courtesy and interest for longer.

She heard him return, speaking softly in his own language to the horse outside.

'If it means so much to you, I won't. I'll let you choose when to tell him.'

Sigrun gave a whispered thank you and began her customary prayer before eating. Sir Gui came in. He nodded briefly at the women, wrinkled his forehead at Sigrun's display of devotion, then settled on to the pallet, ate his food and wrapped himself in his cloak, intending to sleep.

'I don't think you should be so scared of him,' Aelfhild murmured, rolling close and wrapping her arms around Sigrun as they had done as children. 'He may be our enemy, but he seems trustworthy, and he may be fearsome to look at, but I think he would make you a fair husband.'

'He's argumentative and rude and he frightens me. If I had to marry I would want someone gentle,' Sigrun whispered. 'He'd make a better husband for you.'

'Me!' Aelfhild exclaimed. She lowered her voice hurriedly. 'Why would I want anything to do with him?'

'For the reasons you gave me when you say

he would make a good husband for me, which you've just seen fit to ignore. Besides, he doesn't scare you. I've seen how you look at him and how he looks at you in return.'

With this disconcerting pronunciation Sigrun rolled over. A blush crept across Aelfhild's cheeks and neck, and further down until her chest felt as though it could boil water with the heat it gave off. She had not been aware of looking at the Breton in any particular way. The thought that Sigrun had noticed something she had not made her resolve to be more guarded. Even a bride who did not want her husband would not be happy to see someone else flirting with him.

Despite her exhaustion from walking and riding so far, Aelfhild lay awake long after dwelling on Sigrun's words.

A sob welled inside her and she bit her hand to smother it. However much Sir Gui might show interest in her and might coerce kisses from her, he would never throw over a noblewoman to marry a bastard of unknown birth. Even though Torwald had seemed fond of her, she doubted with hindsight that he would ever have married her, had he lived. Sir Gui should rightfully transfer his attention to Sigrun, something Aelfhild preferred not to consider. Sigrun's gentle nature and beauty would inevitably cause her husband to become attached to her. Love must surely follow in time. Though Sigrun currently recoiled from Sir Gui, once she had experienced the kisses that had left Aelfhild's head reeling, marriage would become a pleasure, not an endurance. It was right, and fitting, but the thought of watching it happen was excruciating.

Any dreams she might entertain were futile. She curled up in a ball to try to vanquish the jealousy that soured her stomach and convulsed as sobs racked her body. Hot, bewildering tears spilled on to her cheeks. She should feel only hatred towards her enemy and certainly shouldn't weep over him, but could not dismiss him from her mind. She would not have expected a man such as him to cause her heart to pound, but perhaps such things were not a choice after all.

Chapter Eight

Aelfhild was awoken by Sigrun pulling frantically at her arm.

'There's something wrong with him.'

Aelfhild rubbed her eyes and pushed herself upright, hearing the low guttural snarls interspersed with a tangle of words she couldn't understand that were coming from Gui's bed. It was still night.

'He's just dreaming,' she grumbled. 'Go back to sleep.'

She pulled her blanket over her head, intending to follow her own advice, but Gui gave a sob of such despair it tore her heart to shreds. She sat back up. Gui was thrashing around, head twisting from side to side, groaning like a boar trapped in a net.

'Wake him up.'

'You do it. He's your husband-to-be,' Aelfhild whispered.

Sigrun folded her arms and shook her head. 'He doesn't know that,' she pointed out. 'Besides, I don't want to touch him.'

Aelfhild sighed. 'You'll have to sooner or later.'

Sir Gui gave a sharp cry and arched his back, slamming down again on to the straw mattress. Aelfhild shivered, wondering what horrors he might be seeing. She could not leave him to suffer through the night.

She crawled across the room to kneel beside his cot. In the dim light of early dawn she could see his face. Sweat had matted his hair to his brow and cheeks and his eyes were screwed tight shut as he fought whatever night demons held him captive. He looked more vulnerable than she had ever seen him, more even than when he had stood naked and unarmed in the river. Her heart filled with sympathy for his suffering, but close behind it was a thrill that she was seeing this side to him that he had previously concealed. If Sigrun saw this, perhaps she would lose some of her fear of him. She opened her mouth to call Sigrun across, but then closed it, wanting to be the one who he saw when he awoke.

'Wake up,' Aelfhild murmured, leaning over him.

He didn't respond so she reached a tentative hand to his cheek and brushed the hair back.

His skin burned to the touch like a man in a fever. His chest rose, muscles swelling beneath his loose tunic. Aelfhild spread her fingers wide, longing to trace the path of them and feel the strength in him for herself. Instead she blew gently across his face, hoping that her cool breath might wake him or at least ease his temperature a little and make him more comfortable.

Gui's arm came up abruptly, lashing out with a force and speed Aelfhild could never have anticipated. The metal rivet on his glove caught her on the eyebrow, drawing blood, and the flat of his forearm landed across the side of her face.

Aelfhild had received whippings from the prioress as punishments for some disobedience or other, but no one had ever struck her in such a manner. Lights exploded in her head. She cried out in pain and surprise as tears filled her eyes. There was no fear, she realised when she thought about it later, understanding instinctively that he had not intended to hurt her.

Gui's eyes flew open at the sound of her cry and locked on to hers, but from the glazed expression that filled them Aelfhild doubted he was really seeing her. His shoulders slumped and he murmured something wordlessly, then closed his eyes once more. Before Aelfhild could move away, Gui's arm wound around her back and she found herself clasped firmly to his chest. She tried to pull away, but Gui's arms were rigid and his embrace too strong. In sleep he had made her his prisoner. His nightmare appeared to have passed because now he lay still, breathing with a regular rhythm.

Faced with pulling free and perhaps causing his nightmares to resume or staying where she was, she decided lying in Gui's arms until he released her of his own accord was the most sensible option. She heard Sigrun settling back on to the blanket at the other side of the room and almost laughed at the absurdity of lying with her friend's betrothed while the bride lay so close and seemingly uncaring.

Aelfhild's face throbbed from the blow he had given her and she felt lightheaded. She reached her fingers to examine her temple and was reassured when they felt sticky, but not soaked in blood. The wound was not too serious, though from the throb of heat that coursed through her face she expected to have a bruise come morning. She wriggled into a more comfortable position, lying on her side with her body pressed against his and one leg crooked over his, her pelvis jutted against his hipbone causing heat to surge within her. For want of a better place to put it, she laid her hand across Gui's chest and her head found a space in the hollow between his neck and shoulder. Her breasts pushed against his side where the broad chest began to taper to his taut belly. His deep breaths caused his chest to rise and fall and each movement caused a pulse of excitement to shoot through her body.

She had never realised muscles so firm and powerful could provide a bed so appealingly soft and welcoming. Any wife would willingly lie in such a bed and it upset her more than she expected that she was not to be his wife.

When she awoke, Gui's arms had slackened as he slept and he no longer held her tight. She wriggled free from his embrace, leaving him unaware that she had spent the night anywhere other than the pallet she shared with Sigrun.

Guilherm woke early, feeling more refreshed than he could remember. Instead of leaden heaviness, his limbs felt relaxed and the habitual ache of his jaw from clenching his teeth was absent. The straw pallet was thin and lumpy so why he should be without his usual hazy memories of night terrors was a mystery. Perhaps it was simply that exhaustion had claimed him more deeply than usual. A faint scent of something familiar but indefinable clung to his clothing. He breathed deeply, hoping to capture the source and give it a name, but nothing came to him.

When the women emerged, he was waiting outside the shelter leaning against a tree. He'd spent a lot of time waiting for them over the past day or two, he reflected as he drew his cloak around him, shivering. The cold and damp reached inside his skin, clutching at his bones. The weather was colder with dark clouds rolling over the dales bringing the threat of more rain. Tonight they would have to find proper shelter even if it meant pushing the women harder than any of them would like.

They greeted him with weary yawns. They, too, must have slept badly. As Lady Sigrun passed him Gui noticed an angry bruise that he could not remember seeing before.

'You've hurt yourself!' he exclaimed.

Her hand flew to her face. 'It's nothing,' she said curtly.

Head down, she made to move past him, but Gui took hold of her wrist. Reluctantly she let him draw it down from her face to see what she was hiding. There was a cut on her eyebrow and the beginnings of a black eye.

'Tell me what happened.'

'Sir Gui, I am not yours to command in such a manner,' she exclaimed.

Her words were a dagger in his throat. A nobleman would behave better than this and that was what he was pretending to be. He was acting from concern, but didn't have the graces or manners he needed to make himself likeable. At least she would welcome Gilbert as a husband when she finally met him. Her hair was not tied back in the band she wore. He brushed it back, cupping her chin so he could see better.

'I don't recall you hurting yourself yesterday. Was this from when we fought?' The idea he might have hurt her was insufferable. 'You seem angry.'

She gave him another long stare. 'You did not hurt me when we fought. If I am angry, it is because I'm tired from a poor night's sleep.'

He gave her a slight smile. 'I understand that. I rarely feel rested.'

She bit her lip and looked as if she was about to speak, but said nothing and gently removed his hand from her cheek before shouldering her bag and walking away.

The prospect of a day tramping across the wet countryside lay heavy on their shoulders and they were all equally disinclined to talk. They made slow progress and his hopes they would be prepared to march once they reached the road vanished. The women trudged side by side while Gui led the horse ahead of them. He kept close watch on the pannier in case Lady Sigrun tried to investigate it further, then admonished himself for his unjust thoughts. She hadn't given him reason to suspect she would pry into his belongings.

He recalled the way he had spoken to Lady Sigrun the previous night with angry words and his conscience gave a lurch. His reaction to her discovery of his beloved bow must have seemed far in excess of what was necessary. No wonder she had taken offence at his questioning. When a fine rain began to fall he slowed and fell in beside her as she picked her way through the tangle of roots that made progress so slow.

'I loathe the weather in this country. This miserable drizzle that passes for summer seems never ending at times.'

He gave her a rueful smile he hoped would engender fellow feeling for their shared discomfort. She pulled her cloak tightly around herself and drew the hood up. 'So why did you come here? And why don't you leave if you hate it so much!'

'I came because my lord's father commanded me and because my lord asked me. And because I wanted adventure. I stay because—' Gui's stomach churned as homesickness flared. He missed the endless vibrant green of the fields and the waves that crashed on to the rose-pink boulders of the shore. Leaving seemed awfully tempting.

'I don't know why I stay. Sometimes I wish I had not, but the attraction of escaping was too great.'

She looked surprised. Perhaps she, too, wished to escape her life. Or perhaps just to escape her marriage. He held his hand out to her.

'I was harsh with you last night and doubtless you thought my response an overreaction.'

She looked at him impassively. 'I have not known you long enough to know what is an overreaction and what is your habitual behaviour. You might always be so severe when opposed.'

Gui sighed inwardly. He was beginning to recognise the confrontational manner that he suspected was habitual to her. Worse, he suspected she was correct and that there was nothing to him beyond the anger and resentment at the lot he had drawn. He hoped not and resolved to prove otherwise.

'You might be right, but mayhap I could convince you otherwise. I will explain soon. Not now, but when I have the luxury of time. Until then, I regret that my words offended you.'

Her face softened a little. She walked beside him and said nothing more, but when he caught her eye she did not look on him with such hostility.

* * *

By the time they reached the road they were all damp to the knees from pushing through the undergrowth. Gui announced the two women would ride together and their reactions were exactly what he had come to expect. A flicker of eagerness crossed the face of Lady Aelfhild while Lady Sigrun began to loudly protest that she would rather walk.

'You're going to do as I tell you,' Gui said firmly.

'Why don't you ride?'

'What?'

She marched up to him, and put her hands on her slender hips. 'You said we would take turns, but you haven't even put your foot in the stirrup.'

'I can walk faster,' Gui protested. 'I'm used to marching.'

'I don't think you like riding any more than I do,' she said.

Challenge filled her eyes. Her soft lips widened in a smile that was so triumphant Gui had to resist covering them with his own to banish it. He gave her a stern look, slightly unnerved that she had read his feelings so well and wondering what other sentiments she might also perceive.

'Do not push me, my lady. I've got an empty belly and wet feet and I want a proper bed. We're going to put the miles behind us today. You'll get on to that horse if I have to pick you up and put you in the saddle myself!'

She looked outraged. He heard a snort of amusement that unbelievably had come from her companion. Their eyes met and for the first time he saw humour he had not thought she possessed. She ducked her head the moment she saw him looking and turned to Lady Sigrun.

'I want to go home and I want to do it quickly,' she said. 'Do as he asks, please.'

Lady Sigrun bunched her fists in her skirts. She looked from one to the other and shook her head. 'I cannot fight if both of you are in accord. Very well, I'll ride.'

Her voice was full of resignation, but she looked almost pleased to see Gui and her companion both demanding she submit. She baffled Gui.

'Would you prefer to be in front or behind?' he asked.

'Let my companion decide,' she said. 'Help her mount first.'

Gui helped Lady Aelfhild on to the horse, conscious that Lady Sigrun was watching her future husband putting his arms around another woman. He reached his arms for Lady Sigrun, feeling too eagerly the anticipation of touching her, but she stalked past him to the horse and began trying to climb up without his help. Gui watched her struggle briefly, enjoying the view of her rear it gave him. She had needed his help the day before and would need it again.

'Allow me.'

He bent his knee to provide a mounting block. She hesitated before placing her hands on his shoulders and rested her foot on his thigh. He reached out to steady her, catching hold of her by the waist and spreading his fingers wide over the soft curves beneath her skirt. She made a small noise just on the edge of his hearing and jutted her hips forward a little to regain her balance, tightening her hold on his upper arms. Gui spread his fingers wider, further down, tracing the shape of her buttock and thigh. He lifted his eyes and found she was staring down at him, her lips slightly parted.

'Are you ready to ride?' he asked boldly, wondering if the words had a double meaning in her language, too.

She blinked and held still for an instant before taking hold of the saddle and twisting round. Exhilaration raced through Gui. Her movement had brought her hips close enough that Gui would be able to bury his head in her skirts if he moved his head only a little. An image filled Gui's mind, so utterly indecent but tantalisingly sensual it made him physically weak with lust. He yearned to trail his lips across her soft belly, to work his mouth methodically down until he reached the cleft between her legs and part them with feather-light kisses until she was immobile with ecstasy.

The woman was capable of setting him on fire without the slightest awareness. He was glad her skirts hid his face because if she guessed what he was imagining, she would surely never allow him to touch her again! He struggled to his feet and took hold of the bridle, unable to meet her eyes.

They began the climb up into the hills and his unease continued. Gilbert had no claim on Gui's innermost thoughts or the direction his heart went in. He was, however, unsure how he would be able to look his friend in the face as he handed over the woman who filled his mind with fantasies of such exploits that would make the most experienced woman cry out in abandon.

Guilherm succeeded in keeping the women on horseback for longer than expected, but once they reached the brow of the hill he could no longer dissuade them from easing themselves wearily to the ground and loudly complaining about aching legs. It was fortunate the weather had changed and the heat of the previous days was only a memory because otherwise their thirst would be greater and the journey much harder.

The ground was flatter beyond the descent with the vale spreading beyond. This was where the greatest part of King William's destruction had taken place. The two women stood in shock, staring at the land where once there had been a thriving village. When the inhabitants saw the travellers arriving dressed in their fine clothes they surged around them, pleading for aid. Gui's first impulse was to reach for his sword, ready to defend the women if they looked in danger of being mobbed, but there was no violence. The people were too weak, too defeated to think of such a thing. William had succeeded in killing the spirit of the north. Gui allowed the women a moment to consider what they were seeing before he joined them unobtrusively.

'We need to move on,' he said gently into Lady Sigrun's ears. 'As you can see, if we want to find shelter tonight our choices are limited.'

Lady Sigrun shivered. Her eyes filled with tears that made Gui's heart twist. He was consumed by the urge to draw her to him and let her cry out her grief, but sensed she would not welcome his touch. Not his, or any Frenchman. Gui reached over and wrapped her cloak around her. The only contact he dared to make. She leaned against him briefly and he shuddered from the closeness, aware of every part of her that brushed against him.

'They told us in the priory that William laid waste to the villages everywhere. You warned me and I'd heard the tales. I didn't realise it was this bad, though. There's so much death. The world will never be the same. How could you do this?'

Tears brimmed in her eyes, but to accuse him personally of such a thing could not pass.

'Don't insult me, my lady. I played no part in what was committed here. It appals me to see it just as it does you.'

He strode away and kicked at a burned piece of wood that lay by the side of the road, giving vent to the disgust and helplessness that surged within him at what he saw.

'Bern kaoc'h!'

'Why does it anger you so much? Surely you can't care so much what happens to the people you conquered.'

'This was good land once, there was no need to ruin it. That was meaningless. It makes me angry to think of the lost opportunities. The ground will recover, but it might take years to become fully useful again. A decade even and that makes me furious.'

'You sound as though you know a lot about it.'

'My father worked the land, back home in Brittany. I didn't want to follow his path so I left, but perhaps there is soil in my veins as well as blood.'

'Then why do you keep fighting?'

'I don't fight any more. I haven't since—since the final battle where Harold was defeated.'

'Why not?'

Her eyes burned with curiosity. He realised with a start he had opened his heart to her far more than he had to anyone in recent memory. He started walking, setting a fast pace. Lady Sigrun had to practically run to keep up and he slowed a little. She caught him by the arm. Her touch sent a shiver racing up his arm, every hair on his arm standing on end.

'What have you done since the war ended?' she asked curiously.

Got drunk and grieved over his lost hand.

Wasted the life he didn't know what to do with.

Clutched at the promise of a patch of land in return for assuming a false identity.

Gui looked around. Although the vale lay purple with mist before them, the land they were walking through consisted of rolling hills to either side covered in sparse heather rather than the yellow gorse he remembered from home. The sea must not be far beyond the steepest and most barren-looking hills off to the left. The shore couldn't be anything as beautiful as the pink granite of the Breton coast, but Gui had the sudden urge to see the surge of the waves. Once he had delivered the women to Gilbert he might go see it, or he might go home.

But home to what? A scrap of land in Brittany where he could toil alone, live alone and die alone? What appeal was there in that? But what other prospect?

He had no intention of telling her any of that so strode on.

Alone as always.

Until this point the hamlets they had passed had been small and isolated, but now they were beginning to discover what had once been larger settlements and the devastation was apparent wherever they looked. Beggars lay by the roadside, calling weakly for alms. The ruins of houses and farm buildings became more frequent. Each one tore at Gui's heart as evidence of the destruction his King had ordered, but he had no food to spare and no way of helping. Lady Sigrun and Aelfhild did what they could, even if a sympathetic word was all they had to offer. It made for slow going.

After she had stopped to give a draught of their diminishing water supply to the third old woman who called for alms, Gui insisted there was time for no more. She caught him by the arm as he strode ahead, hard at first but when he stopped her fingers loosened but remained on his sleeve.

'Most of these people did nothing to oppose William, but they suffer just the same. How can you be so cold hearted?'

Her touch set the hairs rising on his skin, but her expression was like a slap to the face. The accusation stung. He'd hardened his heart. He had to. Gui kept walking, refusing to meet her eye.

'Because I have to be. If I stopped to help everyone I saw, I wouldn't have even reached York in the first place.'

She made a noise of disgust.

'If you're no longer a soldier, they aren't your enemy. There's no reason not to help them.'

'It's very wearying constantly having to explain and persuade you to do as I ask. Just for once could you do as you're told without arguing? It isn't a loss of face to accept the advice of someone who knows better.'

Lady Sigrun looked at him scathingly. 'And is that what you would look for in a wife? Someone meek and compliant who will obey your every command?'

'Not at all! I would wish—'

Gui broke off as the conversation sent him down dangerous roads.

'What do you wish?'

He looked back at his friend's wife-to-be. She was staring at him with an expression of raw and unconcealed hunger. It shocked him that anyone would look at him that way and for the woman he craved to be doing it made him weak with longing. His earlier hunger had calmed in his belly from an inferno to a warm glow, but Gui knew it had not been extinguished completely. She should not be looking at him with any intentions or expectation.

'You want a woman with a sweet nature. Someone gentle and obedient, not argumentative,' she told him with a roll of her eyes that demonstrated the opposite. 'All men do.'

Gui shook his head. Gilbert would choose a woman like that, someone who would be uncomplaining while he went hunting or threw her money into rearing horses. He glanced down the road to where the companion was leading the horse. A woman like that would suit Gilbert better than the short-tempered human gorse bush who lit the fires in Gui's loins.

'What I wish does not matter, but someone who would not fight against everything purely on principle would be welcome.' Their shoulders were touching. Without looking Gui could sense where their bodies would brush against each other with the smallest movement. The limbs closest to her felt more alive and more sensitive than the rest of his body. He found it unsettling to be so acutely aware of where she was in relation to him. He spoke briskly in case his voice betrayed the desire he should not be feeling.

'Your compassion does you credit, but my concern is keeping you safe and getting you back to Haxby alive. If we stop to help everyone we'll never get there and the longer we're out in the middle of nowhere the less chance we have of finding shelter.'

'We'll find shelter. We have so far.'

'By luck! If you think a half-rotted barn or thrown-together tent in the forest is going to keep you warm when the weather changes then you have your head in a dream. I can't help everyone, but I can care for you and that's what matters!'

She raised her eyebrows at his outburst. He swallowed to moisten a throat that had become unaccountably dry.

'I care about getting you safely back to your mother's house,' he amended.

'Of course, your bride must arrive for her wedding safe and sound.' She stiffened. 'Don't worry. You'll get your bride and she'll be the compliant, dutiful woman you want. There's no fear about that.'

He touched her arm, but she shrugged him off.

'If you don't want to help that's up to your conscience, but I won't ignore what your people have done to mine.'

She left him standing and caught up with her companion.

'He's selfish and uncaring.'

She didn't bother to keep her voice down. The words were meant for him as much as her companion. The women linked hands and stomped ahead, leaving Gui with a burning sense of unfairness. He was right and she was wrong. However much the plight of these people tugged at his heart it was impossible to help everyone. So why did the judgement of a woman he barely knew cut so deeply?

Chapter Nine

Towards mid-afternoon they came across the ruins of another settlement. Gui remembered it from the outward journey and his spirits lifted a little. Not far beyond was an inn that had survived the carnage, having been used by the army on their march north. They would be able to find refuge for the night there.

'We can stop to rest. But only a short while,' he cautioned.

A band of men was lying by the road. Without waiting to see if Gui would allow it, Lady Aelfhild knelt at the head of one, holding the water bottle to his lips. Lady Sigrun investigated what at first appeared to be a bundle of rags, but which proved to be a man. He reached out a hand and whimpered a plea for aid through cracked lips.

Lady Sigrun pulled back the blankets covering him, but recoiled in horror at what lay beneath, choking in shock. Gui strode over to see what had caused her distress.

The man wore a ragged jerkin and only tattered *braies* covering his nakedness. He had no legs below the mid-thigh. Vomit rose in Gui's throat and his head spun as the sight of this loss drove the strength from him.

He dropped to his knees by Lady Sigrun's side. He drew the blanket back up and over the man, then pulled Lady Sigrun to his chest.

She struggled and tried to look back, but he clutched her tighter. Gui closed his eyes. Dreadful memories he was powerless to ignore threatened to consume him. He passed his hand over his brow, the man's plight affecting him in ways the others calling for aid had not. Gui had no idea how the man had come to lose his limbs, but understood the agony he must have suffered during and after the loss.

'Don't look. You don't need to see that,' he murmured gently.

He held Lady Sigrun tight, imprisoning her in an embrace from which she could not break free and witness more of the horror that confronted them. She slipped her arms around him, her fingers clutching at his waist, and burrowed against his chest. Her breasts crushed against him, her breath came in short bursts, caressing his neck.

Gui stiffened, breath seizing in his throat at this unexpected gesture. He swore he could feel the thump of her heart against his. Gui was unable to recall the last time anyone had offered him solace. He would have stayed holding her for ever, but other matters called his attention.

Gui looked over her bent head to the stricken man. 'How long has it been?'

'Since the start of the year,' the man wheezed. 'The soldiers started it when I tried to stop them burning my home and the frost finished the job.'

'We have to help him,' Lady Sigrun pleaded. She twisted against Gui, bringing her arms about his neck and gazing into his eyes imploringly. 'I have medicines I brought with me from the priory. I could help with his pain.'

'Pain. Yes, I'm done with pain,' the man croaked. His eyes were dark circles in a face of ash. He had seized on her words like a drowning man clutching a rope. Gui closed his eyes, reliving his own agony after the loss of his hand. He buried his head against Sigrun's hair, concentrating on the sweet scent that lingered there. It tugged at his mind for some reason, comforting for no reason he could explain.

'How much of your draught do you have?'

'A little. It won't help for long, but it will help.'

'The lady says she can give you an end to your

pain for a while,' Gui told the man in case he had not understood. 'Will you let her help you?'

The man nodded weakly. 'An end. I want an end to the pain.'

His voice had a note that Lady Sigrun most likely missed, but that Gui had heard before. It filled him with foreboding. He'd used that tone himself under circumstances that made him quake to remember. He could not meet the man's eyes, knowing if he did he would see the same thing he had once begged for.

Gui realised his embrace had loosened, but Sigrun had made no move to escape. His heart tugged and he reluctantly unwound himself from around her. She didn't understand what the man hadn't spoken aloud. Gui had the means to answer the plea. Whether he had the resolve was uncertain.

He crouched beside the man, staring at the ground between them. He felt a hand on his shoulder and looked round into her trusting eyes.

'Please help him, even though he's your enemy. Do it for me, if not for him.'

This man had endured suffering that Gui could only begin to imagine that made his own pale into insignificance. Gui's own craven pleading for an end came back to haunt him now, shaming him. A hand was nothing in comparison yet he had begged to be delivered instantly from the pain he believed was unendurable. He wondered if he would still have begged for death if Lady Sigrun had been offering solace.

'Go find your medicine,' he whispered.

She did as instructed and returned with the small pot.

'I made it only a week ago. It should still be potent.'

'You made it yourself? Are you an apothecary?' Gui asked in surprise. Momentarily forgetting the severity of the situation, he eyed it with interest. He hadn't known she had the ability to create such things.

'I'm learning the skills,' she answered with a touch of pride creeping into her voice.

He took the pot from her hand and opened the lid to inspect the contents. It was about three-quarters full of roughly ground powder that prickled his nose.

'I'll show you how much to give,' Lady Sigrun told him. 'You need to mix it with water.'

'I know what I need to do,' Gui growled. She looked shocked at his tone, but he couldn't do what he had to if she was there to witness it. 'I understand how to help him. I don't need you here to watch over me.'

Her face fell. Remorse tightened his chest at

the thought he had wounded her. He sprang to his feet and drew her to him, bending his head until their foreheads touched.

'You've done enough to help,' he said softly, putting his lips close to hers. 'Take the horse and your companion. I'll catch you up when I'm done here. I won't be long.'

He put his arm about her shoulder and walked her firmly to her companion. He waited until they were out of sight before squatting next to the man on the ground. He was not much older than Gui. He had the fair hair and complexion of the people from the north of Europe, similar to the women. They, too, had come bringing violence to the people of England once, but raiders and invaders had become settlers and traders. He wondered if Lady Sigrun considered that when she railed against him and the rest of the men who came over with William.

'My companion's compassionate heart does her credit, but she does not have a realistic view of the world.' He weighed the small pot in his hand. It was a light thing, but at this moment it contained a life.

'A dose might buy you a day of relief. The whole jar used sparingly will give you no more than a week.'

The man wheezed. 'That's not what I want. I want an end for good. Can you do that for me?'

'I can give you what you want, if you're sure.'

Gui drew his sword and held it in front of the man's eyes. Fear filled them, replaced by an expression of peace, even yearning and the doubt in Gui's heart began to disappear.

The man nodded, whispered something beneath his breath, then tilted his head back to give Gui a clear aim at his throat. Gui rolled his sleeve up and cradled the man's head in the crook of his left arm. He passed the blade swiftly across the man's throat, making one deep, clean cut. The man jerked and gasped. Gui's cheeks stung and he became aware tears were running freely down his face at the death of this stranger who would have been his enemy. The man's back arched, then much quicker than Gui expected he lay still.

Gui held him until the blood stopped flowing. There was no way to bury the man so he wrapped the body in the man's cloak and carried him to the middle of the field where the remains of a shed stood. He piled as many rocks as he could around the pitifully small body to ward off carrion for as long as possible. He'd have wanted someone to do the same for him.

He strode after the women, flinging his arms out to release some of the agitation that filled him. As he grew closer he walked with his head down and cloak pulled tight around him. They were waiting for him at a fork in the road, anxious faces.

'Did you help him?'

'Help him?' he repeated, absentmindedly. She rested a hand on his arm. Her touch should have fired his senses, but he felt tainted by what he had done.

'Did something go wrong?'

'Nothing went wrong. I helped him as he asked. He's in no more pain.' He still could not meet her eyes, the half-truths searing his conscience.

'I knew you had a kind heart.' The joy in her voice tore him to shreds. She wrapped her arms round him and kissed his cheek impulsively. He tried not to flinch from her, but could not stand the hypocrisy of knowing she was praising him for something so far from the truth.

'Did you leave him with enough for a second dose?'

He whipped his head up, finally looking her in the face. She moved her hand from his arms and rested it on his chest at the spot above his heart. He jerked back as if she had stabbed him. Such a gentle touch was more than he could bear under the circumstances.

'Lady Sigrun, grant me a favour. Don't speak to me for a while!' His voice was harsh, but he felt at the limit of his tolerance.

'You're angry with me!'

He heard the shock in her voice. It wasn't fair and he knew it. She had offered to stay and administer the draught and he had not let her. He touched her cheek, but now she recoiled and he was startled to see his hand trembling as he withdrew it. He didn't blame her.

'No, not with you. Not with anyone, or perhaps with everyone. With the world as it is. Let me walk in peace with my thoughts.'

He passed the jar to her and stalked off before his composure cracked completely.

They trudged on in brooding silence and Gui anticipated a miserable night ahead. The rain had been heavier here and thick mud clung to Gui's feet and legs, making his boots heavy. He could only imagine what discomfort the two women were in with their wool skirts caked almost to the knee and growing heavier with each step.

To prove Lady Sigrun wrong about his dislike of riding, he mounted the horse, but decided on balance he would rather prove her right than sit atop the lurching beast while they walked at his side. He caught her expression as he swung himself down and his keen eyes did not miss the triumphant smile that flashed across her lips. He bowed his head in acknowledgement. She looked hastily away, but with a smile on her lips. His heart, heavy with grief for the death of the stranger, lightened a little.

From then on Lady Aelfhild rode the mare while Gui and Lady Sigrun walked side by side, but whenever he tried to address her she turned away, pretending she hadn't heard him speak. There was visible tension to her expression and figure that there had not been before he had harshly rejected her company upon his return. Why had he been unable to take her in his arms when she had greeted him so warmly? He was so unused to company he had no idea how to respond when affection was given.

The inn came into sight just as the sun began to sink below the hills. Gui did not know who had owned it before the conquest, but the new owners were from the bottom of Normandy; close enough to Brittany for their accents to stir homesickness in Gui's belly and make him once more long for home. The establishment was small and basic, but was crammed with guests. He passed the time while he tried to secure beds in imagining himself the owner of somewhere similar, content with his lot in life. It seemed far too unobtainable that it soured his mood, as did the leers and catcalls of a quartet of rough-looking vagrants who loitered around the door exuding an air of menace. Lady Aelfhild looked ready to burst into tears while Lady Sigrun glared back poisonously.

Gui's accent found favour with the landlord and they were grudgingly directed to the stable where they could bed down on straw pallets in the room alongside the horses. This suited Gui perfectly. Many of the other guests were his countrymen and soldiers, and he did not want to risk meeting someone who knew the real Sir Gilbert.

'Regular customers?' He nodded towards the vagrants.

The landlord's face darkened. 'Unfortunately yes. Wild men. They live in the ruins of a farm on the York road and prey on travellers. They deal with slavers and outlaws.'

Gui eyed them surreptitiously. 'I thought the scourging had dealt with men like that.'

'Some vermin always escape the snare.' He poured Gui a drink. 'Stay away from them. Keep your women away.'

Gui downed it quickly. Removing the women from the presence of the unpleasant men would be sensible. They eyed Gui with open hostility and the women with undisguised lust as the trio walked past.

'Greedy Norman *nithing* doesn't need both of them.'

Lady Sigrun whipped her head around. 'Breton *nithing*!' she sneered at the rat-faced troublemaker who had spoken. She linked her arm through Gui's while the fingers of her other hand shot to the *seax* at her waist. Gui resolved to remove it from her at the earliest opportunity.

The skivvy brought a meagre but hot bowl of stew and coals to light a small fire within a circle of stones. All three fell on the food gratefully. Lady Aelfhild spoke her customary prayer and rolled herself into her cloak on the pallet closest to the wall, leaving Gui and Lady Sigrun sitting alone. The stable was warm and smelled of sweet straw. A fuller belly and the prospect of a comfortable mattress lifted Gui's battered spirits. He could stand Lady Sigrun's muteness no longer. He had instructed her to leave him in peace with his thoughts so it was up to him to break the silence.

'Will you drink with me?'

She looked at him suspiciously. 'I'm not thirsty.'

He poured wine anyway and passed it to her.

Their fingers brushed as they circled the cup. Sigrun took a sip and returned it. Gui turned the cup and put his lips on the rim beside where hers had been. If she noticed she made no comment.

'We have to keep each other's company until York so we could pass the time getting to know each other a little more,' he suggested.

'Only until York! Do you intend to absent yourself after that?'

He recalled that he was supposedly her betrothed and suggesting he would be leaving was an error. He ignored the insult to him that her hopeful tone implied and the equally disturbing sensation of sadness that enveloped him.

'I simply meant it seems a shame not to use the time we have together,' Gui said, handing the cup back. 'I would like to know you better.'

'What if I feel disinclined to know you?' She took another drink and passed the cup back into his hand. 'You transform from stern to silent to fierce for no reason I can tell, and though you say you will explain you never do. I don't have the patience for that when I'm only in your company under duress. But very well, as your whim now appears to be conversation rather than solitude I shall oblige: a question for a question.'

She sat, tucked her legs under her and faced

him. 'I'll go first. Why do you carry a bow you won't use?'

She sprang the question on him with the speed of an arrow loosing from the bow. Gui was glad of the wine.

'An odd choice of question,' he said eventually.

'You became so angry when I found it. I want to know why.'

He knew this moment would come. Better he told her than she discovered the truth by accident. He had given her enough unpleasant surprises in their short acquaintance already. He remembered the look of horror on Lady Sigrun's face when she had believed she had bent his hand out of shape without him suffering any ill effect. He glanced to where Lady Aelfhild lay, already asleep.

He edged nearer to Sigrun until she was close enough to touch. He was glad the light was fading and only the glow of the small fire lit the stable so he would not so clearly see the revulsion crossing her face. He held his left arm out before him and steeled himself for her reaction.

'I don't use it because I no longer can.'

He untied the laces, slipped the glove from his wrist and pulled the sleeve of his undertunic back to reveal the wrist that ended where the hand should be. He cradled his arm briefly, loathing the sight of the scarred and puckered skin. It looked worse than usual thanks to the scratch left by Lady Sigrun's brooch pin, which was still red and sore.

'You see, I'm not so far from being the monster that you first thought me. I carry my bow because I cannot bear to destroy it even though I'll never use it again.'

Lady Sigrun's eyes were fixed on his arm. Gui pulled the cuff down before the sight of it turned her stomach completely. His jaw clenched, waiting for her to turn away in revulsion. He'd seen the reaction enough times, but this time more than others it mattered. *She* mattered.

'Oh…' She gave a quiet sigh, but it was of perception, not disgust. Then her eyes shot to his. Piercing blue and skewering him to the spot.

'Was it a punishment?'

Gui prickled at the insult. 'Do you think I'm a thief?'

She looked away abashed, muttering apologies. Nausea filled Gui's belly as the sounds and smells of battle threw themselves at his mind with an intensity that left him reeling. The ghost of Gui's hand twitched and long-gone fingers curled round the string of his bow. The first time it had happened he thought he had gone mad, and the sensation still alarmed him. Sweat slicked his brow. He drained the wine and refilled the cup, reliving the gut-wrenching terror of the war.

'It was in the last throes of the battle. I can't even claim glory for a courageous act. I slipped in the crush to retreat down the hillside and was caught among the horsemen. A hoof crushed my hand and half-severed it. It was a stupid accident. Undignified and unnecessary.'

'Why didn't you tell me before? Why keep such a thing as that a secret?'

She had no understanding of the shame he felt or the revulsion at his own body for making him less than a man or she would never have asked such a thing.

'It is my secret and my choice of when to tell. Everyone has secrets—even you, I'll wager.'

She looked away. Gui wondered what nerve he had struck to cause the reaction. He stowed the thought away, determined to wheedle it out of her if he could. Gilbert would appreciate knowing all the facts after all.

Unexpectedly Lady Sigrun gave a quiet chuckle, shaking her head as she did.

She laughed!

Gui's cheeks burned in humiliation. He turned away with a snarl and started to push himself to his feet, wishing he had never shared his dreadful secret with her, but he felt her hands on his shoulder, catching him by the sleeve and tugging him back. Her eyes were imploring and she knelt up with hands outstretched. Her face was a picture of mortification.

'Oh, no, I'm not laughing at you. Please don't think that, Gui,' she exclaimed. She knelt and clutched Gui by the arms. A *frisson* of excitement rippled through him, tightening muscles and sending blood pounding through him.

'In the water—I thought—'.

'You thought I was a goblin or a dwarf, didn't you? When I scared you in the water you must have seen my arm without really understanding what it was.'

'Perhaps.' She bit her lip, then grinned, but as she had said, it was at her own foolishness rather than mocking him. 'It was all a bit of a jumble. I don't know what I saw.'

Her hands slid slowly up his arms, fingertips skimming lightly across the cloth of his sleeves and raising them to brush against the skin beneath. The tension left Gui's body, replaced with a growing excitement at the sensation of her hands on him. She had not screamed or recoiled in horror as he had expected. She was kneeling so close that he could dip his head forward and kiss her.

'When I drove my pin into your hand it seemed impossible. When you touched my—' Her cheeks coloured and she moved her hand to her breast. Gui ached to touch it himself, fingers, lips and tongue exploring the small mounds, but he could not allow himself to respond despite the yearning that consumed him. It took great effort, but he knelt before her, arms hanging limp by his side.

She lowered her arms, sat back on her heels and folded them. She gave him a long stare, her blue eyes boring into him, giving Gui the uncomfortable impression she could read his past etched on to his heart.

'I'm only a man,' he breathed. He examined the glove in his hand. It looked more false than he had allowed himself to believe. He slipped it back on to his wrist. 'Nothing magical or otherworldly, only a padded glove and a face that would scare an unsuspecting woman.'

'Only a man,' she repeated almost absent-mindedly. Her eyes flashed from his hand to his face and her lip twitched at the corner. 'Your face isn't so terrible. It was the combined effect of your hair masking your face and the way the water fell from your body…'

She tailed off, lowering her gaze, then looking

up at him through her pale lashes. 'You are very alarming when you're wet, you know.'

Her words said *alarming*, but her eyes said something else. It wasn't often directed at him these days, but Gui had lived long enough to recognise desire when he saw it. His throat tightened and the burning need to touch her came over him again.

'Do I alarm you now?' he asked quietly.

'No, you don't.' Her lashes fluttered once more and she raised her gaze to his. 'It's sad.'

Gui's stomach twisted.

'Don't pity me,' he warned. 'I don't pity myself. I did once, but now I accept my lot in life.'

'Do you? I'm not sure.'

His first reaction was a swelling of rage coupled with indignation that she could doubt him. His fist clenched, but she was studying him with such candour that it was as if she could see into his troubled heart. He could not deny it in the face of such scrutiny. He moved closer to her, pulled by unseen ropes that wound themselves around his chest, tightening until he could barely draw breath.

'No, I don't. I carry my bow because I can't bear to destroy it even though I know I'll never draw it again. It gnaws at my soul every time I touch it, but there is nothing to be gained in pitying myself.'

He looked past her, his voice tailing off to a husky growl, and blinked to rid himself of images that plagued him every night. He spread his arms wide with both hands raised to demonstrate the uselessness of his body, then began to pull the laces tight, fiddling with them in the ritualistic way he had developed. Thinking of the injury still made him feel sick to the stomach.

'Do you need help?'

'I can manage. I've done it often enough,' he snapped. He caught his tone and realised how abrupt he was being. He resolved to temper his anger after she had pointed it out to him.

'I mean I'm well practised,' he amended more gently. 'I do not naturally use my right hand, but I've learned since I have no choice.'

She watched as he finished securing the ends of the laces.

'You expected me to run in fear or cry, or something like that, didn't you?' she said. 'I've spent my time in the priory tending to the sick and ill and I've seen worse than that. Like that poor man this morning. I'm not a child or a silly girl.'

He raked his eyes over her, every part of his body acutely aware she was not a child.

'That's why you helped him and not the others, isn't it?' She smiled sweetly. 'You understood his pain and it stirred your compassion.'

She had leapt from one subject to the other quite naturally but Gui's throat constricted with a lump the size of his missing fist. She didn't suspect what he had done. Her belief in his goodness was disconcerting and misplaced, but his relief at learning that was immense. Gui smiled through clenched teeth.

'I understood his pain and couldn't leave him to suffer.'

It was a truth of sorts and seemed to satisfy her because she smiled. Her eyes were growing heavy. Soon she would want to sleep and Gui would be left to face the night. He rubbed absentmindedly at the swollen scratch on his forearm and an idea came to him. She had sprung the question on him and now he intended to catch her unawares with one of his own.

'I answered your question so now it's my turn to ask one.'

Suspicion flitted across her face. 'What do you want to know?'

'I want to know about your brooch.'

Chapter Ten

Aelfhild drew a sharp breath.

'That—that isn't a question.'

Gui watched her with the eyes of a hawk sizing up its prey. 'Then I'll rephrase it. Tell me, why does your brooch matter so much to you?'

'Why do you want to know?' she asked.

He grinned and his eyes crinkled at the corners, giving him a roguish yet attractive expression. 'Curiosity. The same as you. You reacted so strongly when I refused to give it back.'

She chewed a fingernail and considered lying, but after the honest answer Gui had given and the risk he had taken by sharing his secret she felt unable to be so treacherous.

'It was given to me by someone I cared for. Someone who is dead.'

'A man?' He started forward. 'Did you have a lover?'

Gui's voice had an edge to it that confused Aelfhild until she remembered that he thought she was his bride-to-be. No man would wed a bride who had spoiled herself with another man. Sigrun had been as virtuous as any mother or husband could wish. When he discovered the truth of the matter Gui would not be disappointed at his bride's conduct. Aelfhild's had been no worse than that of many women either.

'He was never my lover in the sense you mean. He was—' She was about to say he had been 'Sigrun's brother', before remembering Gui knew Sigrun as Aelfhild the foundling with no family. 'He was a friend of my brother.'

Gui began examining the design of the brooch, rubbing his fingers over the surface.

'So your lad gave you this as a love token and you use it as a weapon?'

He turned his left arm over to reveal the scratch on his forearm. She hadn't realised how deeply she had cut him. 'I used it as a fishing hook. You made it into a weapon when you scared me.'

He had good arms, toned and muscular, with a covering of soft hairs that were lighter in colour than the hair on his head. That only one ended with the hand it should was tragic. The red

wound on his left forearm stood out against flesh
that was less tanned than his throat and face.

'That looks sore.'

He shrugged, but the corner of his mouth
twitched, giving the lie to his indifference. 'A
little, but I've suffered worse as you know.'

'It needs cleaning.'

'I've been doing that,' he said with exaggerated patience. 'You saw me in the river.'

Boldly, Aelfhild grabbed his left wrist and
pulled it to her. Knowing there was nothing in
the glove made her stomach squirm a little, but
she was determined not to hurt his feelings by
letting him know. She took her mind off it by inspecting the scratch closely. The skin around it
was hot to touch. Not a good sign.

'You need to treat it properly before the wound
begins to fester.'

'Perhaps you're right. To die from bad blood
when I've survived the war would be a cruel
trick of fate.'

Aelfhild delved into her bag and pulled out a
small clay pot. 'Let me help. I made this for one
of the old men in the village for a sore on his leg,
but I won't get to use the rest on him.'

'Something else you made yourself?' He
sounded impressed and she glowed with pride.

'The sister at Byland was starting to teach me

how to blend the plants and herbs. It was more fulfilling than spending my days on my knees or washing the linen. I won't miss most of my time there, but I will miss that.'

'You didn't want to enter the priory, but you're unhappy you left?'

The urge to confide in him rose within her, tales spilling out of the whippings she had received, the stifling piety, a burning need to explain how desperately she craved the brief moments of escape she so rarely won.

'I didn't choose to enter. I didn't choose to leave. It's the lack of freedom to decide for myself I resent.'

'I understand that,' Gui said, his face grave. 'You don't have to do this for me.'

He had removed his outer tunic and the fine linen undershirt hung loose, the neck unlaced and giving her a glimpse of the dark hair that fanned across his chest muscles. She tore her eyes from them.

'It was my fault you were hurt. It's my responsibility to mend the harm.'

'Is that an apology for attacking me?' Gui asked. He tilted his head on one side and gave her a wide grin.

'No, it isn't. You're fortunate it was only a brooch and not a knife. I'm not sorry I defended myself against you. I'd do the same if anyone attacked me. I'd do it to *you* again if you tried to take liberties with me I didn't want you to take!'

A blush was rising to her throat. She tried to imagine a liberty she *wouldn't* want him to take, but her imagination failed her. She took hold of his arm again and laid it across her lap. He gave it without resistance. He slid closer until they were kneeling together, his legs either side of hers, firm against her thighs. She ran a fingertip lightly along the side of the scratch from his wrist towards the crook of his elbow, then back down the other side. Gui shifted his weight. His thighs gripped tighter, grinding against her and causing a ferocious throb deep between her legs that radiated outwards. She brushed her hair back, conscious that the skin around her neck felt warm to the touch.

Gui was waiting patiently while she fussed. Aelfhild turned her attention back to her task. She dipped her fingertip into the pot and drew it out covered in the greasy substance. Pressing gently, she smeared a thin layer of the ointment over the scratch. The muscles in Gui's arm tensed beneath her fingers as they moved in small circles up and down from wrist to elbow.

She took her time rubbing it in, longer than necessary if truth were told. She dipped her finger back into the pot and repeated the application, transfixed by the feel of the firm muscles and supple skin her fingers were exploring. Gui remained perfectly still as she worked her way up and down the length of his arm. The ointment was cold, but Aelfhild's fingers grew warm, heat spreading through her hand and along her own arm until it was burning with the same fierceness as the scar. When she drew her hand away it trembled.

Gui ran his forefinger along the route her finger had taken, gliding it over the oily flesh that was slick to the touch. His eyes were thoughtful.

'Does it sting?' Aelfhild asked.

'It makes my flesh tingle all along my arm.'

Aelfhild concealed a smile. The ointment did no such thing. Any such effect that Gui noticed must be caused by the same sensation that had caused her flesh to ignite, how her body awoke at the slightest contact with his. Something was growing between them that should not be allowed to develop, but any resolve she had to deny it disintegrated as soon as she came into his presence once more.

'You have a useful skill and artful hands.' Gui slowly ran his fingers once more over the wound with a sensuous concentration that made Aelfhild's heart stop as she imagined it was her flesh he caressed. 'You should keep learning after our wedding.'

She glowed at his praise. For the first time since leaving the priory it struck her that she might have a future worth thinking of once Sigrun and Gui married. That thought caused waves of desolation and jealousy to wash over her. She dropped his arm.

'I'm finished.'

He ran his right thumb along the path hers had taken. 'Thank you. The arm will heal even if the hand will not, unless you happen to have an ointment that will restore the hand or find me a new purpose in life?'

'A man is more than the weapon he wields. You could learn another weapon.' Gui hunched his shoulders, his mouth twisting down. Anger flared in Aelfhild's belly as she wondered why she was even advising the man who should be her enemy to take arms again.

'Torwald died at York in the first skirmish of the Aetheling's rebellion. If he had grown into manhood he could have been a great warrior, but he never had the chance to become one. The rebellion came too soon. You have your life, which is more than he has!'

Gui fumbled for the wine cup and drained it in one. 'Perhaps your lad would have done great things as you say. Perhaps he was lucky he died when he did.'

Aelfhild jerked forward with an angry gasp, furious that Gui could suggest Torwald was better dead. However much her heart pounded whenever he touched her, she could not allow such a ghastly verdict to go unchallenged. Gui held up his gloved left arm to forestall the protests that sprung to Aelfhild's lips. She let them die there. The sight of his handless wrist was fresh in her memory and curdled her stomach. It had taken a lot of self-control not to recoil from him when he had revealed it. He reached for her hand. She gave it unwillingly.

'I mean no disrespect to your lost love. I told you before, war is not a game, though many young men believe it might be. A thousand men, each trying to survive, knowing they must kill to do so. You don't have time to think or feel. You have to follow orders and pray you survive the carnage.' He spoke in little more than a whisper as if forcing the words out was a physical effort.

'Your lad never had to suffer the terrors of living through a full-scale battle and the nightmares that come afterwards. Some may call him fortunate that death spared him that rather than made him live with the memories for ever. Or the scars.'

Aelfhild looked at Gui's glove. He rolled his sleeve down and drew his arm back beneath the folds of his cloak with an expression of pain that made her want to weep. Life under any circumstances was preferable to no life at all, wasn't it? Memories of Torwald tipped her into melancholy. Bright, beautiful Torwald with his laughing eyes and easy manner could not have been more different from the man who sat beside her.

'Would you rather have died than lived with one hand?'

He was silent for so long as he stared into the depths of the fire she began to think he hadn't heard her. When he looked up his face was bleak and barely recognisable.

'At first, yes, I wished to die. When the surgeon explained he would have to take what was left of my hand I almost drove his blade into my heart.'

His voice cracked. He closed his eyes and dropped his head into his hands. He'd told her he didn't pity himself but he had been lying.

'Was the pain so great?' Aelfhild asked softly. 'I can't even imagine it.'

Aelfhild placed her hand against his cheek. Two days' growth of beard scratched her palm as she gently raised his head. His jaw tensed, the muscle tightening enticingly beneath her fingers.

She wanted nothing more than to run her fingers over it, further and further down over the strong throat and firm chest, to learn the shape of the body that had tormented her since the river.

Gui grimaced, his scarred lip twisting. 'The pain was bad, but that was not the worst of it. It was the knowledge that I wasn't what I had been and could never be again. What is an archer who can't hold a bow? I'm a man with no purpose. I no longer fight. The first time I raised my fist to anyone since the battle was when I fought off your attacker yesterday.'

'Was that really only yesterday?' Aelfhild murmured. 'It seems longer. I feel as though I've known you for days.'

'You have, I suppose.' He grinned. Shadows played a game of chase across Gui's face, accentuating the angles. He was alarming to look at, yet the imperfections gave him a vitality that had been lacking in Torwald's handsome demeanour. 'We had met before, don't forget. If we had recognised each other in the river events might have been different.'

Light filled his eyes. He laced his fingers through hers and lowered her hand, resting it on her lap. 'If I had known who you were when you came to me in the priory, I would have behaved better. I wouldn't have teased you, or made you kiss me. Then perhaps you would not have run from me.'

'Yes, I would!' Aelfhild said indignantly. 'I might still have stabbed you, too.'

Gui raised his eyebrows. He gave a chuckle, which Aelfhild found impossible to resist. For a brief moment they were friends. Perhaps something more, because she saw his eyes widening and desire written clear across them. She glanced away, sitting back on her heels and fumbled for the wine goblet. Gui stared into the flames and poked a stick in deeper with slow precision.

'I don't think I could fight even if I wanted to.' Gui looked back at her, his expression as dark and foreboding as the grave. 'The weapon doesn't matter. I can't fight at all. Not because of my hand but because—because I'm terrified at the thought of going into battle again.'

He whispered his final words in a voice so thick with shame Aelfhild had to struggle to hear them. He drew his knees up, crossing his legs and looking back into the glowing stones.

'The surgeon gave me a drug to make me insensible to the pain when he performed the amputation. He assured me I would know nothing of what happened. He was right in that because my mind was so full of visions and terrors that I barely noticed him working. The nightmares started then and they've never stopped. Every night is the same and every morning I wake exhausted and dreading the next.'

He broke off with a moan of despair that tore at Aelfhild's heart.

'What happens in them?'

His skin had turned pale. Aelfhild gave a soft sigh of sympathy, remembering the way he had writhed in his sleep as if bound in a net.

'I'm dying alone, suffocating among the dead. I call for help, but I have no voice. No one knows I'm still alive and there's no one who cares enough to look. I know no one will come for me.'

She suppressed a shiver at the ghoulish picture he painted, but worse was his belief that he had no one to care for him. He looked so vulnerable and alone. His anguish was unbearable. She slipped her hand into his, desperate to make him understand that she cared.

'That's why you cry out in your sleep.'

'I do?' He looked at her sharply, his gaze spearing her. 'I thought I was silent.'

'Last night you woke us by crying out. I tried to wake you, but you were dreaming too deeply.'

'Why?' He looked confused. Was he so unused to kindness that he suspected a dark motive? She hugged herself, not daring enough to put her arms around him.

'It upset me to see you in such a way and I wanted to help. You were speaking in Breton, I think, and shouting. You seemed so distressed and were thrashing about.'

She broke off in embarrassment and looked down, aware how intensely he was examining her. He narrowed his eyes, then put his hand to her face and ran his fingers softly across the swelling beneath her eye. His touch fanned fires in her belly.

'Did I do this to you?' His voice was rasping and filled with dismay as he stroked his thumb across the curve of her cheekbone.

'You lashed out unexpectedly. I wasn't quick enough to move out of the way.'

He whipped his hand back as if her skin had become molten iron. He held his hand before him, then bunched it into a fist, glaring at it in loathing.

'My lady—forgive me. I didn't know. I would never willingly harm you.'

He swept round and bundled her in his arms, crushing her to his chest and burying his head in her hair. His embrace was fierce and unexpected. Aelfhild cried in a mixture of astonishment and longing as the breath was forced from her. She felt him grow rigid. He unwound him-

self from around her and stared at her with horror on his face.

'I'm not fit to be around civilised people.'

Abruptly he pushed himself to his feet and
stalked to the door. He leaned against the frame
and faced into the darkness, shoulders hunched
and head down. A solitary figure, the embodi-
ment of sorrow. Aelfhild cast a look at Sigrun,
who was in a deep sleep. She crept to where Gui
stood. His broad shoulders tensed as she neared
him. Her step faltered. He glanced over his shoulder at her then looked into the forest once more.
She edged closer, slowly as one might approach
a semi-wild animal.

'I know you didn't mean to hurt me,' Aelfhild
said softly. 'You stopped after that and seemed
to sleep peacefully from then on.'

Perhaps she had been responsible for bringing
him that peace. She hoped so.

She wished she could tell him how she had
spent the night in his arms, but such a thing was
beyond the bounds of propriety. A wife might
boast of easing the troubles of her husband, a
betrothed couple might even share a bed with
enough bedclothes between them to prevent indiscretions, but even if that was true, Aelfhild
was not his bride and she was in danger of forgetting that she was merely playacting as such.

She could not resist hunting for one treasure for herself. She rested her hand on his shoulder.

'Were your dreams as bad last night?'

Gui shivered, but cocked his head to one side, his eyes thoughtful. 'Now I think of it I woke feeling more peaceful than usual. I remember the sky seeming brighter this morning.'

'I'm glad.' Aelfhild smiled. She touched the bruise that still throbbed occasionally. 'I don't mind this if it served some good.'

'I mind. It's best if I sleep away from you for the rest of the journey.' Gui briefly clasped her shoulder, making her heart skip a beat. 'I'm going to check everything is secure. There were some rough-looking people out there and I want to make sure they stay away.'

Gui removed the brooch from his cloak and turned it over in his hand, making it dance between his fingers. He stopped; the brooch paused halfway between his first and second fingers.

'Here,' he said. 'I've kept it for too long. It's time I gave it back.'

He extended his hand. Aelfhild reached eagerly out, but stopped before she took the brooch. It had been a present from Torwald and now she was receiving it again from another man. Curiously this added to rather than detracted from the value of the brooch.

'What's wrong?' Gui asked. His voice was gentle, concerned, a little puzzled at her reluctance to take back what she had demanded before.

'I'm thinking of the night he gave it to me. He took a kiss in exchange.' She gave Gui a half-smile, a little embarrassed at her foolishness.

Gui's eyes widened. He took a step closer to her and Aelfhild realised what he must think.

'Oh! No! I didn't mean—' Her cheeks flamed at her blunder. 'I can never say the right thing!'

'I know what you meant and what you didn't mean.' He spoke without mockery or judgement, but his voice was low and gruff. The look in his eyes caused Aelfhild's stomach to flutter like the first shivering of water coming to the boil. She felt her mouth curve unbidden into a shy smile and watched Gui's grave eyes follow the movement of her lips. His mouth twisted in response, the scar drawing to one side. The cauldron in Aelfhild's stomach bubbled with an energy that was both frightening and exhilarating.

'Here. There is no fee for returning it.'

He held out the brooch once more, not between his fingers, but resting in his open palm. Instead of taking it immediately Aelfhild brushed her fingertips across his palm, feeling the hard callouses at the base of his fingers. She heard him draw breath, a sharp inhalation of surprise that tailed away into a sigh, though his hand remained steady. His fingers closed over hers, the brooch cold and hard between them. He circled his thumb over the back of Aelfhild's hand before running it lightly across her knuckles. It was a small gesture, but one that caused the cauldron to boil over, spilling heat through Aelfhild's veins and causing her heart to stop beating.

She looked up to find Gui watching her intently. Unconsciously they had drawn closer to each other so their elbows were bent and their linked hands were raised between them at chest height.

'Did you love your lad deeply?' Gui's voice was keen. His eyes bright.

A week ago she would have said yes. Now she hesitated before answering. 'I thought I did at the time. I think I confused his interest and my appreciation at being noticed for love.'

Something stirred inside her, a sense that something greater was in command of her. If her heart was capable of love, Torwald had tapped on the door, but Gui was in the process of kicking his way through it.

'I think love is something else,' she murmured. 'Something stronger.'

His eyes crinkled and she shivered in response. Excitement bubbled deep within her as she realised how much she wanted him to kiss her. She leaned towards him, tilting her head and realised he was doing likewise. Goosebumps rose on her skin.

She parted her lips a little, skimmed her tongue around to moisten them. She might have excused the movement to any onlooker as instinctive, but could not pretend to herself this was anything other than deliberate. Gui's scarred lip twitched into a smile, causing a deep halfmoon to appear at the corner of his mouth. Aelfhild's fingers itched to touch it. Would it be hard against her lips or as soft as the rest of them promised to be?

Gui inclined his head, tilting it a little to the left and drawing closer still until his face filled Aelfhild's vision. He gazed at her with such open desire Aelfhild was incapable of thought. Her mind emptied of every desire other than the urgent need to feel his lips on hers. She raised herself on to her toes, leaning closer and closing her eyes in anticipation. His arm slipped around her waist, drawing her towards him while his hand found the back of her head, cupping it gently. His lost hand should have repelled her, but the lust that pounded through her limbs at his touch overwhelmed any other sensation. She cleaved to him, winding her arms about his neck and pressing the full length of her body against him.

In the dark room Sigrun sighed and rolled over. Aelfhild's blood froze. She pulled away, just as Gui's lips brushed across hers, leaving a trail of heat that was unbearable to deny yet impossible to allow. She opened her eyes and looked at Gui as if a veil had been drawn back from her face. Shame made her belly writhe like a nest of adders. Love was not for her. Not with this man. It couldn't be when he belonged to Sigrun. He was not free to kiss her. He might believe that his bride had suddenly become willing to grant him favours and enter into indiscretions before their wedding night, but his true bride lay not a dozen paces from the shameful incident that had nearly taken place.

'We mustn't,' she whispered. She was going to weep. The tears were smarting in her eyes and her throat was tightening. 'I can't. I'm so sorry.'

Gui's demeanour changed. His body stiffened and the keen light in his eyes faded. His fingers tightened around hers, then he slipped his hand from her neck. He bowed his head, then stepped back, passing the brooch into her possession as he did. He did not demand reasons for her sudden change or press her further to resume what they had begun. If anything he looked more guilt-ridden than Aelfhild at what had nearly taken place.

'You have nothing to be sorry for. I swore I would not touch you and I broke that vow. I'm going to make a short patrol. If I wake you with my cries tonight, leave me to my dreams.'

He walked away.

'To your nightmares, you mean,' Aelfhild called. 'I can't do that, not when you've told me how you suffer.'

He turned, his expression nailing her to the spot.

'You care whether I am troubled?' His voice was low, brimming with wonder.

'I do.' Aelfhild stepped towards him, reaching out, but the stiffening of his shoulders—of his entire powerful frame—made her step falter and she dropped her arms to her side. 'I don't know why I should, but it pains me to think of it.'

'Then that is a tragedy for both of us. I bid you goodnight. Do as I said, for both our sakes.'

He gave a smile so gentle and sad that it made tears spring to Aelfhild's eyes. She yearned to console him and be comforted in anticipation of the nights she must spend alone while he slept in the arms of his bride.

Gui squared his shoulders and walked from the clearing without looking back, the blackness

of the woods enveloping him like a cloak. Aelfhild returned to the stable and lay down beside
Sigrun, who slept peacefully, unaware of what
had almost happened. A worm of conscience
burrowed into Aelfhild's stomach. She should
have felt more guilt than she did, but Sigrun did
not want Gui. Why, then, should Aelfhild not
have taken what she wanted, when she had seen
plainly on his face that he wanted it as much as
she did?

She should never have begun the deception,
that way Gui would never have thought he had
the right to look at her as he did, with open interest and the assumption that before long he would
be entitled to claim what he wanted.

He did not know, she felt sure of that, in spite
of his strange words, but every day they drew
closer to Haxby was a day closer to the deception being uncovered and Aelfhild being forced
to admit she had no claim on his growing affection. Quite what would happen after they had
revealed their plot was something she could not
begin to contemplate.

She'd agreed willingly to the deception. More
than willingly—eagerly, because it meant she
could spend more time in the company of the
man who fascinated her so greatly. Her blood
sang as it coursed through her veins whenever

she caught him looking at her and when he had taken her in his arms.

She thought of Torwald whom she had grieved over. That love seemed small in comparison. Had she ever loved him as a woman could love a man or was it a girlish infatuation? The sensation that had been molten iron when the young man had stolen a kiss now felt like no more than the barely warm embers of the hearth at midnight.

She stifled a sob that rose unexpectedly in her throat, drew her blanket over her face and was unable to say which man she was mourning most: the one she had lost or the one she could never have.

She listened for Gui's footsteps as he returned from his patrol, forcing herself to stay awake. She heard him enter, hesitate, then settle at the other side of the room, far away from where he had originally sat.

Far away from her.

She clutched the brooch tightly in her hand, holding it close to her heart, and fell into a miserable sleep. When Gui's moans woke her, the sound of his torment and despair, and the reason behind it was too much to endure. She hesitated before disobeying his orders and vowed only to stay a short while. She crept silently to lie beside the sleeping man, nestling against him. She laid her hand on his chest, drawing as much comfort from the racing, powerful thump of his heart as she hoped to give him in return.

Chapter Eleven

'*My lady!*'

Gui's words echoed in his ears. Not his lady, though; he did not have the right to claim that endearment. His stomach lurched, feeling once again the trace of Lady Sigrun's fingertips moving gently across the skin of his arm. Lust pounded through him, making him swell as the recent memory of her slight body, crushing against him and urging him on, consumed him. He leaned back against a tree, drawing deep breaths of night-chilled air into his lungs as he sought to master his despair.

He should never have allowed her to soothe his sore arm with her medicines, for what had her touch done but create a deeper, aching wound in his heart that no ointment could salve. He should never have become engrossed in an exchange of confidences or allowed her sympathy for him and sorrow for her lost love to burrow under his skin. He should have hurled the misbegotten brooch at her feet and left before he had allowed himself to be beguiled into almost kissing her.

Guard your heart, he told himself; knowing it was already too late. He was lost in a labyrinth of emotions he would never escape.

He craved sleep, but stormed into the forest, patrolling around the inn before returning to circle the stable like a guard dog. Voices drifted from the inn, laughter and anger, singing and shouting. Gui wanted none of it. He only wanted the woman who lay inside. When he could no longer withstand the drooping of his eyelids and the insistent throb of weariness that pummelled his head, he slipped back inside the stable. If the women were awake they gave no sign of it and Gui resisted the urge to check, knowing that if Sigrun awoke and turned her captivating blue eyes on him he would find it impossible to resist taking her in his arms and damning them both for infidelity.

He settled himself as far from them as possible and wrapped his cloak around him tightly, contriving to pinion his arms to his side in the hope he would not flail about.

Perhaps his exhaustion would mean he would sleep without disturbance and without causing her to wake. If he cried out tonight, would she try waking him again?

The knowledge she had tried to ease his suffering made his heart swell. That she saw something in him beyond the scars and disfigurements was barely comprehensible. He inhaled; recalling the odd scent that had confused him that morning and which he now knew was a combination of the herbs that Lady Sigrun had bathed in and her own scent. Knowing she had embraced him while he was defenceless and unaware of her presence made him weak with desire. To know that she had been hurt as a result tore him apart. He fought sleep for as long as he could and as he felt his limbs grow heavy he forced himself to think of her face like a talisman, hoping against hope that this might ward off the nightmares and give him the respite he craved.

Gui woke, hoping in vain that Sigrun had ignored his instructions and he would find her in his arms. He could not be blamed if she chose to ignore his instructions, as she so frequently did, but to his disappointment there was no body nestled close to his, no head on his shoulder. Gui's body felt rested, but his heart was as ravaged as every morning so he assumed she had obeyed his instruction and kept away from him. The slight trace of her scent on his skin made him wonder. After the turmoil of the night before he could have slept like a babe and still woken with a heart aching from loneliness.

He pushed himself up on to his elbow and peered in the dim corner where the women were sleeping. Sigrun was where she had been the previous night, facing towards him. Invisible hands caressed his heart as he imagined they were husband and wife, lying alongside each other. To wake each morning alongside such a vision would make the day worth greeting.

They should be on the road soon, but both women looked so peaceful he could hardly bear to disturb them. Now he studied them there was a strong likeness around the eyes and nose. Sigrun had described her companion as an unknown foundling, but now Gui wondered if the relationship was closer than that. Had Herik fathered both girls, but denied ownership of one to spare the feelings of his wife? It would not be the first time such a thing had happened.

As always Lady Aelfhild's face bore a placid and slightly troubled expression. It would not have looked out of place gracing a marble statue in a cathedral, but it transformed her beauty into something equally lifeless. Even in sleep Sigrun had a vitality her more beautiful companion would never possess. She would never do for Gilbert. Gui wondered if Gilbert would be content to marry the bastard daughter rather than the true heiress, then felt guilty for plotting to give away Lady Sigrun's birthright.

He gazed at his heart's desire for a little longer, knowing it would be his last time sharing such intimacy with her and committing the vision to his memory. He pulled on his boots and slipped out to beg breakfast from the inn.

The morning was peaceful, but evidence of the drinking that had gone on long into the night was everywhere, as men lay sprawled across tables still deeply asleep. The party of men who had insulted Gui and his companions were slumped in a heap and Gui gave serious thought to giving them a swift kick to the head while they slept, or at least stealing their boots in a petty revenge. He did neither, but located some bread and carried it back to the women.

'My lady, are you awake?' he called softly, kneeling beside Lady Sigrun.

She moaned softly and rolled on to her back, pulling the thin blanket tighter round herself, leaving only the outline of her form visible. Her hair clung damp to her cheeks and fell across her eyes.

'My lady, we need to go.'

She moaned softly and rolled her head a little towards him, her sensuous lips parted as if inviting him to wake her with a kiss. Gui's heart began to race as he instinctively bent his head closer then caught himself. He stepped back and spoke loudly. 'Lady Sigrun, Lady Aelfhild, wake up. I've brought bread.'

His tone roused Sigrun where soft words had failed. Her expression became belligerent as she was torn from sleep. Gui waited outside while the women did whatever it was women deemed necessary to make themselves presentable. Lady Sigrun emerged first, but only to ask for water so they could wash. Gui suppressed a sigh and made his way to the well, returning with a pail. He passed it over, acutely conscious of the way their fingers met on the handle. He pretended not to watch as Lady Sigrun dipped her hands into it and ran them across her face and creamy neck. He wished he had a bucket to throw over himself to douse the flames that rose in him as her fingers moved further down towards the neck of her tunic.

She finished and Gui strolled over to join her. She stiffened, holding herself uncertainly with an awkwardness in her manner that had not been there previously. Gui realised she was as edgy around him as he felt in her presence.

'Did you sleep…?'

'How was…?'

They both began speaking at once. Gui held a hand out to indicate she should continue.

'How is your arm this morning?' Lady Sigrun asked. 'Did the ointment help?'

He rolled his sleeve up and examined the scratch, suppressing the shiver that raced over his skin at the memory of her fingers exploring his flesh.

'I believe it did. Thank you.'

Lady Sigrun rummaged in her bag and found the jar. Gui plucked it from her hand, unwilling to risk the touch of her fingers awakening the treacherous response of his body once more. He applied it quickly and rolled his sleeve back down, adjusting the laces that bound his glove to his wrist, and glanced at her out of the corner of his eyes. She was watching him eagerly, eyes darting from his face to arm and back again in a manner he found unnervingly exciting. He was not used to being scrutinised so openly without hostility.

He looked over his shoulder to where Lady Sigrun's companion was rolling blankets. The woman was deeply engrossed in her task and humming tunelessly, her beautiful face serene. Gui's heart lurched, wishing the woman struggling with fury before him could find such peace. Wishing he could himself.

'Your companion seems happier today,' he remarked.

Sigrun looked around. 'She does. I'm surprised, I admit. She wanted to stay at Byland.' She gave a deep sigh. 'I should never have forced her to leave. It was selfish of me.'

'She was happy there?'

Gui thought back to the oppressive atmosphere and the domineering prioress. He couldn't imagine anyone willingly choosing such a life.

'She was. I went unwillingly into the priory, but to her it was a true sanctuary. She folded in on herself after the rebellion, wanting only to deny the world's existence.'

'You both saw the same horrors during the fighting. What did it do to you?'

She looked him square in the face, lifting her chin defiantly. He already knew the answer and his heart sank to see the ferocity flare in her eyes.

'It made me want to fight. I would have stayed in Haxby if I could. I'd have gone to York, too, but Torwald wouldn't let me go.'

'He was right to do so,' Gui said firmly. The hairs on the back of his neck stood on end. He was jealous of even her dead love. How could he ever bear to see her with a living man, even his friend?

'If I loved a woman, I would do everything in my power to stop her putting herself into danger.'

'But what if you didn't have the right to command her?'

His stomach plummeted. He didn't have the right, but the longer he spent in her company the more he craved it. He should walk away now and speak nothing more to her until they arrived at her mother's home.

'That would be a burden I would have to bear,' he muttered. 'You should try to find peace. I prefer the side of you that heals to the one that wants to fight.'

He spoke without condescension, but her fists curled and he regretted his words instantly.

'Fine words coming from a man who refuses to fight any more!' she exclaimed. She tossed her hair back with a flourish. 'What if I prefer the side of me that can defend myself?'

Gui sighed in exasperation at this show of belligerence. 'Must you be so fierce? You aren't a shieldmaiden from your tales and there is no need to try to convince me that you would fight the world at any opportunity!'

This determination to crave violence needed quashing once and for all. He reached out and took the bag from her hand, dropping it with the ointment jar on the ground.

'Come with me,' he ordered. 'We have business.'

Gui's face took on an expression that chilled Aelfhild's blood. Not even when he had described his nightmares had he looked so grim. She shook her head.

'I'm not going anywhere.'

His hand whipped out and he seized her by the upper arm.

'What are you doing!' she exclaimed. She twisted her arm, but he held tight, stepping towards her as she pulled back. His hand encircled her arm, fingers almost meeting thumb, and she was unable to loosen it. His grip wasn't painful, but he clearly had no intention of setting her free.

He led her round the corner of the building, released her and took two steps back, holding her gaze. The mood had changed. The affectionate, tender moment when they had shared confidences the previous night might as well never have happened. The brief, fervent clinch seemed beyond imagining. There was no passion in him now, only danger that flowed from him like a torrent over the rocks.

Aelfhild's scalp prickled with a mixture of anticipation and apprehension.

'Attack me.' He gave her a stern look. 'As if you mean it. As if I was your most hated enemy.'

She had been mistaken. The swell of attraction she had felt between them was still there, but it was overlaid with an anger that clouded the distance between them, thick as smoke.

'Don't be foolish. I don't have time for games.' She spun on her heel to go back to Sigrun, but Gui blocked her path.

'I'm not playing games,' he growled. 'If you want to go back, you'll have to go past me.'

The blood began to thump in Aelfhild's ears. 'I'll scream if you don't let me past.'

'You hope someone else will come to your aid? Would one of your shieldmaidens have called out for her servant, or do you hope one of the drunken brutes who mocked you yesterday will spring to your rescue?'

'I don't want to fight you,' she answered. She was lying. The complacent look on his face filled her with rage. The derision in his voice made her burn. She wanted nothing more than to rip him into pieces and stamp on the remains until he was a sticky mess on the ground.

'I could hurt you.' She tried to stop her eyes

flicking to his missing hand, she really did, but he saw the direction in which her eyes slid.

His expression darkened again. 'I'll risk it. Get your claws out, little kitten. I'll try to dodge them.'

Aelfhild tensed, cheeks flaming at the taunt. She bent her knees and raised her bunched fists. Gui dropped his arms loosely to his side. He bowed his head, shoulders dropping and broad frame relaxed. Aelfhild leapt forward, arms flailing, and aimed at his chest. Gui leaned away and her blow glanced off his shoulder.

'A good start, what now?'

She aimed at his jaw, then his belly, then chest. He did not strike her back, but ducked and blocked her blows. She moved around him in a frenzy. Her breath grew faster, while he barely moved and looked as unruffled as when he started. He was toying with her.

'Fight me properly,' she cried.

'I'll fight properly when you do,' he taunted. 'You'll wear yourself out. Look where you're aiming. Put some force into your blows and for the sake of your thumbs keep them outside your fists!'

He barked instructions as if he was giving her a lesson. Aelfhild hurled herself at him with both fists raised. Before she could land the blow he had seized her about the waist from behind with his right arm. She jabbed an elbow back. In an instant he had slipped his hand into the gap she had created between the crook of her elbow and her back, pushing his arm between their bodies and leaving her unable to pull her arm forward. He brought his left arm round, using it for the first time, and wound it around her waist. She flung herself backwards with all her weight. Gui grunted and staggered, but did not fall or release her.

Aelfhild twisted and bucked, kicked and writhed in his arms and finally went limp with exhaustion. He loosened his grip, which gave her the opportunity she had hoped for to twist her torso around. She gave a cry of fury and brought her free hand round to clout him open palmed on the side of the head. He took the blow with a laugh, tossing his dark curls back.

'You aren't hurting me. You might as well submit now.'

'Not if my life depended on it,' Aelfhild snarled. She kicked out at his knee and heard his first genuine gasp of pain.

'Enough!' He spun her around to face him, half-lifting her off the ground. Her legs caught in her skirts and she kicked out to untangle them. Her balance was off. She felt herself lunging backwards and flung her arms round his neck. He stepped closer. Both arms came around her waist and he pushed one foot between hers. Their legs were entwined, bodies pressed together from groin to chest. Aelfhild felt a hardness pressing against her crotch and realised he was deeply aroused. A growing, aching heat began between her legs and spread out in all directions through her legs and belly, shocking her into realising he was not alone.

He shifted his right arm to her upper back and leaned closer until his cheek brushed hers. The scrape of his growing beard against her jaw caused fires to ignite in her breast. She gave another twist of her body in an attempt to break free, but her struggle was half-hearted and only succeeded in squashing their lower halves closer together and causing her breasts to grind against the swell of his chest. Her limbs turned to water.

'Do you submit now?' Gui demanded in a low whisper. His breath was hot on her collarbone, his words coming in soft bursts of air that made the hairs on the back of Aelfhild's neck lift and cause her to shiver. She stood motionless, fearing that any further movement would result in their bodies becoming even more intimately bonded and he would realise what a thrill she felt at being in his arms.

He must have interpreted her silence for resistance because he drew her closer, tightening the arm encircling her waist.

'You fought well but as you can see there is no way you could have seriously hurt me. Even maimed and useless as I am, I could have stopped you any time I chose.' He cradled the back of her neck with his hand, spreading his fingers wide in the fall of her hair, and brought his lips closer to her ear.

'It was just a game to you!'

'Yes,' he breathed. 'A game. An exercise to demonstrate how little you really understand about a battle. Did you like playing it? To other men it would not be a game and you would be hurt or worse.'

A sob of humiliation and despair forced itself unbidden from Aelfhild's lips. Gui tilted his head, his lips searing a streak of heat along Aelfhild's flesh from earlobe to cheek.

'Lady Sigrun, do you submit?' he asked again, his lips now at the edge of her own.

'I submit,' she breathed, turning her head so their mouths were aligned. She could feel his breath on her lips, soft and teasing, hot enough to bring a flush to her cheeks. She parted her lips and ran the tip of her tongue rapidly over the soft mounds to moisten them and tilted her head slightly to the side. The movement was small, but enough to bring their mouths fully together in the way it almost had the night before.

Now, however, there was no Sigrun lying close by to prick her conscience. She pressed her mouth to his greedily, desperate to sate the need that coursed through her. His lips were hot and firm, igniting flames within her core. He drew a sharp breath as his lips enclosed hers. It drew the air from her lungs and felt to Aelfhild as though he was drawing her soul within him, claiming it for his own. She gave a low, keening moan.

Gui stiffened at the sound and released her, uncoiling himself from around her and staggered away. His eyes were distant, but he blinked as if waking from a dream and turned his attention fully on Aelfhild. She reeled as she felt once again the full force of his attractiveness drawing her towards him.

He had bested her with ease. Her pride burned, but her body cried out that there was no shame in being conquered by a man such as this. Would he conquer his bride in their bedchamber with such skill and thoroughness, too? How could any woman regret becoming the lover of a man who could awaken such unseemly fantasies simply by shrugging his shoulders? Her lip trembled and she stared at the ground between them. Their situation struck Aelfhild as so monstrously unfair. Sigrun didn't want Gui, she recoiled from the thought of even having to speak to him in horror, and such a display of strength would have her fainting away whereas Aelfhild desired him so badly the craving was agony. And Gui for his part…

Aelfhild raised her eyes to meet Gui's. He was looking at her with an expression now so full of concern and so tender it broke her heart.

'Did I hurt you?' Gui asked.

Aelfhild shook her head, a hand clawing at her throat and stealing the words. She couldn't speak the ones she wanted to in any case; to tell him what effect he had on her when he held her so intimately and that if it really were she who was bound to marry him she would do it willingly and with elation in her heart. She twisted her hands together, biting her lip until she was happy her voice would be steady.

'Only my pride, and realising that I have no means of defending myself.'

He walked to her and smiled down with a gentleness that was so different to the fierceness he had displayed he could have been a different man.

'Don't be downhearted. I meant it when I said you fought well.'

He glanced downwards. His fine brown surcoat was rumpled and his cloak had slipped askew. Aelfhild felt a prickle of satisfaction to see there was at least a little visible evidence of his exertion and that she had left her mark on him. He shrugged his cloak back into place with a shrug of his shoulders and Aelfhild's stomach did cartwheels. A wicked, indecorous desire to press her body once more against the hard, muscular chest that lay beneath the fine wool tunic overwhelmed her.

He flipped the hair back from his eyes with a quick toss of the head, then reached out and brushed the hair back from Aelfhild's cheek, tucking it behind her ear. Aelfhild swallowed, acutely aware of the singing of her skin where his fingers brushed her cheek. 'You have me to defend you for the time being. I'll keep you safe until York.'

'And afterwards,' she said, summoning a faint smile.

His jaw hardened. 'Of course.' The veil came down across his eyes once more. 'We need to be on the road. Your companion will be wondering where we have got to.'

He gave a polite nod and left her standing alone.

Aelfhild ran her fingers through her hair and pulled the neck of her dress into shape. She picked up her bag and the jar of the ointment where he had discarded it. As she returned the ointment to her bag her eyes fell on the jar of medicine he had used to help the soldier. The contents had barely been touched and she felt her legs go from underneath her. The amount Gui had taken would barely have touched the edge of pain such as that.

'He lied,' she whispered to herself.

He had left the man to suffer despite what he had told her. She had trusted him, but now began to wonder if she knew anything about him at all.

She looked to where he stood trying to make conversation with Sigrun. He was waving his arm towards the horse and talking with an easy smile on his face, as if he had not recently been bodily restraining Aelfhild or kissing her. He seemed unmoved by what had taken place.

Had their kiss been a game to him as their fight had been? If she had not insisted there would be no intimacy until after marriage she might have discovered the truth, however many difficulties that would lead to.

He veered between charm and darkness and

she had no idea which side would triumph at any particular moment. She had allowed herself to grow fond of him and that had been a mistake. She would have nothing more to do with him. She threw her bag across her shoulder and stalked to them.

'Let's go.'

'Will you walk with me, my lady?' Gui asked. His eyes were warm and soft and the sight tore into her. How much of the warmth was false? She looked at him coldly and stalked away. He caught up in four paces.

'How have I offended you so quickly?'

'I checked my jar,' she snapped. 'It was full. You lied to me about helping that man. How could you leave him to suffer, after what you have suffered?'

'I didn't leave him to suffer.' He whipped his head up, glaring.

'But you didn't give him the powder. What did you do?'

'I did what he asked me to do.' His face had gone white. His fist bunched and his words by the fireside came back to her in a rush. He had craved death when he had lost his hand.

'Did you murder him?' Her voice was ragged.

A look of rage crossed his face. 'Murder is a serious accusation, my lady.'

'That isn't an answer. Did you kill him?' She spat the words, unable to believe he could really have done it.

Gui took too long to answer. 'I took his life. He asked me to release him from his pain, begged me to do it and I could not refuse.' His voice was gentle. Soothing her. It raised her hackles to be talked down to in such a way and knowing he had deceived her made it so much worse.

'I thought you were showing compassion, but it was just pretence.' She felt her eyes fill and ran her hand angrily over them. 'You said you wouldn't fight again!'

He caught her by the shoulder, spinning her round to face him.

'I said I couldn't bear to fight in battle. I never said I wouldn't take a life. If you can't see the difference, you're a fool!'

'Then I'm a fool who wants nothing to do with you!' She tore her arm from him. She stalked to where Sigrun was lingering, looking worried, and side by side the women walked past the inn where other travellers were beginning to make their way to the road. Aelfhild ignored the lewd mutters from the group who had shown interest the previous night and stalked ahead. She felt Gui come alongside her, but kept her head resolutely down, refusing to acknowledge his existence and he in turn made no attempt to speak to her.

'What is wrong with you?' Sigrun asked. 'What were you and Sir Gilbert doing behind the barn?'

'Nothing!' Aelfhild said, too quickly to be convincing. Sigrun looked startled. Aelfhild took a long breath to calm her voice. 'We were only talking.'

'And now you're not speaking at all.'

The rowdy group of travellers who had insulted Gui overtook them, driving a dilapidated cart. They catcalled, but Aelfhild was in a foul mood now and shot them an evil glare.

'No. I'm sorry I told you to try to get to know him,' she told Sigrun. 'We'll keep to ourselves until we get to Haxby, then try our best to persuade your mother to change her mind.'

'Change her mind!' Sigrun clutched Aelfhild's arm tightly enough to cause pain. 'Change it how? She hasn't agreed—has she?'

Aelfhild cursed inwardly at her error. 'I thought you were better not knowing. It would distress you.'

'You *lied* to me!' Sigrun tore her hand away. 'How could you do that?'

'Sigrun, please let me explain.'

'Leave me alone,' Sigrun cried. She stumbled away, leaving Aelfhild standing miserably. She realised Gui was watching. He raised an eyebrow quizzically. She ignored him, trudging on alone.

It was the worst morning of the journey. Everything was dreadful. Her muscles ached. Her belly was empty. Her heart was sore. She had succeeded in hurting her dearest friend and whenever she thought of Gui her mind refused to co-operate, feelings overriding sense. They still had miles to travel. The day could not get any worse.

The attack came at midday, when they were least expecting it. The road had split into two and without consultation Gui led them down the fork that wound through the forest rather than climbing steeply over the high hill. They walked single file, spread out and each keeping their thoughts to themselves.

If they had been walking together one of them might have seen the waiting cart, or might have presented a better defence. As it was, Aelfhild was walking ahead when an arrow thudded into the tree she was walking past. She froze and a figure rushed at her from behind a tree, seizing her around the waist. Aelfhild screamed. She clawed at his arm, wishing she had her brooch to hand, but it was pinned beneath her outer tunic.

She heard Gui's roar of anger and Sigrun's panicked shriek mingling with harsh male voices, but there was no time to see if something similar was happening to them. She kicked out, bucked and twisted, and was rewarded by a blow to the face with such violence her head snapped to one side and she was unable to catch her breath. The taste of blood filled her mouth and her lip felt as if it had been split in two. Her knees buckled and she fell face first to the ground. Her mouth filled with soil and leaves and she coughed. The sharp weight of a knee in her lower back pinned her there. A hand jerked her head back by the hair and delivered another blow to the ear that set her head spinning. She understood now the extent to which Gui had held back when he had taken her on in mock combat that morning.

A sack was pulled over her head, stifling her breath further. She felt herself lifted, carried, thrown on to something hard. Terror consumed her, sending her mind darting to the horrific scenarios that might follow, turning her limbs to stone. The world was moving away from her, senses fading and she could do nothing about it. She barely noticed when another body was dumped beside her. One thought was constant and sustained her through the ordeal: Gui would save her. He had to. He had promised. Keeping his face in her mind, Aelfhild slipped into unconsciousness.

Chapter Twelve

Gui was already reaching for his sword when the first ambusher seized Lady Sigrun. Roaring her name, he rushed towards her past Lady Aelfhild, who was standing frozen by the horse. Movement in the trees caught his eye and two burly men were upon him together. A fourth seized Lady Aelfhild. Lights exploded in Gui's head. He felt himself falling forward, the sword dropping from his hand. Sticks grazed his cheek. The shrieks and sobs of the women filled his ears, their distress torture to him.

Before he could right himself a swift kick to the ribs, followed by another to the kidneys left him struggling for breath. He twisted on to his back and kicked out. A boot stamped down hard between his legs, obliterating the world.

Rivers of pain flooded his body, leaving him as weak and mewling as a day-old kitten. No breath in his lungs. Limbs like water. Tears blinding, stomach threatening to empty itself. Even without the pressure of hands forcing him on to his front he would not have been capable of standing, let alone fighting back.

Something thick and heavy covered his head and the world became a nightmare. Arms wrenched behind him and bound. Rope around his feet. Hauled backwards by the feet along the ground. Tunic dragging up to expose his chest to stones and roots that tore at his flesh. Nothing but pain and fear and despair. The certainty that he was breathing his last.

Hands on his body, then he was rolling sideways.

Down and over, fast and steep and uncontrollable, bound legs scrabbling to gain purchase, but failing.

He had the presence of mind to draw his head in to prevent his neck being wrenched or broken and came to rest with a thump.

Then he knew nothing more.

Gui awoke in darkness. He had not expected to wake at all so to be alive came as a relief. He was lying face down on something spongy, making breathing an almost impossible task. He began to pant, but this did no good, merely serving to make him lightheaded. The side of his head felt tender and his left eye was sticky with blood that had trickled and congealed, sealing the lashes together. Wrenching it open caused him to wince, but the sharp stinging focused his mind. He twisted his head back and forth until he felt something slip from his face. Cold air filled his lungs. He gulped to fill his lungs, though the pain in his ribs was immense.

He listened. There were no voices of either his assailants or the women and no sound of other bodies struggling for freedom. There was nothing beyond the usual sounds of the forest. An almost paralysing fear gripped him that the women were already dead. He pushed the thought away before the idea of such a fate caused him to lose his mind and determined to gain his freedom as soon as possible.

His wrists had been bound behind his back. An aching pull in his shoulders and legs told him the ropes binding them had been tied together. Presumably whoever had left him here intended to come back and slit his throat without meeting any resistance. He could smell death, the sickly, pungent stench that had not left his nights alone since he last fought. He was in his nightmare, but this time it was real and he was going to lose his mind and he was going to die.

He bucked and twisted as dread turned his skin clammy. Against all expectations he felt his empty glove shift on his wrist and he went weak with relief. The small mercy was enough to drag him back towards sanity.

For a two-handed man being bound would have been disastrous, but it could prove to be Gui's salvation. Slackening the rope enough to allow two hands to slip free would be impossible, but one hand and a glove that was filled only with padding was another matter. His captors clearly had not noticed that when they bound him, they bound only one hand.

Gui twisted and wriggled, pressed his wrists together and arched his back to draw his feet nearer to his wrists and give the rope some slack. His lacerated chest and belly brushed against the ground and he gave an involuntary whimper that shamed him with its fragility. He ground his teeth against the pain and writhed about until he felt the binding that held glove to sleeve loosen and the glove start to slip. Taking care not to make too many sudden movements he eased his glove over his stump, taking the rope with it. In the years since he had lost his hand he had never once thought there would be a time he would be thankful for that loss, but today it had come.

It struck him that someone might be watching

and sweat broke out across his body. He forced himself to be still, heart racing, and waited to see if he had hastened his death. When nothing happened, still lying on his side, he drew his legs up to his chest and unknotted the rope around his feet. Untangling the rope from his right wrist and from the laces of his glove caused him to waste unnecessary time cursing and devising painful ends for his attackers, but eventually he was free, hurling the tangled mess to one side. He reached for his sword and found it missing. The *seax* he had taken from the vagrant by the river was also missing.

'*Kac'h!*'

He took a deep breath and struggled to his knees. His ribs and back ached, his grazed belly stung and his poor, maltreated cock felt like it might never wake again from the stomping it had endured. He did his best to ignore the pain that racked his body. He would allow himself to brood over his injuries later once he knew where he was and where his companions were.

He looked around warily for assailants waiting to dispatch him. The sun had not set and the darkness was due to the trees and bushes that surrounded him on all sides. To the right the hill climbed sharply upwards. He recalled rolling downwards and now understood he had landed in a ditch of some sort. He put his hand out to steady himself and felt flesh beneath his fingers. What he saw when he looked down sent him sprawling away with a yell of horror, hand outstretched before him.

A human face. He had been lying on the body of a man. It was not alone. Others lay crumpled in the pit with arms bound as his had been. Some had been there for perhaps weeks, others for longer. Much longer.

Gui's stomach emptied itself. His assailants would not be back to finish him off. There was no need. It wasn't a ditch he had been pushed into, but a grave pit. He retched again, sour bile filling his mouth.

The ambushers waited on the path where it became narrow, then attacked and condemned their victims to slow deaths in this lonely place where no one would rescue them.

Sigrun! Where was Sigrun?

Gui searched the pit, but the women were not there. He sobbed with relief, head buried in his arms. They were not dead, but nor were they here. They had been taken elsewhere and, remembering the way the men had ogled them, the use to which they might be put curdled his stomach.

Every part of his body ached, vengeance consumed his thoughts and his heart tugged him towards Sigrun. Nevertheless, Gui placed the corpses side by side and pulled branches to cover them. This act of reverence was rewarded immediately when he discovered one of the unfortunate men had a short dagger concealed in a boot. It had served the owner no good, but to Gui it might prove the difference between failure and success because, poor as it was, he now had a weapon. He began the slow climb back up to the road, determined to find where Sigrun had been taken if it took him the rest of his days. It was only when he reached the top and found himself back on the path that he realised he had left his gloves. How had his mind been so full of other concerns that he had forgotten them!

He looked over the edge. He could climb back down and retrieve them, but could not bear the thought of returning to the grave. Besides, every moment he delayed reduced his chance of finding Sigrun. Finding her alive.

Don't think of that. She had to be alive.

He scanned the path, searching for any indication where to begin his hunt. In the event, tracking the men proved easier than expected. Cart tracks that were hard to see unless the hunter was looking very carefully led away down the road, but veered off down a track half-covered by tree branches. Gui crept through the undergrowth alongside, keeping low until the path widened into a clearing.

The farmhouse that the landlord had described barely deserved the description of a building. It had no roof, only three walls, and only one of those was full height. Branches and skins provided a roof and wall of sorts. It was a large building by the standards of this country and once it would have been prosperous. The sort of place Gui dreamed of one day possessing. It would have been good land and a good place to live until William tore the country apart. Would the men who lived here have become the wild men they were now if that had not happened, or if they would have lived out their days in peace and happiness? How much were people like him responsible for their acts, too?

Three of the men Gui recognised from the inn lay sprawled around a fire pit in front of the dilapidated farmhouse. They were in the middle of an argument. The fourth—the rat-faced man who had insulted Gui—sat apart.

Sweat broke out over Gui's body as he faced his odds. Four men. Men he had already allowed to insult him rather than confront them. He had faced greater odds in battle, but not for years and when he had been a whole man. He had sworn that life was behind him. Now he was faced with no choice but to fight and that prospect filled him with dread. His hand trembled. He bunched his fist and bowed his head in shame.

He was a coward. How could he return to York and explain to Gilbert what had befallen his bride? Never mind what Gilbert might think. Gui knew in his heart he could not continue to live knowing Sigrun was dead and that he had failed her.

The rat-faced man had something in his hand. With a shock, Gui realised it was his own bow. A wave of cold fury overcame him. Rat Face was firing Gui's arrows at a skin that was stretched between two trees. At such a close range the arrows sliced through the skin and disappeared into the woods beyond. When Rat Face had exhausted his supply he hurled the bow overarm towards the skin and joined the others by the fire, adding his thoughts to the argument.

To see his most treasured possession abused with such contempt turned Gui's blood to fire. His long-gone fingers itched to fire it again, to use Rat Face as his target. He vowed he would hunt out the bow from where it had landed before he left. That was not his main purpose, however, and there was something far more precious he needed to reclaim.

He slunk through the tangled weeds around the perimeter of the clearing until he was level with the side of the building where he saw the outlaws' cart parked a little way off. It was not alone. Gui sagged with relief: the women were alive. He let out the breath he had been holding.

They had been separated, one at each side of the cart. They had been stripped of cloaks, dresses and finery and were clad only in their shifts. Despair and fury at the thought of their violation threatened to unman him. He covered his face in an unsuccessful attempt to block out images of them enduring such indignities and worse. If he had doubts about exterminating the vermin, they were rapidly diminishing.

The women were bound at the wrists with lengths of rope that secured them to the shafts of the cart where a scrawny-looking yoked donkey was tethered. Gui's horse was tethered alongside it. The companion, Aelfhild, was at the side of the cart closest to the building. She was kneeling, seemingly praying, with her eyes shut and lips moving silently. Gui wondered how long she had been doing that. He crawled closer to get a better view of Lady Sigrun. She sat huddled against the wheel of the cart, with her knees tucked up to her chest in a manner that made her look more fragile and slight than ever. Her head was bent down and her fingertips worked furiously but ineffectively, clawing at the rope securing her wrists, trying to get any purchase in order to undo the knot. Her hair fell across her face, but Gui could picture the expression of determination that would no doubt be gracing her face.

Despite the gravity of the situation Gui smiled. Both women were trying to gain their freedom in the way they knew best. He vowed silently that he would be the instrument of their liberation before the night was over.

He moved further round until he had a clear view of the front of the farmhouse. The four men lounged before it as a pot in the centre of the fire gently steamed. A rabbit was roasting on a makeshift spit. Gui's stomach growled and he clamped his arm across it to silence it. He must have rustled because Lady Sigrun looked up, forehead wrinkled as she peered into the woods towards him.

Blood streaked from her mouth to chin. Someone had struck her and split her lip. Her face was flushed with anger, the scarlet dashes on her cheeks giving life to a complexion that was otherwise pale enough she could pass for a corpse. Bile rose in Gui's gut, making him nauseous at the comparison that had sprung to mind. He'd seen too many of those for the sight to be easily forgotten. To imagine this living, breathing woman who had been warm and eager in his arms as one of the dead was horribly unsettling.

Their eyes locked. Her mouth opened. She had the presence of mind to close it again, but her eyes shone with relief and hope. Such confidence that Gui would be her saviour warmed his heart, but a treacherous doubt gnawed at him.

Rage at his own impotence poured through him. For the first time since the conquest and the nightmares he felt the urge to throw himself into battle. These four men had deliberately sent him to a slow, agonising death and he could only imagine what the women had been subjected to. However much he pitied the circumstances these men lived under, he was determined to make them pay for what they had done.

He felt for his sword, but of course it was missing and this brought him to his senses. He needed to plan, not head rashly into a fight that would see them all slain.

He retreated slightly and saw anxiety flash across Sigrun's face.

I'll be back, he mouthed, adding a brief mime he hoped would explain further.

He crept back into the undergrowth and sat on his haunches. He would wait. The men would have to sleep at some point and most likely they would empty their bladders before they did. When that time came, Gui would slip into the camp and free the women. If he could retrieve a weapon so much better.

A weapon! He retraced his path round the camp and further until he was behind the target skin. Arrows littered the bushes and his bow was caught in the low branch of a tree. Stealthily he retrieved them. He ran his fingers over the bow, inspecting it for damage, but it seemed fine. He could no longer fire it, but it fitted into his palm as though it was part of his body. Six arrows were more than enough to dispatch these curs. He had excellent aim and had been swift at loosing arrows one after the other, cutting down the enemy before they even knew he was coming for them back when he could fire his bow, but those days were gone.

He made an exploratory foray into the woods further beyond the clearing, sharp eyes picking out an escape route before returning to his position where he could see Sigrun and she could see him. Her fingers still worked tirelessly at the ropes binding her wrists. Gui could see it was useless—she would never gain purchase at that angle—but he admired her tenacity. When she looked up he pointed to the other end of the rope that was secured to the cart. She shuffled closer to the wheel and turned her attention to that instead. She kept her head mostly bowed, but occasionally she glanced towards Gui. As the dusk became evening he kept the vigil with her.

For the ninth or tenth time Aelfhild slid her gaze to the clump of bushes where Gui was hiding. She had muttered prayers and psalms beneath her breath, less out of piety and more as a way of timing how long it had been since she had last looked for him. It would not do to draw attention to his hiding place by looking too often.

He was still there, though she had to concentrate to pick him out from the depths of the tangles. Good. If she found it hard to spot him clearly when she was expecting to see him, her captors who would not be looking would never notice him if they went that way.

It made sense for Gui to wait until dark, but time had never moved so slowly. Even the long months spent incarcerated in the priory had not dragged in this way. In his place she would have rushed straight into the camp.

And I'd have been slain before I landed a blow.

Impotent fury coursed through her. Only this morning Gui had proved to her how useless she was at fighting. Any lingering doubts had vanished when she had been unable to save herself from being taken. Now her life was in Gui's hands. She glanced again to him and gave a slight smile. His scarred lip flickered at the corner and he retreated a little further into the depths of the brambles. Panic squeezed her chest, stopping her breath, in case he was leaving, even though she trusted he would not.

Aelfhild shifted into a more comfortable position, trying to ease the ache in her legs and back. She tried working again at the knot securing the rope to the cart. Why had she not thought of trying to loosen that end herself rather than wasting time making her fingers numb from clawing at her wrists? The rope was tied high and she could not do it for long before her shoulders ached and the blood left her arms. It was a risk because if her captors saw what she was doing she would be punished. She bent her head, trying to look under the cart.

'Sigrun—Sigrun—' She kept her voice low.

Sigrun was only at the other side of the cart, but Aelfhild couldn't see her. Perhaps Sigrun couldn't hear her, but she didn't dare to speak louder in case she attracted the attention of their captors.

'Aelfhild?' Sigrun's voice was a sob.

'Gui is here. He's come to save us.'

'They were too strong. I saw him fall,' Sigrun answered.

Aelfhild wondered for the first time what had happened to him. Her captors had laughed that he would not come for them, that he would find other women and to a Norman all women were just flesh made for pleasure. In the darkest moments she had wondered if they spoke the truth.

'No, he's here. He'll rescue us, you'll see—'

She broke off as the brawniest of the men walked round the corner of the farmhouse. Her heart seemed to seize. If she had revealed Gui's presence they were all lost and she would blame herself for whatever remained of her life. She should never have spoken. She huddled back against the cart, remembering the violent blows she had received. The man strode towards the cart, one hand lifting up his tunic and fumbling beneath. Vomit filled Aelfhild's throat as what she had dreaded most seemed about to happen and she huddled against the wheel. The man glanced at her, but did not stop. He lurched past to the edge of the clearing and let fall a long arc of piss into the woods with a satisfied sigh. He returned to camp, pausing to look at Aelfhild with an unpleasant glint in his eye.

'Did you hope I was coming for you? You'll have plenty of that where you're heading.' He laughed. 'I prefer more meat than a scrawny slut like you has to offer, but perhaps later, if you beg me.'

He ambled back to his friends, chuckling, and resumed his drunken argument.

Aelfhild began to shake with revulsion. Tears blurred her vision. She sought out Gui, hoping to draw comfort from his presence. He must have heard the man's taunting threat because his face had taken on an expression of unadulterated fury that she had never seen before. He cocked his head towards the man, then slowly drew his finger across his throat. His meaning was clear and Aelfhild nodded her approval. She settled back against the wheel and closed her eyes.

She never expected or intended to sleep. Perhaps it was a combination of the harsh blows she had received coupled with an empty stomach that had weakened her, but she could not stay awake and fell into a troubled drowse. She was not aware of time passing until something jolted her awake. She opened her eyes a little to discover it had grown darker. Owls hooted and creatures rustled in the undergrowth, but the farmhouse was in silence. Something landed beside her on the ground. Something else hit her on the shoulder and made her jump. She peered at the ground beside her and saw a small stone that had not been there before.

She tensed, anticipation throwing off the final confusion of sleep. She looked for Gui in his hiding place in the woods, but could not see him and was so intent on searching him out that when a black-clad figure appeared beside her she could not help gasping in alarm.

A hand clamped over her mouth, stifling her voice, and she was pulled tight against someone's body, head held rigid. The face of the captor who had threatened to return loomed in her mind and she began to draw breath to scream, but Gui's voice whispered in her ear.

'It's me.'

Aelfhild sagged with relief. Gui released the pressure on her mouth. She craned her head to look at him. He had drawn his hood up over his face and wrapped his cloak around the bottom half so all that was visible were his eyes. She looked into them—the familiar deep brown that stirred her heart were currently narrowed and watchful, alert to anything that might happen. He held her gaze for the briefest of moments and the expression softened, then he looked towards the farmhouse and the determination returned.

He had a knife and began sawing at the rope with difficulty. The blade was rusted and almost blunt. Aelfhild pulled the rope taut and eventually it began to fray. She tugged hard and it snapped. The sudden release sent her sprawling back on to the ground with a groan that sounded hellishly loud in the silence of the night.

Sleep-addled mutters of confusion came from inside the farmhouse. Gui swore under his breath in Breton. Someone would be coming to see what had caused the disturbance any moment.

Aelfhild tried to rise to her feet, but her limbs refused to obey. Fear paralysed her, feet as heavy as stone. She began to crawl on her hands and knees towards the cart where Sigrun was still bound at the other side. She felt herself hauled upwards. Her legs buckled, but before she fell she was in Gui's arms and he was half-carrying, half-dragging her from the clearing. He was cradling her like a child, holding her close to shield her with his body as he pushed his way through the tangle of trees into the forest. She struggled against him, fighting to return, but he carried her away, deep into the woods, moving rapidly, ducking beneath low branches and through bushes that snagged at her hair and whipped at her face.

She could not find her voice, unable to protest, unable to tell him he was making a mistake. He was carrying her to safety, but he was going in the wrong direction, taking Aelfhild away from her captors but also away from Sigrun. Away from the bride he should be rescuing.

Chapter Thirteen

'You're safe, Sigrun. I've got you,' Gui breathed. He buried his lips in her hair, murmuring words in his own language she could not understand.

Aelfhild struggled in his arms, finally in possession of her wits. He held against his chest, both arms tightly around her so she could not break free. He was crushing her with the fierceness of his embrace and the determination to bear her away from danger. How could he know he had rescued the wrong woman?

'We have to go back!'

Aelfhild was speaking too loud, reckless in her need to make him understand. He clamped his hand across her mouth again, eyes flying back in the direction they had come from. He ducked under another low branch, leaving the clearing further behind with every step.

They paused behind a clump of brambles, both

listening for sounds from the camp. There were none, or they were too far to be heard. Gui lowered Aelfhild to her feet and at once she started to run in the direction they had come from.

He caught her by the arm and she turned on him with a snarl.

'We've forgotten her!'

'Not now.'

She twisted and faced him in anguish. 'I can't leave her.' She spoke low but urgently. '*You* can't leave her. You don't know what you're doing.'

'We'll get her back, I promise,' Gui soothed.

'We have to go back *now*!'

The rope was still tied tightly around her wrists. She beat both fists against his chest, putting all her strength and rage and fear into the blows. He winced. Aelfhild remembered Sigrun's words and wondered what he had suffered before he came for them.

'I said no.'

His voice was a whip, cracking in the silence. Since they had quarrelled that morning Aelfhild had been struck and threatened, endured hunger and thirst, and threats of violation. His curt response was the final beating. She dissolved into tears.

When Gui's arms came around her she did not object, even though she was furious with him.

He cradled her gently, drawing her head on to his chest, and held her while her tears fell, soaking his shirt. It felt good to be held after the brutality she had suffered. Better than good, if she was honest. She cleaved to him, hating him, loving him, wanting him. The curves of her body found the hollows of his so they fitted together like two figures carved from the same piece of stone.

'You left her behind,' she sobbed. 'You made me leave her. I promised I would take care of her and I didn't.'

'I had no choice.' He held her tighter and buried his face into her neck, his breath teasingly sensuous against her ear. 'I couldn't risk taking you both when you cried out. If they had woken they would have killed us all.'

'Are you saying it's my fault?' Aelfhild pulled away from him, glaring. 'Don't you dare blame me!'

'That's better, I like you best when you're full of fire. I was worried it had been extinguished for good.' He gave a little smile, then grew serious again. 'It isn't your fault; don't think that for even a heartbeat. If I could have taken you both I would, but I had to choose. I couldn't lose you.'

He swallowed, voice growing thick with passion that burned equally in his eyes and made Aelfhild's heart soar.

'Where were you?' she asked. 'I thought you might not come, that you might have left us.'

'Why would you think that?' His voice was heavy with confusion.

'Because we had argued.' She looked at her hands, twisting them together, embarrassed to acknowledge the treacherous voice that had whispered evil little thoughts into her ears. 'Because of what I said about the man with no legs. I accused you of murder. Because you are French and I'm English, and we are not supposed to be friends. But then I remembered I am to be your bride and a lord would not give up the claim to his land so easily.'

'You think I would hold a grudge but still come for you because I get to claim your property?' His voice dripped with anger and hurt. 'Do you really think I am such a poor excuse for a man?'

'No. I'm sorry. I know you're better than that. It was unfair of me.' Her lip began to tremble and she bit it, tasting the dried blood. There was one more question she did not want to hear the answer to, but needed to ask.

'If my companion had been your bride, would you have rescued her first?'

'I would have still chosen you, whatever the repercussions. I came for you because I care for you, whatever you might accuse me of. I would have come even if I didn't care, because that is the right thing to do. I didn't abandon you. It took longer than I would have liked, but I came as soon as I was able.'

His tone reached inside her, invisible fingers caressing her body from the inside, stroking limbs and belly, breasts and crotch, and awakening the overpowering desire to be in his arms once more. She began to shiver with longing and shock.

'Did they—harm you?' Gui asked hesitantly. 'In any way?'

He didn't mean the blows or the shoves, painful though they had been. Aelfhild's mouth twisted.

'You mean did they violate us? No. I feared they might after they had made us take off our clothes and jewels. I think one of them wanted to, but the others wouldn't let him.'

Gui's face grew thunderous as she spoke of the humiliation she had endured, being forced at knifepoint to strip to her shift by the braying, mocking men. A good way of keeping them cowed and frightened, and it had worked. She crossed her arms tightly, suddenly conscious of how much her thin shift might reveal to Gui and wishing she was wearing more.

'They planned to take us to the coast and sell us to the slavers. They told me I would do well for the men who liked young girls and children; that I looked young enough to pass. They said she is worth more to them because she's more beautiful.'

She gave a sob, unable to contain her distress any longer. 'We have to go back now. She'd rather die—she'd rather kill herself—than suffer the touch of a man she didn't choose.'

Gui wordlessly pulled her to him, clasping her tightly enough to squeeze the breath from her chest, uttering soothing sounds until her shaking ceased. She rested her head against his shoulder and closed her eyes, reliving the terrible moments she had thought would never end. He stroked her cheek, running his finger across the bruise that throbbed. After the treatment she had received, being caressed so tenderly made her weak with relief.

'I'll get her back, I promise,' he murmured. 'If they want her for what you say they won't touch her because that will lower the price someone will pay for her. Virgins are worth more. She'll be safe until the morning and I'll go back before dawn while they're still asleep.'

Sleep. Aelfhild's knees began to buckle as exhaustion washed over her. 'Can we rest now, we must be far enough way?' she pleaded.

'A little further. Can you walk?'

Aelfhild hesitated before answering. If she said no, he might carry her again as he had before. The temptation was hard to resist, but he looked as weary as she felt. She needed him to be strong and ready to return for Sigrun. To take advantage was selfish and reckless.

'My hands.' She held them up before her. He looked contrite at having forgotten she was still bound. He sawed at the rope with his rusty blade, supporting and steadying her hands with his left wrist and Aelfhild realised what her eyes had noticed, but her mind had not. The cuff of his sleeve hung loosely over the stump that he usually concealed.

'You aren't wearing your gloves!'

'I had to leave them behind.' His eyes became distant, seeing something she could not.

'But they're important.'

'No, they aren't. They're a vanity, a way of fooling myself and the world that I was normal. It doesn't matter.'

He spoke without regret, but Aelfhild's heart broke.

'We can find them afterwards.'

'I'm not going back there.' His face twisted

and he looked as if he was about to vomit. 'Let's move.'

He held out his hand. Aelfhild took it, mind churning with horror at a place so bad he refused to return to it. Presently they reached a huge fallen tree, roots wrenched out of the ground leaving a hollow.

'We'll sleep here.' Gui removed his cloak and unfastened the bundle that was tied to his back. Aelfhild recognised his bow and hope surged in her breast. They had a weapon she had not known about.

Gui began pulling branches from bushes and laying them across the roots. Aelfhild rushed to help him, tugging at them until they had created a makeshift shelter. They crawled inside and knelt facing each other. Gui rolled his shoulders back, frowning. Aelfhild remembered the way he had winced when she had struck him. She leaned forward and placed her hand on his chest, spreading her fingers wide. He drew an audible breath, but remained motionless. His tunic was sticky, clinging to his body in places and when she moved her fingers upwards to the open neck she felt the ragged skin and crusted blood.

'You're hurt. Let me see.' Aelfhild moved closer. She pushed her hands beneath the tunic, easing it up and over his chest and trying to ignore the speeding of her pulse caused by the tantalising sensation of his bare flesh beneath her hands. He bent his head forward, assisting her in the removal of his clothing.

He was a mess. Even by the dim light of the moon she could tell that he was scratched and bruised from neck to waist. The dark hair that fanned across his muscular chest was matted with blood.

Aelfhild cried out, horrified by what she saw. 'What did they do to you?'

'You don't need to know.' He sounded haunted, his voice as torn as his flesh. 'They'll pay though, I swear it.'

He remained perfectly still while Aelfhild ran her fingertips lightly across his chest, examining the lacerations. His lips parted and closed again. He blinked once or twice and sucked his breath in sharply, whether from discomfort or the same awakening of desire Aelfhild was feeling.

'I wish I had my ointment. It would help with the pain.'

'The pain isn't so bad,' he said. 'I've had worse. I'll be aching for a day or two, but nothing more.'

Aelfhild's fingers trembled. She used both hands now to explore his body, alternately skimming her fingers or stroking with flat palms, revelling in the feel of his broad chest where softness and strength combined. He shivered as she ran her fingers lightly down his sides to his waist, then back together, meeting in the centre of his belly. She felt the tightening of his belly. She dared not move her hands further down. While she could try convincing herself that this was purely an examination, to travel further would remove all pretence. She raised her eyes to meet his, sliding her hand back to rest above his heart.

Gui ran his thumb along her lip, wiping the dried blood from the cut. His eyes narrowed with alarming fury.

'Does this hurt?'

She shook her head, before giving up the pretence and nodding vigorously, wishing she could be as strong as him. Her mouth turned down and the lip began to shake uncontrollably.

'Yes, it does. I can bear it, though.'

She reached out her hand and brushed the tips of her fingers across Gui's mouth, feeling the ridge of his scar. They studied each other closely. Aelfhild's scalp prickled.

'Do you think mine will scar like yours?' she asked.

He cupped her chin, turning her face to catch the moonlight, and ran his thumb over the scar. It throbbed a little, but the pain was nothing compared to the pounding of lust that his touch awoke.

'I don't think so, it's only a small cut. Don't worry.'

'I'm not worried. If it did I wouldn't care as long as I wore it as well as you wear yours.'

'You're wrong there. I look hideous.' He grimaced. 'It twists me into a monster.'

'Don't say that!' She reached out impulsively and put her hands on each side of his face. 'Don't you realise how handsome you are? The scar makes no difference to that.'

His eyes widened. She whipped her hands away, conscious of the liberty she had taken. Running her hands over his naked torso had not seemed as intimate or intrusive.

'It does make a difference, but I don't mind. I've learned to live with it and I've been called worse. You've called me worse yourself! Do I still remind you of a goblin?'

'Only a little,' Aelfhild admitted. 'You look roguish, but you don't scare me now.'

Their eyes never left each other's. Daringly she rested her hand on his chest once more. When she saw his eyes widen she moved it across his shoulder and down his arm, feeling the muscles that were as firm as if they were hewn from rock. Gui's arm came around her waist and lightning speared her from heart to groin. Slowly, cautiously, she slid her hand beneath his arm, round to his back, feeling her way over the knotted muscles along his spine. He slid his hand behind her head, burying his fingers in her hair, drawing her upwards towards him.

She couldn't tell who made the first move, but with a rapidity that took her breath away, his lips were finding hers and they were kissing as they had so nearly done the night before. His mouth was hot, eager, lips tugging at hers, parting them, vanquishing what little resistance she threw up. She met him with equal fervour; leaning in to him, clawing at his back, her tongue greedily seeking his. Kissing Torwald had been nothing like this sensation of utter submission to an appetite that she was unable to resist or command. Great gods! She thought she knew what it was to be kissed, but they had been like children playing!

She raked her fingernails down his back. Both his arms clasped her tightly to him, her breasts brushing against the hardness of his chest, the exquisite scrape against her nipples through her shift setting her on fire. His hand moved to her buttocks, pulling her closer, tilting his hips against her. His erection, rock hard, ground against her and her belly rolled over. He was ready to take her, straining towards her. She pushed up against him until she straddled his lap, fingers fumbling at the laces of his hose. Her head spun with desire and she whimpered softly.

'Please…'

Abruptly he stopped. Lips frozen where they had come to rest beneath her earlobe. He wrenched away from her and dropped to his knees.

'No. Not that. Too far.' His voice was rough. He was shaking bodily.

'Why did you stop?' she asked in dismay. 'What did I do wrong?'

'Wrong? Nothing. You did everything right.' He stared over his shoulder at her, eyes full of shock. He brushed the matted curls back from his forehead. '*Yec'hed dioualez*, woman! Sweet devil! Who taught you to kiss like that?'

'No one!' She looked at the ground, ashamed of what she had done. She had never before lost her head to such an extent and here she was, grinding up against him like a cheap whore, begging him to breach the door that no man had. She should be struck down where she knelt for committing such indiscretions, yet the only thing that threatened to destroy her was the overpowering craving to do it again until the end of time.

'I'm sorry,' she whispered, her voice cracking. 'It was wrong of me. I'm sorry. I shouldn't have let it happen.'

She wasn't sure if she was apologising to Gui or to Sigrun, or to the shade of Torwald. Perhaps to none of them. Perhaps to all. It was the greatest betrayal Aelfhild could imagine, to be kissing Sigrun's betrothed when Sigrun was still captive, to be eager for what would surely follow.

Tears began to flow again. She'd done so much crying and didn't know how she would ever stop with a heart that felt more bruised than the rest of her combined. She shuffled to the furthest corner of the shelter into the darkness and drew her knees up, hiding her head in her lap. She could not look at Gui for fear of seeing the judgement written on his face. When she felt his hand on her shoulder she buried her head deeper.

'Look at me,' he commanded softly. 'Sigrun— look at me.'

She raised her head. He had slung his tunic back on, but left the neck unlaced and she could see the abrasions she had so recently examined. His face bore no condemnation. If anything, the only emotion was sorrow, though why he should regret learning that his supposed bride was adept at raising him to passion was confusing.

'It shouldn't have happened, but it doesn't matter that it did. It was only a kiss. We're both scared and alone. We've seen horrors today that will stay with us for ever. The morning might bring our end. It's perfectly normal for soldiers facing battle to take comfort where they find it. That's all we did; we took the opportunity to share something to remind ourselves we're still living. We did nothing unforgivable, but under the circumstances no one would blame us.'

It did not feel like that to Aelfhild, but perhaps he was right. He knew better than she did, after all. She bit her lip, but that only served to remind her of where his had recently been. He sat beside her and leaned in close so that his head was almost touching hers. He tilted his face slightly towards her and his breath caressed her neck. It was cool on her skin, but each soft exhalation made her burn hotter and hotter within. She closed her eyes and lost herself in the sensations. He could not possibly suspect what effect the simple act of drawing life into his lungs had on her or he would not continue. She needed to move before she found herself unable to, but feared the time had already passed.

'We need to rest.' Gui passed his cloak around her shoulders. 'It's cold and I don't know who else might be out here. I want you by my side tonight. I promise your virtue will be safe and there will be no repeat of what happened. Do you trust me?'

She trusted him; it was herself she could not trust, but she was exhausted and frozen in only her shift and the prospect of a warm body to lie against appealed. The kiss had taken her by surprise. That was why she had so enthusiastically participated. She would not be caught unawares again. She would have more strength.

'You're right, it was only a kiss. It was fear and relief that made us behave so incorrectly. That makes sense.' She shrugged, affecting a carelessness she didn't feel in the slightest. 'I don't know what came over us.'

She lay down on her side with her back to him and wriggled down into the earth, drawing her knees up to her chest. Gui settled himself behind her, moulding his body to hers. He drew his cloak over them both and slipped his arm around her, holding her tight to him. His touch wasn't seductive now, but protective and reassuring. A woman could sleep every night in such arms and know she would be perfectly safe.

'We will rescue her, won't we?' she asked through a yawn.

'Of course,' Gui murmured, his voice close to her ear so that the breath tickled the sensitive flesh beneath her lobe. 'You sleep now, we'll take shifts. I'll wake you when I can stay awake no longer so I can rest.'

Her anxiety eased. They would rescue Sigrun. Everything would be well as long as Gui was there. Comforted by that thought and unable to keep her eyes open any longer, Aelfhild drifted to sleep.

Gui lay awake long after he was sure Sigrun was asleep. Even if his mind had not been racing, the discomfort he felt physically would have prevented any rest. Gradually the arousal that plagued him became tolerable and the urging of his body eased. Even so, he lay as still as possible, knowing that the slightest brush of her body against the wrong part of him would awaken him again. His heart hammered at the thought of how close they had come to transgressing against Gilbert far beyond a simple kiss.

He ground his teeth. It hadn't been simple in the slightest. It had been sanity-ending, life-changing, world-destroying, heart-stopping. No kiss in the future, no woman he might meet would come close to what he had felt when Sigrun had finally come to his arms. He still wasn't sure where he had found the strength to draw back before he had bedded her.

He felt no guilt at what had passed between

them. Tonight he had ignored all the dictates of his conscience. He had betrayed his closest friend, but he did not care in the slightest. He was sure Sigrun would never reveal to her husband what had happened and he intended to take the secret to his grave. He had wronged Gilbert, but no sanction Gilbert could mete out, no recrimination could be as brutal as knowing that the ecstasy he had experienced in Sigrun's arms was to be denied him for ever.

Gui rubbed his eyes, knowing he would have to give in to sleep before long. He was uncertain what hour it was. Had it only been that morning he had taunted Sigrun with her lack of strength, proving she could never best him? What idiocy, when all she had to do was lay her lips on his and he was overpowered more thoroughly than if William's entire army had laid into him as one.

Sigrun slept, her body rising and falling gently. He cradled her like a lover. Gui wondered what she was dreaming of and hoped it was happy. She looked peaceful now, the tears she had shed dried on her cheeks to faint traces. She had cried so easily and he had envied her that release. He wanted to weep, to release the fear and anger and distress and longing that plagued him, but the tears would not come. They never did.

Perhaps they never would again and he would be perpetually denied that release.

When his eyelids began to droop and he had awoken three times with a start, he shook her awake. She came back to consciousness, eyelids flickering, lips parting. He couldn't look her in the eye for fear he would see the same desire as before and be unable to stay strong this time.

'Is it time to go?'

'No, but I need to sleep, just for a short while. You keep the cloak to keep you warm. Wake me before the sky turns pink.'

Gui huddled down and closed his eyes, but found he was no longer so keen to sleep, knowing she was awake and beside him. Her hand slipped into his and the surprise jolted him half-awake, sending every nerve in his body vibrating with love. He smiled to himself as he wrapped his arm around her, drawing her close once more. To miss a moment of time in her company was wasting something precious and limited, but he could not fight sleep any longer.

Tomorrow would bring a rescue and revenge. The day after that would see them in Haxby, where he would have to give her up to her rightful husband. That was tomorrow, however. To-night she was his to hold and dream of.

He savoured the cold air that filled his lungs,

feeling more alive than he had for years. He had lived through the scenario that gave him nightmares and survived it. He had tasted the forbidden fruit and it had been as sweet as he could have wished it to be. She didn't think him a monster and his scars and lost hand meant nothing to her.

Though he could never have or keep her, he would sleep for one night in the arms of the woman he adored. For the first time in more nights than he could remember, Guilherm Fitz-Lannion fell asleep without dreading what terrors the night would hold.

Chapter Fourteen

Gui woke disorientated, unsure why he was lying on leaves and what he was missing. It was Sigrun. She had slipped from his arms without him realising and was sitting cross-legged, attempting to remove the rust and sharpen the knife with a rock. Gui watched her through half-closed eyes, drinking in the sight. Her face was in profile, her expression determined as her hands scraped the blade down the rock.

'Did you wake me?' he asked. 'I don't remember hearing you call me.' *Or feeling you touch me.* Goosebumps raised on his skin as he remembered the pleasure of her fingers on his flesh.

She glanced round and smiled a greeting, eager, then as shy as a bride after her wedding night. It was something that would stay with Gui as long as he lived.

'I didn't. I was going to soon. We have time

before we need to start out and I want you to be at full strength.'

Sigrun had neatly lined up his arrows and bow.

'Everything is ready. We can set off as soon as you like.' She held her stomach and sighed. 'I'm so hungry.'

'Me, too. Those dogs were feasting well enough last night.' His belly ached with emptiness. Gui raised himself on to his elbow. 'Did they feed you?'

'There was an old woman there—a *thrall*, or perhaps she was their mother—who gave us some bread when we arrived after—'

She plucked at the skirt of her shift, straightening it. Gui kept his thoughts to himself about the English barbarism of slave keeping. He was consumed by the urge to take her in his arms again and ward off any danger, but resisted. A kiss after the tumult of the day before might be excused, but in the cold hour before dawn he had no such excuse and did not feel sure he would be able to control that impulse.

'With luck I'll find food in their camp once I've done what I need to.'

'We.' Sigrun folded her arms and jutted out her jaw. 'We'll get her back. I'm not letting you do that alone.'

Gui could no longer ignore the matter that had been worrying him since her rescue. She intended to come with him and he did not intend to let her. He sat up and began gathering the arrows, avoiding her eyes.

'You aren't coming with me. I'm not risking you getting hurt, or captured again.'

'What? You can't mean that!' She tossed her hair back and raised her chin, eyes full of anger. 'You're not leaving me behind. Where you go, I go, too. Besides, I can cut her free quicker. It will be easier for me with—'

She broke off, faltering, and looked away.

'With two hands?' Gui didn't bother to hide his dismay at her words. He pulled the sleeve over his stump, twisting the end and wishing he still had his glove to conceal the unsightly mutilation.

'Yes.' She reached across and stroked his cheek, gazing into his eyes sorrowfully. 'I'm so sorry, Gui. I know that hurts you to hear, but it's true and you know it.'

Perhaps it was her touch that did it, but the anger that erupted inside him at her words grew cold. She was right. She was the only person who had ever been honest with him in that regard and though her words stung he did not *un*wish them.

He covered her hand, closing his eyes briefly as longing for her consumed him.

'If it was a simple matter of untying her and running I would agree to you coming, but it isn't. I don't plan to rescue her and leave them to carry on doing what they do. I plan to put an end to them for good.'

He took the knife from her hand and ran his thumb across the edge. He'd give a lot to have his sword, or even the *seax* instead of this lump of rust. What chance did he really have? What chance would she have?

'You don't have the right to stop me. You're not my husband. Yet.'

Nor would he ever be. Gui writhed in misery.

'Right, no. Responsibility, absolutely,' he growled. 'I showed you yesterday how easily you could be defeated. They proved it to you also. You would only get hurt.'

His stomach tightened at the thought.

'That was different. I had no weapon then.'

'I only have one weapon now.' Gui brandished the knife.

'Wrong! We have two.' She gave him a triumphant smile.

She knelt beside him and reached for the bow at his side. His hand was on her wrist before she touched it, with a speed that surprised even him. 'You're not using that.'

'Why not?'

'No one uses it except me.'

'Then you use it.'

His jaw tightened. 'You know perfectly well I can't.'

He let go of her wrist and picked up the bow, cradling it with the same possessiveness he had held Sigrun with while she slept.

'Then let me try.' She was on the verge of tears now and it was his fault. 'Unless you're refusing out of obstinacy.'

Gui bit back a retort. Was she right? The idea of anyone else using it set his teeth on edge. Sigrun gave a cry of exasperation and jumped to her feet. She pushed her way out of the shelter into the brightening dawn. Gui dropped the bow and flung himself after her, catching her around the waist.

'What are you doing? Anyone could be out there!'

She twisted around; her face was contorted with fury. 'If you won't allow me to use your bow, I'll walk into the camp unarmed and demand her back. I mean it!'

He had no doubt she would do it. And she would die.

'You need strength, a good eye and an accurate aim. How many of those do you have?'

They were as close as they had ever been; close as when they had kissed. The memory sent a shiver down Gui's spine, but Sigrun's face contained no desire now.

'We're wasting time arguing and every word puts Aelfhild in more danger. Please, Gui! I'll do anything you ask, if you'll only do this for me.' Her eyes were imploring, brimming with tears that broke his heart. He released her and bowed his head over her hand, spreading her delicate fingers wide and lacing his through them.

'You could show me. I think you could teach me to do anything.'

Gui swallowed, thinking of the things he longed to teach her.

'Perhaps in time I could train you to hit a target, but as you say, we don't have time now.'

'But I could still fire it.' She was beaming at him now, head tilted to one side, eyes peering through her pale lashes. Seductive. Irresistible.

'Not accurately. If you hit anyone by chance you would only wound them.' He could feel himself weakening and knew she could sense it because her eyes glinted with sudden hope.

'Then that's better than having them unwounded.'

She was surprisingly bloodthirsty.

'Could we do it together?' she suggested.

Gui furrowed his brow, confused.

'You could draw the string and aim, I could hold the bow steady.' She raised her arms and mimed the gesture of pulling back a string. Her stance was dreadful. If she hit a tree when she was standing directly in front of it she would be lucky. Gui looked at the sky. Black was turning to purple, tinged with pink. They were out of time. Sigrun stood motionless. Tense. Hopeful. Determined. He would be incapable of denying her anything she wanted for ever.

'Please,' she whispered once more.

She was braver than he was, ready to fight and more eager in a way that shamed his reluctance. She'd challenged him and argued with him, comforted him and moved him in ways no other woman had. He could not refuse her entreaties, would not deny her right to revenge herself on the man who had mistreated her and play her part in saving her companion.

He took his time before answering, considering the implications of what he was about to say and knowing that once he did there was no turning back.

'I lost the hand I draw the bowstring with. I

think we will stand a better chance if I hold the bow and you pull the cord.'

They moved swiftly, retracing the steps they had taken the previous night. Halfway there they discovered a brook and fell to their knees to gulp handfuls of water and rinse the grime from their faces. Gui raised an eyebrow to Sigrun to check how she was bearing up. She gave him a faint smile and pulled his cloak around her. He had given her the garment partly for the sake of her modesty, partly because it disguised the whiteness of her shift, but mainly because her form was all too apparent beneath the thin shift and the sight of her drove him to distraction.

'I'm glad you stopped me leaving on my own. I would never have been able to find my way back without you.'

He resisted the urge to warn her the rest of her plan was equally foolish. He unhitched the bow from his back and pulled an arrow from the bundle.

'We should practise before we get there. Are you ready to learn?'

He instructed Sigrun how to string the bow, bending the wood so she could slip the loop of cord into the notch. The cord was old and it had been a long time since he had strung it. He hoped the hemp had withstood the damp and would still hold taut when it came to firing accurately.

He gripped the bow in his right fist, feeling a chill at the familiar curve of the wood between thumb and palm, and indicated the arrow. Sigrun picked it up, now looking anxious. Gui had given thought to how this would work. Whatever positions he had tried in his mind, he could not avoid how close they would have to stand.

'Stand behind me at my left. You're going to be my left hand.'

She obeyed, standing a foot length away from him.

'You're going to have to be closer than that, I'm afraid. Much closer. We'll do it slowly. Now, lean your body against mine with your chest touching my back.'

She obeyed silently. Gui forgot to breathe as he felt her press the length of her body from breasts to hips against him. A throb of lust took him by surprise. He gripped the bow firmly, squared his feet, tensed and tried to remember the simple actions that he had carried out a thousand times since childhood, but which now evaded him. He could barely remember the words in his own language, never mind hers!

'Grip the arrow by the shaft, where it meets the fletch. Ease it between your fingers.' He could feel himself turning scarlet as boyhood innuendo came back to him. 'Reach your left arm beneath mine, take hold of the string and notch the arrow level with my right hand. When you draw back the string you'll need to brace your feet and push against me or you won't have the strength.'

Without being asked Sigrun slipped her right arm around him. Her fingers fumbled downwards, tickling unwittingly until they splayed across his belly. Her hips tilted forward, grinding against his buttocks. Gui nearly lost his mind with desire.

'That's…that's good. I mean that's right.' He looked over his shoulder to try seeing if she was equally affected by such intimacy but her face showed nothing but concentration. 'Now, draw the string back as close to my chin as you can. Don't let go until I tell you.'

He steadied himself as she followed his instructions exactly, adjusting his thumb to balance the arrow as he sighted it before commanding her to release it. It worked surprisingly well. The cord was not as taut as Gui would have drawn it when he was still able, but the string snapped against his inner arm with a painful thrum that felt as familiar the greeting of a long-absent friend and the arrow vanished between the trees.

They exchanged a triumphant smile before Sigrun ran to retrieve the arrow and they repeated the process another three times, becoming more accurate with each shot. He would not have the range he was accustomed to and they would be far slower, but they might stand a chance of dispatching at least one of their opponents if they had surprise on their side. That would leave only three for Gui to deal with. It might not be as hopeless as he believed.

He was silent as he led the way back until the farmhouse came into sight. He took Sigrun's hand. They moved around until they could see the opening and knelt in the undergrowth. The cart was where it had been the night before, but the white-clad figure was no longer where she had been. Sigrun gave a soft moan of distress.

'Don't give up hope,' Gui said. 'She'll be inside. They would have moved her as soon as they noticed you were gone.'

He drew her towards him and was dismayed to feel she was trembling violently. He leaned down and kissed her forehead. Her face was grey and her pale eyes were lost in dark smudges. She looked fragile, as if she would disappear with the moonlight when the sun shone on her. Gui wanted nothing more than to protect her from what was to come.

'You said you wanted to face battle. Now is your chance. Are you ready?'

'No. I'm not. I don't know what to do. Gui, I'm… I'm scared.' She turned frightened eyes on him, searching for reassurance he could not give her.

'Do you want to stay here after all? There's no shame if you do.'

'No. I want to come. I want to stay with you.'

'Then stay close by and I'll protect you. If anyone tries to hurt you I swear it will be his last act. Stay by me and do as we planned.'

She placed her hand lightly on his left forearm, where his glove would usually end. 'Gui, are you scared, too?'

He considered her words. His belly fluttered, but it was with anticipation rather than the all-consuming dread that had plagued his nights since Senlac. He had shied away from conflict for years, but now he faced the prospect of his death with serenity.

'No. I'm not.'

He slipped his hand into hers and felt the squeeze of her fingers as they tightened.

'If something does go wrong, if it begins to look as though we—as though I—might not triumph…' He held up his arm to cut off the words that were beginning to form on her lips.

'*If* it looks that way, I want to free your companion and run. You get her and you go. Don't wait for me.'

He drew out the rusty knife and held it out to her, handle first.

'Take this. I hope you don't have to use it on anyone, but if you do, stab hard into the belly or heart. Twist, then let go and run. Don't try to pull it out, or see what is happening behind you. Make your way back to the road and go to the inn. Someone there will look after you.'

'I won't need anyone else to look after me. You're going to survive. We all are.'

She took the knife and gripped it tightly, but her hand shook. She sounded on the verge of tears and Gui felt his eyes begin to sting.

'I hope so, but if by chance I do not, then know…' He looked away, eyes dazzled by a burst of sunlight that speared him between the trees. They began to smart. Were his tears finally going to start falling in front of the woman who had unexpectedly and unwittingly opened his heart? He picked his words carefully, desperate to make her understand the love that consumed him, but bound by his oath not to reveal the truth.

'Know I would have liked to have been your husband. I believe it would have given me the greatest happiness I could know.'

He wasn't expecting avowals of love in return, but her mouth twisted. She drew a sharp breath and turned away, leaving him lost for words. She had been unmoved by their intimacy when practising with the bow and had agreed too readily their kiss had been the product of emotion and circumstance. His heart lurched, wondering if he had misjudged her feelings so badly? Perhaps her heart still belonged to the dead youth who had given her the brooch and whom she still grieved over, or perhaps she still intended, as she had claimed all along, to resist marriage until the bitter end.

He fumbled for the bow and beckoned her to follow him. It should not matter either way, but as he crept closer to the farmhouse, he was unsure if he cared whether he lived or died if he did not have her love.

He would have liked to be her husband. His words tore her to shreds. Even if they survived what they were about to do—and Aelfhild was becoming less certain of this outcome with every moment—she was never destined to be his wife. She had wanted more than anything to answer that she would have been the happiest woman in England to become his bride, but that would serve no purpose. Besides, she had the dreadful suspicion that he had only said what he had because he believed they were about to die. If she admitted her own feelings it was tantamount to acknowledging her impending death.

She watched as Gui crept closer to the farmhouse, moving with elegant stealth through the undergrowth. She drew his cloak closer around herself and inhaled to catch the smell of him on the wool. Her body felt riddled with flames and ice—too big and too small at the same time. The sensation was something she had experienced before when her monthly bleed was about to begin, but never before had she realised what her body was doing. Now she knew it was urging her to couple with a man and this was the man she wanted more than anything to lie with. If she had not been so desperately worried about rescuing Sigrun, she might have considered throwing her virtue away as carelessly as grass seeds on the wind. She bit back a sob that welled suddenly enough to choke her and followed him.

She slipped the rusty knife into her sleeve and joined him. Together they positioned themselves as they had practised. To prevent herself shaking with nerves Aelfhild concentrated on the way Gui's muscles moved beneath his tunic as he squared his shoulders and centred his weight. Her breasts throbbed at the memory of pressing

herself against his broad frame. She pushed close
to him again and tightened her grip around his
waist. No one would ever know how much dis-
cipline it took her not to run her hands across
his body, to explore the contours of his arms
and chest and that magnificent part which had
caused such an alarming response and signalled
carnal gratification she could scarcely imagine.

She reached between his arm and waist and
took hold of the bowstring, leaning into his body.
She curled her fingers round the hempen cord,
drawing back and centring the arrow on the entrance to the farmhouse.

'A little to the left...up ever so slightly... Now
hold it as still as you can.'

Gui whispered his instructions, staring ahead,
one eye closed. He gave a short, low whistle,
then a higher, longer one, followed by a word-
less cry. Aelfhild began to count her heartbeats
as each thud threatened to split her chest open.
She reached six before the skins covering the entrance moved and a figure appeared.

'Now!'

She uncurled her fingers and the arrow sped
towards its target with such speed that Aelfhild
did not have time to close her eyes as she'd intended. The arrow found a home between the
man's ribs. He gave a grunt that sounded dread-

fully loud in the early morning calm, looked down in disbelief and staggered backwards. He fell through the doorway back into the farmhouse and out of her sight.

Vomit rose in Aelfhild's throat. She had done that.

There was no time to appreciate the curious mix of guilt and triumph for long, because Gui was already bending to reach for the next arrow and shoving it into her hand with a hiss. Aelfhild had expected an immediate response from the occupants of the farmhouse, but nothing had prepared her for the shouts of surprise that became roars of anger. She drew the string back and held the arrow poised to release it, but she was trembling with greater intensity. The brawny man who had taunted about raping her appeared, carrying a short sword. Could they be so fortunate that the men were intending to appear one at a time and give Gui the opportunity to dispatch them with such leisure?

No.

As soon as the man was fully through the curtain skins, the bald-headed bearded man followed.

'Now!'

Gui's voice was sharp, taut as the string between her fingers, knocking her out of her reverie. Her aim was less true this time and instead of finding his heart the arrow embedded itself in the brawny man's groin. He shrieked in pain and staggered, but did not fall.

The third man, whose gaunt face and sharp eyes reminded her of a weasel, was out now and scanning the clearing.

'Go round and reach the building from the side,' Gui whispered urgently. 'I'll draw them away. Find Lady Aelfhild and leave.'

She stumbled between the trees round the clearing. Behind her she heard Gui screaming what must be a battle cry in his own language. She looked back to see him hurl himself straight towards the nearest man, who met Gui halfway. Using his bow as a quarterstaff Gui brought it round in a wide arc to catch the scrawny man in the small of his back, felling him. He dropped the bow and pulled an arrow and stabbed at the man's chest. The bald man joined in the fray, swiping at Gui with a short dagger while the one with the arrow embedded in his groin flailed around, his sword in hand and swiping at empty air.

Summoning her courage, Aelfhild ran across the clearing and slipped inside the building. She leaned against the wall, breathing heavily. A high-pitched sob cut through the sounds of battle from outside and she did not instantly realise it was her own name being called. Sigrun was lying in the furthest corner, hands and feet bound, but when Aelfhild moved towards her, Sigrun's head jerked to one side.

'Look out!'

Too late she saw the first man she had shot in the chest. He was lying prone in the centre of the room between her and Sigrun, clutching at the arrow that protruded from below his ribs. His mouth was slack and the agonising wheezing sound he was making would haunt Aelfhild's dreams for many nights to come. She edged round him and he reached out and seized her skirt. She shrieked in panic and kicked out at his hand and face. He finally let go and she stamped hard on his hand and dashed past.

She threw herself on to her knees beside Sigrun and began sawing at the ropes with the rusty blade Gui had given her. A pang of guilt sent her belly plummeting as she thought of him unarmed. Sigrun gave another cry of warning and Aelfhild turned.

She had forgotten about the old woman, but now found herself staring down the blade of a sharp dagger pointing at her face. She began to plead for mercy, but the crone tossed lank grey hair from her wizened face.

'Use this.'

She passed the knife to Aelfhild who received it in astonishment, half-expecting trickery, but the woman simply retreated back into the corner where she had been loitering unseen. Cutting Sigrun free was a simple matter with the better knife. They knelt together, arms around each other, Sigrun holding on to Aelfhild as if she would never release her, sobbing wildly.

'I'd given up hope of you coming. I thought that once he had you safe, why would he come for me?'

'I would never leave you. Nor would he. He's a good man.'

Aelfhild's heart gave a violent thump of longing and sadness, shame and desire as she remembered the way their bodies had become one as they kissed. The infidelity would be her secret shame to bear and a memory to treasure for as long as she lived.

Behind her, the dying man gave a final, bubbling rattle of breath and lay still, drawing her back to the present. She pulled Sigrun to her feet. They ran hand in hand outside, but what Aelfhild saw caused her to cry out in dismay.

The scrawny lout lay unmoving on the ground, the arrow in his chest, but Gui was spread-eagled face down at the edge of the clearing, arms pinioned behind his back by the bald man. He was twisting and bucking to free himself while the man Aelfhild had shot had pulled out the arrow and was dragging himself closer to them, sword in hand, leaving a thin trail of blood on the dirt.

Gui had told her what to do. They had a clear path to the track leading to the main road and no one looked likely to prevent their escape, but she moved towards Gui. Sigrun tugged her back, painfully twisting at Aelfhild's hands to drag her from the clearing. Aelfhild took two steps after her, then stopped, looking back again.

'Come *on*! Why are you stopping?'

'We can't leave him.'

As she watched Gui pulled his hand free and began clawing his fingers towards the final arrow that lay just beyond his reach. The man sitting astride him pulled Gui's head back, then smacked it into the ground. Gui groaned, his fingers clawing at the earth.

'Yes, we can!' Sigrun exclaimed. 'He's our enemy. He is nothing to us.'

Aelfhild stared with horror into her companion's face and saw a stranger. Gentle Sigrun, who never raised a finger in anger, never spoke an unkind word, was lost in the wild-eyed, filth-smeared woman who ground her teeth in anguish and looked on the brink of madness. What further terrors had she been subjected to that would make her say such brutal things, and how could Aelfhild think of making her remain here a moment longer?

But Gui…

He wasn't *her* enemy. He might be nothing to Sigrun, but he was everything to Aelfhild, even if she could be nothing to him once they reached York.

'If he dies here, I'll never have to marry him,' Sigrun pleaded. 'We can go on to York, or back to the priory. We'll be safe.'

After everything she had been through, Sigrun's proposition was understandable. If Aelfhild helped Gui she would be condemning Sigrun to the marriage she currently dreaded, though she had seen enough of Gui to believe he would win his bride's love in time. But if she left Gui to fend for himself and he did not survive, part of her would die, too.

'I'm sorry.' She wrenched free from Sigrun and turned away.

Chapter Fifteen

⁓⁓⁓⁓

Gui's opponent was reaching for the knife at his belt. Gripping his fingers into Gui's hair. Drawing Gui's head back to bare his throat in order to slit it.

Gui's bow was lying discarded where he had dropped it. Aelfhild picked it up double handed and hurled herself across the clearing. She gave a piercing shriek that tore her throat painfully and swung it round. The bow caught Gui's assailant full across the back of the head. He sagged on top of Gui, who rolled over and pushed the man off him. Both men began a deadly race for the knife. A hand seized Aelfhild's ankle and she was jerked off her feet, landing painfully on the ground.

The man with the arrow in his groin had finally reached them. He crawled towards her, dragging at her legs to pin her to the ground. He hissed at her through spittle and blood-covered teeth as he heaved himself on top of her. Almost out of her mind with terror, Aelfhild tried to cry out, but his hands were on her throat and she was choking, unable to breathe, unable to break free, and she had failed to save them at all.

When she next awoke she was being held. Tighter than was strictly comfortable, but not so much that she was in pain or troubled by being restrained. The sensation was comforting.

'Sigrun, my lady, wake up.'

The voice was familiar. It was speaking to her, but that was not her name and she was momentarily confused. She swallowed and now she felt pain. She decided to remain as she was, lying down with her eyes closed, until she could make sense of what had happened.

'Please. Come back to me.'

The voice had an edge of pleading to it now and she knew whom it belonged to. If they were Gui's arms in which she was lying she would gladly stay there for ever, but she could not ignore any entreaty he made so she opened her eyes. Gui was leaning over her. His forehead was oozing blood from a graze and his already broken nose looked swollen, but his brown eyes were full of concern and his scarred lip curved his face into a picture of abject despair. He gave a gasp of relief as their eyes met before his expression changed to one of fury.

'I told you to leave! Why didn't obey me?'

Aelfhild bit her lip to stop it trembling, but heard the concern simmering beneath the anger. She smiled weakly. 'And I told *you* I am not yours to command.'

She tried to continue, but her throat was dry—a combination of the shriek she had given and the hands trying to wring the life out of her that had bruised her throat. Gui put his finger to her lips to stop her speaking, but she brushed it aside.

'If I hadn't come back, you'd be dead by now.'

'As would you, if your companion hadn't picked up a sword!'

'She killed him?' Aelfhild pushed herself upright, pain forgotten, looking for Sigrun. She had been standing behind Gui, but now dropped beside Aelfhild and took hold of her hands.

'I didn't stab him.'

'She hit him with the flat of the blade, but it gave me time to dispatch the one I was fighting and come to your aid. Someone should teach her how to handle a sword properly.' Gui grinned at Sigrun, who smiled back nervously, though with an expression of triumph on her face that Aelfhild had never seen. She seemed less shaken by her ordeal than she had while they were trying to escape. Sigrun embraced Aelfhild. Gui's arm came around both of them and they held each other, heads together in weary relief that the ordeal they had all shared was ended. It was the first time Aelfhild could remember Sigrun willingly touching her future husband, or allowing him to touch her without recoiling.

'Well done, my lady.' Gui held his hand out to Sigrun, who hesitated before taking it and allowed him to bow his head over it. They were comrades, united by what they had done for Aelfhild, and her presence was not needed for them to share that satisfaction. The gulf had lessened between Sigrun and the man she would marry. It was as it should be, but seeing them sitting side by side seared Aelfhild's heart until she felt it might explode from her chest and burn up with grief. She disentangled herself. Leaving Gui and his bride together, she walked into the farmhouse, heart breaking.

There were practical matters to attend to and Aelfhild was good at being practical. She had been raised to serve Sigrun, after all, something she had almost forgotten. Their clothes had been thrown into a pile in the corner on top of rags that had once been clothes before they mouldered. Various weapons were stacked alongside. She pulled her dress over her head and folded Sigrun's. Her herbs had been emptied and the precious jars of ointment smashed with a casual destructiveness that only increased her hatred of the men.

She found their rings and her precious brooch in a sturdy box along with half a slim arm torque of twisted silver and a silver ring. Gui's seal ring was there, too, still on the cord he used to hang it round his neck. She ran her fingers over it and wondered about the fates of those poor women and men who her captors had preyed upon. Their fate could have been hers. She shuddered involuntarily, wondering what Gui had seen that made him so determined to kill the men.

'Take 'em all! No one else has use for them now.'

Twice now the crone had made Aelfhild jump. She hobbled towards Aelfhild, gesticulating at the box. Aelfhild gathered her treasures and hesitated before slipping the half-torque into her bag. The men had hacked pieces off when they needed to, but the amount left was still more silver than Aelfhild could ever have hoped to possess. She contemplated offering it to Gui in exchange for freeing Sigrun from the promise of marriage, but the silver wasn't worth as much as Sigrun's estate by any means. She pressed the silver ring into the woman's hand.

'Thank you for helping me save my friend and for your kindness yesterday. I can't leave you with nothing.'

'You stayed to help your man,' the crone said, slipping the ring into her pouch. 'I was watching. That's good. A woman should be loyal, whoever her man is.'

'He's not my man.' Aelfhild's voice cracked.

'Says you. I saw different.'

'He isn't!' She tried to curb the anger and sorrow in her voice. The woman was trying to be kind, probably, and she had helped Aelfhild to free Sigrun. She curled her fingers into her palms. The nails dug in, leaving red half-moons.

'He can't be mine.'

'Well, he'd like to be,' the woman muttered.

Aelfhild felt her legs giving way at this bold declaration of what she yearned to hear from Gui himself. She turned to see Sigrun standing in the doorway. Had she heard the crone's words? She gave no sign, but perhaps she would not care in any case. Sigrun pulled on her dress, but shook her head when Aelfhild gave her the fine girdle.

'The girdle is yours for now. The rings, too.'

Aelfhild sighed. She was tired of the deceit, tired of the pretence that she could one day respond to Gui's clear affection, tired of seeing the hurt flash in his eyes when she rebuffed him. Most of all she was tired of allowing herself to dream that she might have a future with Gui in it.

'Must we still pretend? Even now after you and he—'

'Yes!' Sigrun took the girdle and passed it around Aelfhild's waist. She turned Aelfhild firmly round to face her and Aelfhild was struck again at the unexpected confidence she had developed.

'He and I are nothing to each other. Just because we worked together to save you does not mean I am willing to marry him.' Sigrun raised her hand to Aelfhild's cheek and tenderly brushed a finger across the bruise. 'We did it for love of you. Both of us.'

Sigrun's eyes flickered to the old woman. So she had heard their conversation. Aelfhild's eyes filled with tears.

'Sigrun, I can't keep pretending. It hurts too much to deny what I feel for him.'

'What you feel?' Sigrun gave her a look of pity.

'I love him. It's wrong and if I could cut the feelings out of my heart with a knife I would do it.'

Sigrun enveloped her in an embrace and held her while tears racked her body.

'We'll be in Haxby tomorrow and then we will tell him the truth. Perhaps he will be willing to accept you as a bride instead. Come on, I can't bear to stay here any longer.'

Gui was calling her. Aelfhild wiped her eyes. She did not share Sigrun's belief. She had no land or wealth to offer to him, but until that tiny flicker of hope was extinguished completely it was all she had to hold on to.

Gui had not been idle. The bodies that had been lying where they had fallen were now laid in a row at the side of the farmhouse. Gui had hitched the sad-looking donkey to the cart and had tethered his mare alongside. The mare was tossing her head and looking agitated. Sigrun walked to it and began talking in a low voice, running her hands over the animal's dirty flanks. Gui watched her, his face thoughtful.

'Is something wrong?'

He shook his head at Aelfhild's question. 'Nothing. I was thinking of a friend of mine. I believe he loves horses more than he is fond of people. They would get on well with each other.'

He faced Aelfhild and looked her up and down. She gazed back fearlessly. His eyes settled on her brooch. The corner of his mouth twitched.

Perhaps he was remembering the night he had returned it to her. They had so many memories to share and they would have to last her a lifetime.

'I didn't mean to get angry at you when you awoke. The idea that you might have died terrified me. Nevertheless, thank you for returning to help me.'

He stepped closer, inclining his head to look at her. The hairs on Aelfhild's neck and arms stood on end, remembering the last time they had stood in such a manner and what happened next. She lifted her head to face him, parting her lips unconsciously. Gui stepped backwards. Away from her. His head dropped.

'What I said to you before we started this, about becoming your husband—'

He was mumbling. Ashamed. Regretting his words as he had regretted their kiss. Disappointment crashed over Aelfhild. She cut his words off.

'You thought we were going to die.' She wished at that moment that she had. 'I understand. Soldiers facing battle, as you explained before.'

He did not contradict her. The old woman was wrong. Sigrun likewise. There would be no more words of affection.

She pushed the seal ring into his hand. He

stared at it dumbly before slipping the cord over his head.

'There are weapons inside the farmhouse. You might want to choose something in case we face further dangers.'

She swept past him before she began to weep, in an attempt to preserve her dignity. She would choose a knife of her own so she could protect herself rather than relying on Gui, but it struck her as she headed to the farmhouse that she had lost her taste for fighting. The brief battle she had been involved in was enough to teach her that she did not have the stomach for such things. A groan stopped her in her tracks. One of the men she had taken to be a corpse was moving slowly.

She cried in alarm. Gui was by her side almost before the sound had left her lips, a questioning look on his face. Aelfhild pointed to the man they had shot in the groin. He was clutching his wound with hands that were red with gore and drawing short, wispy breaths. He smelled foul.

'He's still alive!'

Gui eyed the man coldly, appraisingly. He shrugged. 'He's bleeding fast. Probably inside his belly, too. He'll be dead before noon. He won't harm anyone else.'

He turned away, seemingly happy to have re-assured her that the dying man would present no more danger. Aelfhild caught his sleeve and he knotted his brow in confusion as she tugged him back.

'You can't leave him to suffer.'

The confusion turned to coldness. Hard eyes chilling her blood. 'Can't I?'

'No! Killing during battle is one thing, but that's torture. Don't you have any compassion, even for your enemy? You did it for the man with no legs.'

'And if you remember, you condemned me as a murderer for doing it!'

She hung her head, remembering the bitter accusations, the hurt in his eyes.

'I was wrong to do that and I apologise. But you did it, none the less. You showed him compassion.'

'That was different, he had done me no harm. Do you know how many they've killed? How many they left to die an agonising death? This dog doesn't deserve mercy!'

She thought of what they had done to her and Sigrun, and to the others who had come before. This man would have raped her. He'd have sold her to a brothel without a second care. What did he deserve, after all? But to see Gui so callous chilled her bones.

'They became what they were to survive. If

you let him suffer, then you're no better than they were.'

Gui turned white. He rounded on her, his face fearsome. He looked more furious than Aelfhild could ever remember seeing him. A monster after all.

'No better! When they ambushed us they could have killed me instantly, but they didn't. Instead they threw me bound and helpless in a grave pit filled with the corpses of their other victims.' His voice was a husky whisper, filled with the same agony he had used when recounting his nightmares.

'It would have taken slow, degrading, painful days while I starved to death or the wild beasts attacked. Every moment would have been a greater torture than anything he will endure. How dare you condemn me because I show no compassion?'

He pressed his lips together and looked at her with eyes that had seen terrors she couldn't comprehend. He had been forced to live out his recurring nightmare and she had callously berated *him* for being cruel. His anguish was unbearable to witness and she wished more than anything she could claw her words back.

'Oh, Gui, forgive me. I didn't realise.'

She rushed to him, throwing her arms around

him with a passion that unnerved her. He stood rigid in her arms. She realised he was starting to shake, but fighting with every muscle in his body to hold steady.

'They were bad before his kind came. Bad since birth.'

Gui and Aelfhild turned to face the old woman who had spoken. She had her arm tightly around Sigrun's shoulder. Aelfhild jumped back from Gui, mortified to be caught in such a position by her friend.

'Sons of mine from a husband just as worthless!' She spat on the ground. 'I should have strangled them at birth. I would have pulled them from the womb unborn if I'd known what they would become. Still—' her lip twitched into an unpleasant grin that she bestowed on Gui '—the maid is right. It would do you credit to end this one's suffering. It might ease your mind, too.'

Gui looked from one woman to another. All three nodded in unison. He seemed to come to a decision and heaved a weary sigh.

'Then I do this for you, not for him.'

Aelfhild could not tell which of them he referred to.

'Gui,' she began.

He whipped his head up to look at her. She held her hand out in a gesture of peace.

'Do it only if you think it will bring you peace.'

'You change your mind so frequently, lady. I wish I knew where it would settle.'

He bent beside the man and drew out a knife Aelfhild recognised as his opponent's.

'Do you want the quick end the women think I should give you?'

The man spat blood. 'I won't beg from an *earsling* like you.'

Gui shuffled round to block the man from view. Aelfhild could tell the instant he drew the knife across the man's throat and when the man's life left him from the way he jerked, then grew still.

Gui stood and dropped the knife beside the corpse. He didn't look peaceful. His head was bowed and he looked so lonely Aelfhild wanted to weep. She stayed where she was, unable to forget the cold unyielding body she had tried to embrace.

'It's done. Now, let's be on the way. We can be in Haxby by nightfall.'

Gui stared across the vale. They had been leaving the hills behind them gradually over the day and the flat expanse that now lay before him signalled the end of their journey. Ahead, the road dipped over one final curve, then levelled out. The Galtres Forest loomed ahead. He shifted his weight on the seat of the cart and arched his back to ease the ache in his spine. The board sorely needed some padding, but he could not complain. Even with the discomfort, steering a cart was preferable to riding or walking. It had increased their speed fivefold, which was fortunate as Sigrun and Aelfhild had insisted they could not abandon the old lady in the forest and had taken her as far as a village halfway home.

Sigrun clambered on to the cart and sat beside him. She gazed ahead at the view. They had not spoken beyond civilities since they had begun this final stage of the journey. If anything, she had been deliberately avoiding him.

'It's been a long time since I saw this view,' she mused, more to herself than him. 'It's changed.'

Sunlight bathed the barren earth, turning the scrub and soil to gold and bronze. Gui could picture what it would look like when the land finally recovered. It would never have the beauty of the Breton coast, but he could see the potential for beauty.

'It'll change again,' he answered.

A knot filled his throat. Before he had started his mission he could have made his home here on the land Gilbert gave him and been content with his lot in life. With Sigrun at his side life would have been blissful, but knowing she was out of his reach for ever would make each day a torture to be endured. He tilted his head to better look at the beauty by his side and melancholy filled him, spreading into every limb. A day of partings and revelations like today should be thundery and cold, with lashing rain and screaming winds, not warm and golden.

'It's been a long journey.' Dull-witted remark! She knew that as well as him, but his mind had emptied of everything but the all-encompassing yearning to tell her the truth. He longed to declare his love before her true husband claimed her, but that was beyond imagining so all he could do was speak nonsense like a shy fifteen-year-old.

'Do you want me to take the reins? You must be growing tired.'

He shook his head and gathered them in his hand. 'This is easier than riding one handed.'

Gui had not thought twice about taking it after they had set fire to the foul hovel. The previous owners had no use for it now and he had more than earned the spoils of that battle. He had left the weapons, beyond the *seax* he had reclaimed, a short sword and his bow.

Sigrun glanced down to his left arm, which rested in his lap. He had folded the end of the sleeve over and secured it with a leather cord. The lack of glove unnerved him, but not as much as he would have predicted if he had been asked to give up his false hand voluntarily. Perhaps he would not be so quick to replace it, but would face whatever response he incurred with a challenge rather than hiding cowed behind padding and falsehood. She had not cared about his scars. He was determined that from now on he would not either.

She twisted in the seat, expression pensive. 'What will we find when we get home? Is Haxby as ravaged as the places we've seen?'

'I imagine you will find it mainly unchanged.'

'Of course—she had the bargaining power of a daughter to wed to keep it safe.'

She sounded more at peace with her fate now. There was none of the resentment she had showed when they had met.

'I want to tell you how much I admire you.'

He wasn't sure where the words came from. He hadn't intended to speak and admire was not the word that came close to expressing his feelings. Her eyes widened and he thought he saw anxiety flash across them, but he continued.

'What you did this morning was remarkable. I am not exaggerating when I say I could not have done it without you. You have more bravery than

I could imagine. With a woman like you at his side a man could rule England.'

'A woman like me?'

She blushed, her pale eyes widening. Her lips parted alluringly. She wanted him as much as he wanted her. Incredible though it seemed, he could not deny that he had seen the look in her eyes he knew he wore in his own. To keep the truth from her was cruel. He was supposed to have told tales that made her fall in love with Gilbert, but instead he appeared to have captured her heart. He felt a touch of pride that it was he who meant the prospect of marriage was not as unbearable as it had been, but an immense pit of sadness threatened to consume him. The sense of betrayal that she would feel when she discovered he was not to be her husband would be all the greater.

Gui took her hand, examining it as if it was the most interesting thing in the world. It was small and cold, like the hand of a child, with rough fingers and nails cut short. She didn't possess the hands of a pampered lady, but of someone who was prepared to do what needed to be done and wasn't afraid of working. They were hands that dug roots and plucked flowers, then ground them to powders. Hands that would fashion a fish hook from a brooch and stab a man through the arm, then soothe his wounds with the same gentle touch. He remembered them on his body, the nails scraping deliciously against the bare flesh at his waist and chest. His chest tightened.

'Yes, like you. Courageous and strong. Fair minded and compassionate. Passionate and... and...'

He swallowed down regret that he would never discover just how passionate she might be, that the brief glimpse when he had kissed her the night before had only opened his eyes to the possibilities. That would be for Gilbert to do. He would be the one to claim her virginity and introduce her to the pleasures of lovemaking. Gilbert would help her discover what a man liked and in turn teach her what drove her to the edge of reason with passion. Another man would fully awaken the senses that Gui had glimpsed stirring within her when they had kissed. She would learn the sensual power she could wield in the arms of another man. The knowledge consumed him entirely, threatening to spill over in an outpouring of grief and jealousy.

'With you by his side a man could do more than win a fight over a bunch of ruffians. He could conquer the world.'

'Is conquest what you still desire?' she asked.

Gui's whole body cried out that it was. Not for

conquests of worlds, but of the woman at his side. Resisting her last night, when her body had so clearly been calling to his, had been the hardest thing he had done. Merely holding her hand and sharing this quiet moment drove him to torment with the yearning to claim her. Even dreaming of what he was imagining was a betrayal of his friend and of Lady Sigrun herself. He placed her hand gently back at her side, as if it were the most delicate of jewels, and gave her a smile.

'No. I did once, but I know now I'm not made for war.' He rolled his head from side to side, then gazed into the distance. 'This morning was my final battle. Those men deserved to die and I'm glad I was the instrument, but I want peaceful days and nights not plagued by dark dreams.'

'Do you think your dreams will ever leave you?'

He had slept well the previous night despite the rough ground. The thought that he had found peace in her arms was unendurable when he knew he would never do so again.

'I don't know. I hope so, one day. Whether or not they do I want an old age of contentment, not fear or strife.'

She smiled. 'You're not old.'

'No, but I plan to be one day. It won't happen if I keep fighting. I wanted adventure and the chance to make my fortune.' He held his left arm up. 'Instead I lost a hand, gained a headful of sights that haunt me at night and little more.'

'Little more. Is that what you think? You've gained a bride and her lands, a home in England that should have belonged to another man. After everything you have seen and done you dismiss that as a small matter!'

Her voice was cold, her expression withering. He'd been talking of himself, thinking of the small portion of land that Gilbert had promised for bringing her to York, not the swathes of land Gilbert would claim himself, but of course she did not know that.

'You misunderstand me.'

She tossed her hair back and glared at him. Gui was confused at her sudden vehemence until she spoke again and this time he could hear an edge of a sob in her voice. 'I'm sure when your marriage day comes your bride will understand the value you place on her property and self. Women are born to expect nothing more from life and it's better she knows from the outset that you care nothing for either!'

He could not lie any longer. He would lay the whole deception open and to confess the feelings that consumed him. They did him no credit, but he could not remain silent any longer. Would not, despite his vow to Gilbert.

'We need to discuss your betrothal.'

She cut him off with a violent wave of her hand, her face twisting in misery. 'Not now! Please, I can't bear to talk about that.' Her face crumpled. She pushed herself to her feet. Gui caught hold of her skirts, holding her back. A flash from her eyes made him release her. 'Do not ask me to speak of it!'

Humiliation and confusion coursed through Gui. He had thought she was falling in love as deeply as he had. Now she recoiled from discussing a marriage she should no longer dread if she believed he was her intended husband.

'As you wish, my lady.'

Sigrun climbed off the cart in a swirl of skirts and joined Aelfhild. The companion spoke, glancing towards him. Sigrun shook her head. She glanced over her shoulder, saw him looking and her expression changed from anger to what he could only interpret as sorrow. Her eyes shone. Gui's throat tightened as he realised they were wet with tears.

They had shared confidences and secrets, and last night she had offered herself to him, begged him to take her. The night had been a frenzy of emotions, but perhaps on her part only caused by the situation they had found themselves in. There was no reason to expect those emotions would outlive the journey. He had told her as much when he lied to calm her shame, though he had not believed a word himself.

He wondered how he had so badly misjudged the situation. He could not see any reason why she lurched between meeting his desire with equal force and rejecting him completely. Perhaps she did not care for him after all. Perhaps being married to anyone was too big a hurdle to overcome. Perhaps she cared and the thought he did not value her for herself had wounded her heart too greatly.

He consoled himself that she would find out before the day was done. Then she would understand that even though he could never have her, his devotion was to her alone, with no regard to her lands or status.

It was small consolation.

The countryside continued to roll past, changing subtly from curving hills to the flat plain of the vale where York and Haxby lay. King William himself could offer Gui everything that lay before his eyes and it would not be enough to keep him there if he could not have Sigrun. The smallholding that Gilbert would grant him was generous and tempting, but it was a poor exchange for having to live close to the woman he loved and watch her build a life with someone else. It would be unbearable if Sigrun and Gilbert were miserable, but watching them grow to love each other would be equal agony.

He let the miles pass beneath his feet in a fantasy of returning to Brittany, but taking Sigrun with him. Only a fantasy because although he might trespass against Gilbert to the extent of stealing kisses, he had more honour than to steal away his friend's wife.

He would deliver Lady Sigrun to her home, exact a promise from Gilbert to treat her in the manner she deserved, then go back to Brittany and begin again the life he had abandoned, keeping the memories safe in his heart of the woman who had once seen the possibility of the man he could be.

Chapter Sixteen

Finally they were home. Aelfhild had longed
to return here for as long as she had been in the
priory, but now she felt no joy at her return. The
last league or two had felt as long as the rest of
the journey put together. Although the daylight
lasted longer at this time of year it was a relief
to see the torch burning in the doorway of Herik's house.

Gui drew the cart to a stop a little way from
the door. No one moved. No one spoke. No one
made eye contact.

Dogs barked. Someone would come out before long to find out who was visiting at such a
late hour. Wearily they clambered from the cart
and, arm in arm, the two women began to walk
to the home they had left so long ago. Halfway
to the door Sigrun stopped and returned to where
Gui stood methodically securing the reins to a

fence post. Aelfhild realised she was holding her breath, blood pounding as she watched to see what would happen. Finally Sigrun inclined her head to Gui.

'Thank you for bringing us home safely, Sir Gilbert. We are in your debt.' She glanced at Aelfhild and a look passed between them. Aelfhild knew what it was costing Sigrun to speak so openly to her unwanted husband, even with her newly discovered confidence, and in turn Sigrun would know what the end of the journey would mean to Aelfhild. 'You are welcome in our home.'

'I thank you,' he said, his voice lifting in surprise.

She gave him a shy smile, cast a look of sorrow and sympathy at Aelfhild and walked away to take her bag from the cart. Aelfhild stood rooted to the spot, her belly churning. Was the welcome Sigrun's way of acknowledging her identity and accepting the marriage or did she still intend to resist it?

Aelfhild raised her head to see Gui was staring intently at her, his expression grave. She took a step towards him, but her foot faltered. She longed to touch him, to throw herself into his arms with admissions of her love and kiss him once again until they were both incapable of standing. But that was not her right. She tried to smile, but her mouth felt frozen. She smoothed down her skirts that were crumpled from the journey and adjusted the rings on her fingers for the final time. Soon she would have to return her fine disguise to its rightful owner, along with the husband. Her heart was being ground into pieces small enough to make into rissoles, but she smiled bravely. Since she had refused to discuss marriage and had left him on the cart alone, no words had passed between them.

'We should go inside. Lady Emma will be waiting.'

His response was a shrug. He appeared in no hurry to enter the house and claim the reward that had been bestowed upon him. Still he did not speak or move, only gazed on her with those eyes like dark pools she could drown herself in.

They had started the journey as adversaries, but over the days that had followed they had grown so much closer than was acceptable or advisable. Now they were strangers once more.

It would make it easier for him to forget her and transfer his developing feelings to his rightful bride, but she did not think she could bear to see that happen. The thought of the priory was like a shroud enclosing her, but that was where she would return rather than stay here.

There was no point delaying. If he were not going to move, then she would have to be the one. Sigrun was waiting by the door. Aelfhild nodded curtly at Gui and turned to go.

'Wait.'

She stopped, heart in her throat.

He crossed the ground between them in three strides, reached his hand out and clasped hers. His thumb bent round between her forefinger and thumb, pressing in the back of her hand until both began to shake. His grip was strong, holding tight for far longer than was necessary or appropriate. They didn't look at each other and spoke no words, but the strength of the bond between them was so great and apparent no other communication was necessary.

She squeezed his hand, her slender fingers lost in his great palm. The force of this substitute embrace made their arms tremble. The unspoken passion and devotion that would have taken a dozen frenzied kisses to express passed through his hand to hers and back again. Why they were saying farewell in such a manner when only she was certain it would be a parting was something she did not understand.

Reluctantly Aelfhild released the pressure of her fingers and slipped free. He offered only a little resistance, but enough for her to treasure. She walked away, head held as high as Sigrun's had been, and joined her mistress. Gui walked past them and hammered on the door until one of the menservants opened it and bade them to enter.

The room was brightly lit by torches along one wall. Lady Emma was sitting on the dais at the furthest end, eyes closed, listening to the musician who played at her feet. She opened her eyes as the travellers entered.

Gui strode forward and swept a deep bow, lowering his head humbly. 'My lady, I have returned your daughter to you.'

Lady Emma barely acknowledged him. She rose from her seat and pointed a finger at Sigrun. She looked incensed.

'Explain why you have brought my daughter back dressed in the manner of a servant!'

Her clear tone rang through the room. Gui's head snapped up.

'What!'

He looked from Aelfhild to Sigrun, then to Lady Emma. His eyes settled on Aelfhild again. She felt herself shrink under his gaze. She could not meet his eyes, but looked at him surreptitiously from beneath her lashes. His face was incredulous.

'This is your daughter? Are you sure?'

Lady Emma treated the question with the contempt it deserved. 'I gave birth to her. Credit me with the sense to recognise her.'

Her scathing reply didn't seem to disturb Gui. In fact, he was smiling broadly, his black eyes sparkling with unspoken glee. Aelfhild felt herself go limp with misery. He didn't care that she was not the one he had to marry. He looked ecstatic at the thought of Sigrun as his bride. Her eyes filled with tears and it took all her strength not to run from the hall.

Sigrun ran and embraced her mother. They were equally tall, equally striking. Aelfhild heard Gui let out a low murmur of comprehension as the two women stood side by side. He was seeing the resemblance now.

'Aelfhild and I swapped identities so I could avoid having to spend time with him. He didn't know.'

Gui muttered under his breath in Breton and she wondered if he was angry at the deception.

Sigrun carried on boldly speaking to her mother in a manner she never would have previously. 'It was my idea. I don't want to marry Sir Gilbert and he doesn't want to marry me. He loves Aelfhild. They love each other.'

Sigrun stopped to glance at Aelfhild and Gui who finally acknowledged Aelfhild's existence.

His broad frame was tense. If he agreed with Sigrun's words, he gave no sign.

'You wouldn't be so cruel to all of us, Mother,' Sigrun continued. 'Please say you won't.'

Lady Emma was rarely surprised, or rarely permitted anyone to see it if she was. The discovery that Aelfhild had been masquerading as her daughter had seemingly not daunted her, but now she threw her head back and gave an exasperated sigh.

'Are your senses addled, Sigrun? I don't know what lies he has told you, or why you have all spent the journey deceiving each other, but this man is *not* Gilbert du Rospez!'

A ringing began in Aelfhild's ears, drowning out all other sounds. Not Gilbert. Not Sigrun's husband-to-be.

She could see Sigrun's lips moving and Gui— Gilbert—who knew what he was really called— opening his mouth to join in, but she couldn't make out a word they were saying. She couldn't breathe. The smoky air was choking her. She turned and bolted from the Great Hall and out into the darkness. She leaned her elbows on the low fence post and buried her head in her hands.

The implications of that revelation were too great to consider. He was not bound, but was as free to marry as Aelfhild. Her heart soared, then fell to earth with a thump when she thought of how she had deceived him. The passionate embraces had been from a man who thought his beloved was wealthy. To marry her, he would need to be prepared to marry a woman with no name or family and no dowry. What man would want to marry her as she was? She shivered even though the breeze that caressed her was balmy and smelled of sweet summer grass, then closed her eyes, weary and confused.

As soon as he felt it polite, Gui left the woman he must now think of as Lady Sigrun to argue with her mother. Let her plead and bargain to be released from her marriage to Gilbert; the outcome held no interest to him. His heart was dragging him elsewhere. The only thing that had stopped him rushing straight to the side of—of who? He still thought of her as Sigrun—was that he was unsure of the reception he would receive. He wasn't the knight she had believed him to be and he had nothing to offer her, but neither was she the noblewoman he had imagined.

He made his way out of the house and joined the slight figure leaning on the fence. She stared straight ahead and didn't even acknowledge his presence. He would have to say something to provoke her.

'You lied to me.'

That got her attention. She spun to face him, eyes full of fire and challenge.

'I didn't lie! *You* named me as Sigrun when you caught me! You made the assumption because of what Hilde had told you. I just carried on the deception.'

It was a fair point. He had jumped to the conclusion. 'But you didn't bother to correct me.'

She pursed her lips. 'You lied, too. To Hilde and all of us as soon as you arrived at the priory. All the time we were travelling you were lying.'

'Not all the time!' Words of affection he had spoken rushed back to him. 'Only my identity and you cannot hold that against me as you did the same.'

'I can if I choose!'

He laughed and heard the weariness in his voice that contrasted with the belligerence in hers.

'When Gilbert and I first came here Lady Emma told us that her daughter was compliant and gentle. That alone should have given me reason to realise you were not the woman she described.'

She bit her bottom lip, drawing it in between her teeth as she considered his words. Gui leaned on the fence and gazed at her. His whole body was starting to tremble with the urge to take her in his arms as he had done the previous night. He wasn't sure if she would allow it, but he suspected the balance was tipping in his favour.

'What is your real name? Are you Aelfhild?'

She nodded and glanced towards the house. She was still guarded, unwilling to unbend, while Gui for his part was determined not only to unbend her, but to vanquish any resistance and claim her for himself.

'I didn't expect the journey to be so dangerous,' he remarked.

'Didn't you? You told me it would be hard.'

He sniffed. 'I mean dangerous for me. I found that despite my intentions to keep my distance from you I couldn't. You're in my head and under my skin. When I thought I'd lost you it was unbearable. I'd have followed you across the world to get you back.'

Her mouth grew wide. He realised how intense he sounded.

'The whole journey here has been almost unendurable; to be close to you all day and every night, but thinking you were claimed by another man. Wanting to touch you, but being convinced I didn't have the right.'

She dropped her head modestly. 'When you kissed me I didn't want you to stop. I'd wanted you to do it for so long. Then I felt so ashamed. I thought I was the wickedest woman in England for behaving in such a way with Sigrun's betrothed, even if she didn't want you.'

He put his hand on her shoulder and felt the shiver that raced through her.

'I'm very glad you weren't meant for Gilbert. You wouldn't suit each other at all. You're full of fire and that would overwhelm him. I think he will be happier with Sigrun.'

'She will have to marry him, won't she?' Grief crossed her face. 'All our deception won't change that.'

'I imagine so. But he's a good man and I will stay here to make sure he treats her well. You could stay here, too, to make doubly sure.'

'To live as her companion or stay with Lady Emma, who will have to give way to her daughter once they marry?' She wrinkled her nose. 'I've trespassed on their charity my whole life, I'd rather not any longer.'

'I don't mean with them.' Gui's stomach turned over as nerves threatened to overcome him. 'I agreed to play the part of Gilbert because he promised me a portion of the land he will gain by marriage. It was my only chance to gain status and wealth, and to build a life for myself now I can no longer fight.'

She looked puzzled so he continued at a rush.

'I wasn't sure if I was going to take his offer, but now I am. I want the land. It'll be years before the ground heals and yields what it can and the work to bring it back to life will be hard. There has been so much destruction caused by French hands and I need to play my part in atoning for that.'

He was acutely aware that she was saying nothing and that he was making his offer sound less unattractive with each word. He smiled widely, no longer conscious of the fact that his lip twisted. *A roguish air*, she'd once called it.

'I'm expressing myself badly. I'd like—I *want* you by my side while I do it. To do it with me.'

'To help you?'

He swallowed, took a breath to steel his courage and went down on his knee before her. 'As my wife.'

She turned pale and her face grew solemn. Gui feared the idea was abhorrent to her. 'You want to marry me? But we lied to each other. What start to a marriage is that, knowing that we both deceived each other?'

'It's an honest start,' Gui said with a grin. 'Better to wed knowing what we're both capable of than find out a year or more into the match.

But there won't be any more deceptions now, I promise you that.'

'You do know I'm not rich like Sigrun is? I have nothing to offer you. I don't even know who my family were.'

Family. Gui's heart skipped a beat. Something he had never thought to possess for himself. He closed his hand over hers.

'You have yourself. That's all I want. My heart is in your hands. You're under my skin and in my blood. Reject me now and you will crush the life from me. Tell me before I die with anxiety, could you love a man such as me? A man who isn't whole. An archer who can no longer use a bow, who wakes in the night full of terror. A *dweorgar* who can scare a woman half to death? Will you have me as your husband, scarred and broken as I am?'

She flung herself down into his arms, almost knocking him off his knees, slight and small as she was.

'Of course I'll have you and you're not broken to me. You're brave and kind, and you're perfect as you are. I wouldn't change a thing about you. I love you.'

Gui staggered to his feet, drawing Aelfhild with him. He wrapped his arm around her, his left arm, the useless one which he now understood was more than adequate to hold a woman to him, and brushed his right thumb across the curve of her cheek. She gazed up at him with eyes that confirmed her words were the truth. Her pupils grew large and he caught the way the corner of her mouth flickered. He drew her closer.

'I can kiss you properly now and I will. There is nothing to prevent me now I know you aren't bound to my friend. Nothing to prevent either of us.'

She looked at him with eyes full of joy and desire. Gui could no longer hold back. He drew her to his chest, lifting her to meet him and kissed her with a frenzy that she returned in kind. He slid his right hand down the curve of her spine to rest above the softness of her buttocks and heard her muffled gasp of pleasure as he spread his fingers wide. She pushed against him, hips tilting forward in a manner that drove him to the edge of reason. She desired him as much as he wanted her. He broke off kissing long enough to whisper in her ear.

'You're mine now, my sprite.'

'And you are mine, *dweorgar*.'

Aelfhild threw her hands round his neck, drawing him down towards her into another kiss that was deeper, longer, unending and yet only the start of their life together.

There would be matters to settle, questions to answer, and no doubt obstacles to overcome but they could wait for now. Their days would be hard, but their nights together would be endless bliss. Gui gave himself over to the dizzying pleasure of their kiss, knowing that with Aelfhild by his side and in his heart, he was whole at last.

Epilogue

One year later

Shoots were starting to appear in the furrows. Gui bent and pulled out a few weeds that were greedily trying to claim the good soil from his crop. He worked his way along one strip until he reached the end, then stretched and leaned against the wicker fence that separated his land from Gilbert's. He wiped the sweat from his forehead and surveyed his work. Pale green in colour and in some places barely visible among the soil, the shoots were small and weak for now. With care they would grow strong and the crop would survive, and Gui had all the time he needed to ensure that would happen. He would finish the weeding by the end of the day.

He heard humming and turned to see Aelfhild making her way back from Sigrun's home, a basket of bread over one arm. His heart swelled and he opened the gate, hastening to meet her. He enveloped her in a hug, pulling her towards him and almost lifting her off her feet. She giggled.

'Careful, I'll drop the bread or end up on the ground,' she said in mock severity. She lowered the basket to the ground and flung her arms around his neck to stop herself falling backwards, which gave Gui an idea. He leaned over her so that her legs entwined with his and there was not a gap between their bodies. He allowed her to drop a little until she squealed, then caught her before she truly fell. He lowered her to the ground on to a patch of grass at the edge of the field, settling beside her.

'I've been working hard all morning,' he murmured into her ear, taking pleasure in the way she squirmed with delight. 'I think I should rest for a while before I weed the rest of the field. Will you join me, Wife?'

The word brought a lump to his throat, as it always did. His wife. His land. A home he had never dreamed of owning and a woman he had never hoped to possess. His nights were more peaceful now that he shared a bed with Aelfhild, who had decided that the best way to ensure he slept was to make demands of him that left him exhausted and barely able to move, but he still woke anxiously, expecting to discover this was the dream and the nightmares that were fewer now were the reality.

She rolled on to her side and wrapped her arm around him, nestling close and wiggling her foot in between his.

'When you say "rest" I hope you don't plan to fall asleep, my love.'

She bit her lip coyly and gave him a look of such innocence that it was all Gui could do not to tear his hose off there and then.

He contented himself with stroking his fingertips down Aelfhild's cheek.

'You've got mud on you now.' He grinned. He ran his fingers down her neck, tickling the hollow of her collarbone and slipping his fingers inside the neck of her dress.

'So have you,' she murmured, tugging his tunic loose of his belt and sliding her hands underneath to scrape her fingernails against his belly, causing him to swell with lust.

'More mud. It's gone everywhere, all over your dress.' He sighed, nuzzling into her neck. 'What shall we do about that?'

He took hold of the end of the cord at Aelfhild's shoulder between his teeth. A few pulls would undo it and would allow him to tug the dress down and reveal the skin-tight linen shift beneath. She withdrew her hand from beneath his shirt.

'You'll behave yourself, for a little while at least, while I tell you my news.'

Gui obediently stopped his attempts at undressing her, though left his hand where it was. In truth, he was always interested to hear of Sigrun and Gilbert and suspected Aelfhild was admitted to more confidences of their marriage than he was.

'Is Gilbert returned?'

'Last night, with the mare from Durham he was hoping to buy. She's in foal. Sigrun says she's beautiful and they plan to breed her to the bay stallion next. They talked of little else. I could have not been there for all they would have noticed.'

'Horses, always horses,' Gui remarked, thinking how the meek, almost silent woman he had brought home had blossomed and found a kindred spirit in Gilbert. 'She was happy to see him return?'

Aelfhild nodded and slipped her hand around Gui's waist. 'I think she was. She's liking him more and more. I think it helps that his return means she no longer has to have Lady Emma staying with her for companionship.'

Gui laughed and noticed Aelfhild's eyes were also gleaming.

'It's often said a shared annoyance at a mother-in-law can unite a husband and wife,' he said.

'We're fortunate not to have that worry at least,' Aelfhild agreed.

They had no worries, and no outside influence could unite them more than the love and pleasure they drew from each other, but the mystery of her past still troubled Aelfhild at times.

'That was thoughtless of me. We may never know, but we can keep trying to discover the truth.'

Part of him was still convinced that Herik had fathered her on someone and that Lady Emma might one day be persuaded to yield the secret. Aelfhild put her finger to his lips, replaced it with her lips far too briefly for Gui's liking and smiled.

'You are my family now. Which brings me to my news.'

'I thought you'd told me everything,' Gui said, idly running his hand along the tempting contours of her thigh and buttocks, and drawing her skirt slowly upwards.

'I told you their news,' she replied. 'I haven't told you mine. Ours.'

She rolled on to her back, trapping Gui's arm beneath her and gazed solemnly into his eyes.

'Gilbert's mare won't be the only one to give birth next year.'

She took hold of his hand and placed it on her belly. He looked from her face to her stomach, which was to his eyes as slender and flat as always.

'You mean...'

'I'm with child.'

A sob burst from Gui's throat. Tears blinded him. He couldn't help it and cared nothing that anyone might hear or see the proof of his joy. Aelfhild's eyes were glinting, too. He wrapped his arms around her with infinite care, cradling her tenderly, and rested his forehead against hers.

A child. His wife was carrying his child. He said it out loud and she gave a soft laugh as he gazed at her reverentially.

'It's true, my love.'

'You should be resting! You need to lie down! And to think I was about to...'

'I know what you were about to do.' She laughed again. 'We still can. It won't be many months before I grow too large, so we had better make the most of the time we have, don't you agree?'

He intended to protest that such a thing might

be too dangerous, but she dropped her hand to his knee and began to walk her fingers slowly up his inner thigh until he had no further thought of objecting. She lay back on the grass, spreading her arms above her head and giving him a sultry look he was powerless to resist. Gui lay down and began to kiss her, tenderly at first, but with an increasing passion that she met and matched eagerly until they were unable to hold back any longer and joined together in a jumble of hastily pushed-aside clothes.

Afterwards they lay in each other's arms while the sun moved lazily across the sky. Gui yawned, sliding his eyes to look at Aelfhild who slept in peace. He should wake her. He should return to his work. He did neither, but closed his eyes and settled back to dream of a future full of life and promise.

The weeding could wait.

* * * * *

COMING SOON!

We really hope you enjoyed reading this book. If you're looking for more romance, be sure to head to the shops when new books are available on

Thursday
28th June

To see which titles are coming soon, please visit
millsandboon.co.uk

MILLS & BOON

Coming next month

ONE WEEK TO WED
Laurie Benson

Charlotte's gaze dropped to Andrew's lips just as a giant boom reverberated through the hills. They both turned towards the house to see more colourful lights shoot into the sky and crackle apart.

'I'm thinking about kissing you.' He said it in such a matter-of-fact way, as if the idea would not set her body aflame — as if the idea of kissing this practical stranger would be a common occurrence.

Charlotte had only kissed one man in her life. She never thought she would want to kiss another — until now. Now she wanted to know what his lips felt like against hers. She wanted him to wrap her in his arms where she would feel desirable and cherished. And she wanted to know if his kiss could be enough to end the desire running through her body.

He placed his gloved finger under her chin and gently guided her face so she was looking at him. The scent of leather filled her nose. There was no amusement in his expression. No cavalier bravado. Just an intensity that made her believe if he didn't kiss her right then, they both would burn up like a piece of char cloth.

It was becoming hard to breath and if he did in fact kiss her there was a good chance she would lose consciousness from lack of air. But if he didn't kiss her…

She licked her lips to appease the need of feeling his lips on hers.

He swallowed hard. Almost hesitantly, he untied her bonnet and put it aside. Gently, he wrapped his fingers around the back of her neck, pulling her closer, and he lowered his head. She closed her eyes and his lips faintly brushed hers. They were soft, yet firm, and she wanted more.

Continue reading
ONE WEEK TO WED
Laurie Benson

Available next month
www.millsandboon.co.uk

LET'S TALK
Romance

For exclusive extracts, competitions
and special offers, find us online:

f facebook.com/millsandboon

⊙ @millsandboonuk

🐦 @millsandboon

Or get in touch on 0844 844 1351*

For all the latest titles coming soon, visit
millsandboon.co.uk/nextmonth